BL
my

Real Life & Liars

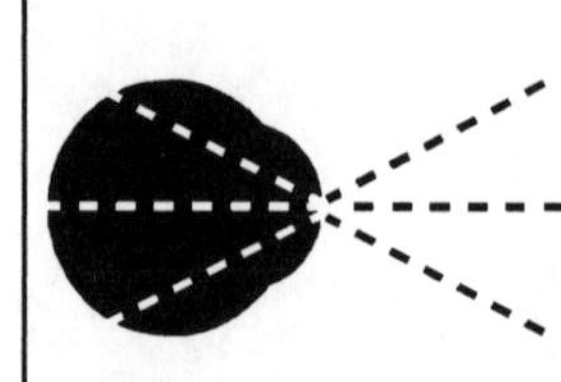

Real Life & Liars

Kristina Riggle

KENNEBEC LARGE PRINT
A part of Gale, Cengage Learning

Detroit • New York • San Francisco • New Haven, Conn • Waterville, Maine • London

Kennebec Large Print® Superior Collection.
The text of this Large Print edition is unabridged.
Other aspects of the book may vary from the original edition.
Set in 16 pt. Plantin.
Printed on permanent paper.

LIBRARY OF CONGRESS CATALOGING-IN-PUBLICATION DATA

Riggle, Kristina.
Real life & liars / by Kristina Riggle.
p. cm. — (Kennebec Large Print superior collection)
ISBN-13: 978-1-4104-1971-2 (pbk. : alk. paper)
ISBN-10: 1-4104-1971-1 (pbk. : alk. paper)
1. Breast—Cancer—Patients—Fiction. 2. Parent and adult child—Fiction. 3. Family—Fiction. 4. Domestic fiction. 5. Psychological fiction. 6. Large type books. I. Title. II. Title: Real life and liars.
PS3618.I39387R43 2009b
813'.6—dc22 2009027021

Published in 2009 by arrangement with Avon Books, an imprint of HarperCollins Publishers.

Printed in the United States of America
1 2 3 4 5 6 7 13 12 11 10 09

To my husband, Bruce
You made me believe, then you made it possible

ACKNOWLEDGMENTS

Contrary to the stereotype of writer-as-loner, I'm a pack animal, and thus have many people to thank for their assistance in the creation of this book.

Thank you to my agent, Kristin Nelson, and my editor at Avon, Lucia Macro, plus the rest of the team at HarperCollins, for loving Mira as much as I do and giving me a chance to share her with the world.

The following people helped me with research. A huge "thank-you" to Kristine Nelson for meteorological expertise, Ann Kuipers and Tim Jenks for information on natural health, and Keith Cronin for insight into the music-publishing business. Several people helped me research breast cancer, including Susan Sorensen, Executive Director of Spectrum Health Regional Cancer Program Dr. Mark Campbell, Sharon Roberts with Susan G. Komen for the Cure, Dr. Cheryl Perkins, Spectrum Health Director of Radiation Oncology Mary Mencarelli, R.N., and Dr. Jane Pettinga, whose fictional diagnosis talk was invaluable. I also owe a debt of gratitude to the National Comprehensive Cancer Network.

I consulted these books in my research: *Just Get Me Through This: The Practical Guide to Breast Cancer* by Deborah A. Cohen with Robert M. Gelfand, M.D., and *Straight Talk about Breast Cancer, From Diagnosis to Recovery,* by Suzanne W. Braddock, M.D., Jane M. Kercher, M.D., John J. Edney, M.D., and Melanie Morrissey Clark.

Thank you so much to my first readers, Eliza Graham and Barbara Sidorowicz, for their wise critiques and for making sure the Escalade didn't magically move from one place to another (or mysteriously change into a Hummer.) Thanks to Jill Morrow for service as sounding board and amateur therapist. I'm grateful to Becky Motew, and Mark Vender, for his consistent support, no matter the continent or time zone.

I couldn't have accomplished this without the support of my writer friends, those I've befriended online and in living color. Their commiseration and expertise are beyond price. I'm also terribly grateful for the support and cheerleading from Denise Taylor and the crew at Schuler Books and Music.

Thank you to Mrs. Dykema, though I knew her as Miss Zagers at Townline Elementary. She was the first one to teach me the "show, don't tell" rule, and about the joy and necessity of revision. It was in her class that I first felt like a writer.

To my family and friends, I can't tell you how much your support has meant to me. Thank you to my sister, Kimberly, my parents, John and Jan Riggle (my first editors and my first typist), and all those who cheered me on and took me seriously as a writer, long before I was an "author." I love you.

All happy families are alike;
each unhappy family is unhappy in its own way.

FROM *Anna Karenina* BY LEO TOLSTOY

Part 1
Homecoming

Chapter 1
Mirabelle

My tea tastes so fresh, and this joint is so fine, I might melt right into the red-velvet cushion and run down the walls into a silvery pool on the floor.

Sure, I'm a little old to be toking up. Five years north of sixty. So sue me. It's been a rough couple weeks around here.

The kids — actually, just my oldest, the other two are dragged along under the wheels of her train — are throwing us an anniversary party. By tomorrow night they will all be here, with spouse, children, suitcases, plus the usual petty arguments and festering resentments.

And I thought my being a hippie would free them of all that crap. The joke's on me.

"Mira!" calls my husband from the kitchen. "Mira?" he says a second time, maybe realizing how frantic he sounded.

"In here!" I know he will follow my voice and check on me, and ask me some ludicrous question like where the spatula is when he knows darn well. Lately, he can't let me out of his sight for very long. It's like living with a toddler again. I'm surprised he doesn't come into the bathroom while I'm taking a dump.

But then, didn't I long for this, his fervent attention? As they say, be careful what you wish for. It's like some sort of medieval fable, where a wish has been granted with a horrible catch in the bargain.

In the echo of all this deference rings that horrible fight, when he turned into someone else, something alien possessing him such that I've never seen in forty years. I take a deep drag from the joint and shake my head a little, shaking away the memory.

Max pokes his head into the study, and I place my joint carefully in the ashtray on the seat next to me. He's got Einstein hair this morning. His sandy-colored curly mop sticks up on each side, but he's bald in the middle. His spectacles are on top of his head, and his ratty red bathrobe hangs open over his boxers and T-shirt. He doesn't mention the marijuana smell or the joint smoldering next to me.

"Honey, are you all right? Where's the egg beater?" he asks.

I turn my head to the side and blow out a

stream of smoke, slowly. "We don't have one. Use the whisk."

Max comes over and plants an urgent kiss on my cheek, and another on my lips, before heading back out to the kitchen.

The phone rings, and I unfold myself to answer it. Max is likely so involved in beating eggs or on a whisk reconnaissance that he doesn't even hear it. Ah, the absent-minded *artiste.*

"Hello?"

"Mom! Good, I caught you. It's not too early, is it? Great, listen I wanted to ask you about the flower arrangements, he said he doesn't have enough lilies if you can believe that nonsense so I wondered . . ."

And so on. I couldn't give a goddamn. I pick up the joint and breathe in again, smooth and deep. I preferred daisies for the party, but Katya said they were too common, practically weeds.

Heaven forbid I love a weed. I should make myself a bouquet of dandelions. No, a crown of dandelions, better yet.

"Mom? Are you listening? I asked you about the freesia."

Exhale. "Sure, sweetie. That sounds nice. So, are you sure you want to stay in a hotel? We can put sleeping bags on the floor, and the kids would be just fine."

"No, I don't want to trouble you," she says, which I translate to mean, No, my kids hate staying at your house because you don't have cable.

"If you insist. Love you, see you tonight."

How did my eldest daughter get so wrapped up in material things? Freesia, lilies, twinkle lights wrapped around fake trees, and crystal goblets. Why does she give a damn?

Myself, I shopped at thrift stores, wore clothes my best friend Patty sewed for me. The same for the kids, though Katya never let me forget the great torment she suffered as a result of wearing something that wasn't — oh, the humanity — brand-new.

Katya never saw me obsess about looks. She didn't see glossy fashion magazines with starved models languishing on sun-bleached beaches. I never competed with the neighbors for bigger, newer, best.

We all have the best-laid plans for our children, and they go and ruin it all by growing up any way they want to. What the hell was it all for, then?

At least she's healthy. They all are, thank goodness for that. My sweet, misunderstood Ivan, and Irina, my butterfly, flitting through life.

The morning sun slips over the houses

across the street and pours into my study, setting my maple rolltop desk in a halo, glinting off the brass nameplate that Max bought me when I landed my teaching job at the college. I had it in my office at first, but it looked so grand and pretentious in my tiny cubbyhole that I brought it home to my rolltop, where it's been ever since.

MIRABELLE ZIELINSKI, it says. I would have preferred to use my full, legal, hyphenated name, but I'm sure *Mirabelle Delouvois-Zielinski* would never have fit.

When I started that job, full of vigor and bright-eyed with promise, I could not have reckoned that more than thirty years later they'd be trying to hustle me out the door like a drunken party guest who stayed too late.

The soft morning light illuminates my filing system of piles all over the place. Each pile has a specific purpose, mind you. Maybe I should start real files. Someone else, someday, maybe soon, will have to sort through all this. I should do it myself. Throw everything away that's unnecessary, which is to say, everything.

The sun brightens the wine-colored walls to a sassy red, like stripper lipstick. I sip some more of my tea and enjoy soaking in the memories locked in the framed photos.

I hate studio portraits. I put those up in the hallway for strangers to admire: my grandson Taylor standing next to a big plastic number two in a miniature suit with a clip-on tie. Granddaughter Katherine with an Easter basket, wearing a dress that is so fussy I itch just looking at it. Visitors say, "Oh, what a beautiful family you have," and I do, but their beauty is not in these created moments.

I much prefer that photo, there, of Taylor with his finger up his nose and his eyes crossed. It gives me a warm buzz to recall that moment when he did it, and I almost peed myself with laughter. And it suits him even now, because he can't quite get serious. I hope he never does. And there's my little Kit, up to her knees in mud in my backyard, mud on her hands, arms splayed out, missing a front tooth. Katya sits in a lawn chair nearby, knees pressed together primly.

Maybe I should get a portrait taken, before I die.

Max won't say the word "die." As if he's terrified that speaking the word aloud would be some kind of totem and cause that fate to fall on me like an ax. But I know those ravenous cancer cells don't care what we say; they will do as they please.

How oddly like grown children.

I stub out the roach, then climb out of my window seat and stretch. I step over Bartleby on my way to the bathroom for my morning shower. She meows at me, her gray tabby tail straight up, indignant. "Oh, hush. Max already filled your bowl." Another meow. "For heaven's sake, it's no different when I do it, you fussy old brat."

She storms off, inasmuch as a thirteen-year-old tabby can storm.

Max wanted to name her Savoir Faire after the villainess in the book he was writing at the time. I said the cat would just get called Savvy, and he wrinkled his squishy nose and let me name her. So she became Bartleby, after Melville's famous scrivener, who simply "prefers not to" do anything at all. So feline, that attitude.

I pass through the kitchen, the screened-in porch, and out the back door to test the feeling of the air. It's the only kind of weather forecast I bother with. I'm not one of those people who have to know the humidity or discuss the barometric pressure, like Katya. She can't leave the house without listening to all three local weather forecasts, watching the Weather Channel "Local on the 8s," and now that she has the Internet on her phone, she checks it all day long, too. She even knows what dew point is, and can tell you all about it, if you ask her, which I don't.

It's early, but the sun is strong, the air already feeling like summer. The tulips haven't even turned brown yet. Seems like just last week the forsythia bloomed.

I walk to the front of the house, glancing at my flower beds as I go, on my way to say hello to the Big Tree.

It's a maple, and just as tall as the house. Maybe taller, but who can tell from my vantage point? It's been known as the Big Tree since Katya was old enough to form the words. We've had picnics under it, taken family portraits in front of it — Max running to get back in the frame, the camera on a tripod with a timer — and it was our family meeting place if we ever had to flee a fire. It was "safe" in tag, where the kids closed their eyes and counted for hide-and-seek. Max did hang a tire swing from it once, but the rope was so long, and the tree so close to the sidewalk, the kids kept whapping pedestrians.

No kids play around it now. This old tree stands stately and alone these days. So I make it a habit to come out every morning, just so she doesn't feel lonely. I brush my hand across her cracked and peeling bark and walk around her trunk until I find it: the one time any of the kids ever carved in the tree. It was Ivan. "IZ and PT" inside a heart. I don't remember now who "PT" was. I do remember scolding him for defacing the tree, then regretting it immediately, as his face crumpled up in shame. Love makes a person do stupid things.

Well, it's time to get dressed. We're having company today.

In the shower, when I scrub my breasts, I remember Dr. Graham telling me I have to get one lopped off. The left one. The sinister one. She didn't say "lopped off," of course. She said they would probably need to "take the whole breast," and I puzzled over the meaning of that for a moment until I felt the word "mastectomy" like a battering ram to my gut. The tumor is too large for my little boob, and right behind the nipple, too, so the whole wicked thing has to come off. I gathered that much before I backed out of the office, hand over my heart as if she were ready to leap across her desk with a scalpel right then. I think that was only ten days ago, but it might have been ten years, or maybe ten minutes. Time goes slippery on me when I'm high.

Yep, there it is. The lump I found over at Patty's house. Patty's newest grandson was there, little baby Sam. I gathered him up to my bosom in the instinctual way all mothers do, and when he squirmed against me, I thought, *ouch,* and then, *that's odd.* It stayed merely "odd" until I dared probe that spot, alone in our bedroom, my eyes following a crack in the ceiling. Still I left it alone, until I noticed the other one like a marble under the skin in my armpit.

That'll teach me to neglect those mammograms. Not only is cancer eating up one breast, it's the "invasive" kind, with "poorly differentiated" edges, which, I think, is bad. That lump in my armpit is a bad sign, too. Cancer cells could be racing through my body even now.

I step out of the shower, towel off, and grab my fluffy, purple robe off the hook. I towel-dry my long hair and finger-comb it. That's all the attention I'll give it today. Anyway, Max likes it long and loose like this.

I go to our bedroom and pull open the enormous wooden wardrobe, like right out of that C. S. Lewis book. I choose my favorite summer dress, an olive green thing with shiny metal beads sewn all around the neckline. It hangs like a sack and feels so good, it's like being naked.

I should ask to be buried in this. Katya

would be horrified, because it's not at all appropriate. Ivan wouldn't want any part of that decision, nor would Max. Death and fashion together — not a male specialty. Irina would argue with Katya just out of habit.

No, it would be selfish for me to dictate what happens after I'm dead, when it couldn't possibly matter to me. I'm being greedy enough by daring to set the agenda of my own demise.

If I have to go down, fine. But I'm going down with both tits swinging.

CHAPTER 2
KATYA

She bends the wheel gingerly to the left, as if to make the Escalade sneak around the corner.

"Mom?" asks Chip from the backseat. "Where are we going?"

Damn. Katya squirms and chews on her lip. "What?" she says, pretending not to hear, buying herself another moment to come up with a suitable lie. Since when do the boys peel their eyes off their Game Boys?

"This isn't the way to the grocery store."

"Just a wrong turn," Katya answers. "Would you like a snack?" One eye on the road, the other on the passenger seat, she fishes her emergency snack provisions out of her giant Coach bag and stretches her arm back to toss the boys a packet of cheese and crackers. As Chip and Taylor take the bribe-and-distraction treat, eyes back on their Game Boys, Katya feels her SUV swerve alarmingly right, and she yanks it back into the lane.

Katya thinks this is a wrong turn, after a fashion, to be driving down her old boyfriend's street. Wrong as in stupid, not to mention, pathetic.

And still she keeps going.

After all, it's not like Charles could take the moral high ground while underneath his secretary.

She's lost track of the times she's done this, accidentally on purpose swinging by Tom's house. First it was just curiosity: Was the rumor really true that he'd moved into her town, right into her subdivision? The first time, she hadn't seen any clues on just a casual drive past about who was living there at all.

So, she'd had to drive by three more times before she caught a glimpse of him trimming the hedges out front, have mercy, shirtless.

Now that the boys have started actually paying attention, she would have to avoid Tom's street unless they were all in school. And with summer fast approaching, that meant she'd soon have all three of the children home.

Why did that thought make her chest constrict and her pulse race? Hadn't she been juggling her graphic-design business in her home office since Chip was pulling up to stand, long before they were all in school all week for most of the year? With children old enough — mostly old enough — to be shooed away while she was working, summer should be Easy Street, compared to breast-feeding Baby Tay while Chip took a crap in his training pants and she wooed a client on the phone, pregnant with Kit already.

Her cell phone goes off, sparking snorts and muffled giggles from the backseat. It blares, *Don't you wish your girlfriend was a freak like me* . . . Katya throws a fiery glare at her boys while she answers the phone. They are always changing her phone's ring tone, and she doesn't know how to change it back. She'll have to wait for Charles to get home.

"Kat's Cradle Design, Kat speaking."

"Yes, Mrs. Peterson, this is Forever Floral calling . . ."

Katya barely listens as she rounds onto Tom's street and stares at his two-story home, designed to look like a Swiss chalet, but with a two-car garage stuck onto the side. Her breath catches in her throat when she spies a dark figure in an upstairs window pull back the curtains to look right at her car.

She barks at the florist, "Look, just get the damn freesia, they're not that expensive, and I don't really care if it's more than what we talked about. Get it done."

She throws the cell phone on the floor of the passenger seat and guns the motor away from Tom's house, and maybe away from Tom himself, staring out the window to see his old girlfriend idling past.

She glares at the boys again through the rearview. "If you mess with my cell phone one more time, I'm taking a hammer to both of yours, I swear to God."

The boys smirk and roll their eyes. Katya's shoulders slump, because she knows they've heard "one more time" a dozen times a day for their entire lives.

Katya is always holding out hope they'll behave, just this once.

The boys thunder through the front door of her home, casting off backpacks and rancid sneakers like shedding a layer of skin. They rumble off to their bedrooms, no doubt to immediately boot up their laptops and instant message all their friends about God only knows what.

Katya looks with dismay at their beefy retreating backs, knowing she should feed them healthier food, knowing she should make them exercise, and knowing that despite Charles's protests to the contrary, they are not big-boned. In fact, as toddlers, they were slim, pinballing around the house from one disaster to another.

She stoops to grab up the things they've dropped, and curses at yet another scratch in the hardwood from a backpack zipper. She checks the family organizer dry erase board on the refrigerator. Kit isn't due to be dropped off for another twenty minutes. Just enough time to check her messages and return calls.

Message one, from Charles. "Hi, honey, I'm running late tonight and probably won't make it home on time. Oh, and I'm golfing with Roger tomorrow, just so you know. Bye."

Katya jams her thumb into the machine's DELETE button. He knows damn well it's her parents' anniversary party weekend, or he bloody well should. It's all she's been talking about for weeks. Shows how well he listens. Just like the kids.

Message two, from Irina: "Hey, Kat? It's me. Um, I have to, um. I wanted to talk to you, but you're not home, and I'm out of town, so never mind. I guess I'll see you at Mom's. Hope you're OK."

Messages three and four are from clients, demanding changes that are out of scope of their original contracts. These return calls will require a minimum of a half hour each, as Katya will effect her most persuasive purr to convince them to cough up the money or shut the hell up.

Message five, from her brother, Ivan. "Hi, Kat. Just wanted to ask if I was supposed to bring anything to the party. I can't find my notes. Oh, and just so you know, Barbara's not coming. Don't ask."

No, Ivan, Katya thinks, I know better than to ask a man to do anything even vaguely related to social obligation. Some of her friends didn't speak to her for weeks after the one year she let Charles handle the Christmas cards. And one of those few he did send out went to the Goldsteins, with a trumpeting angel and a manger, no less. She'd told him about the special card for them, with a snowman and innocuous "Seasons Greetings" at the top of the pile. Katya seems to remember he sent that one to his own parents, who strongly disapproved of such a secular card on such a holy day.

In other words, don't trust men to do the slightest thing right.

Katya kicks off her mules and scowls at her chipped pedicure. How did that happen with her wearing shoes all day? She turns to attack the dishes she left over from her own lunch, when she'd gotten ambitious and whipped up a salad. She pulls open the dishwasher and curses out loud. It's full of sparkly clean glasses and her elegant plates, and a fork smeared with peanut butter has contaminated all its nearby flatware. "You'd think a man who runs his own successful corporation could recognize clean dishes," she mumbles. Katya knows it's too much to ask that he empty the bleeding thing.

She stacks the dishes much harder than necessary. The peanut butter knife galls her more because it's the one thing awry in her kitchen. Her granite countertops gleam, her stainless-steel refrigerator reflects the afternoon sun coming in from the breakfast nook, and if she were prone to do such things, her utensils and pots hanging from the rack above the center island would sound like wind chimes if she brushed them with her hand.

Once, she saw a refrigerator magnet at her mother's house that said, "Boring women have clean kitchens." Katya was deeply insulted.

Katya winces as the front door bangs open into the wall behind it. She refuses to put one of those ugly doorknob cushions on her ivory wall with the gold sponge-paint effect that she slaved over for a week.

"Mom! I'm home!" Kit saunters in, hips swaying much more dramatically than they should for a girl of eleven. Katya rebukes herself again for ever letting her watch MTV. And when she gave in to her plea to wear "only lip gloss," it somehow crept into blush and eye shadow, too.

Katya slams the dishwasher shut with her hip. She knows what the other mothers say about her daughter, but they don't know how strong-willed the girl is, and if Kit had her way, she'd be in hip-huggers and crop tops. She got all her grandmother's determination with none of her hippie values about wearing no makeup and growing out your leg hair.

Kit pops one hip out to the side and blows a bubble with her gum.

"How was your day, dear?" Katya asks, hoping Kit won't answer.

"Oh my God, Bella was so mean to Emma, and I thought Emma deserved it . . ."

Katya starts dinner preparations, making commiserating noises and not listening, keeping one eye on the television, where she has turned the Weather Channel on with the sound muted. She can't keep track of this grade-school drama, and she can't quite believe it has started so soon. Bella, Emma. Another of her friends is named Imogene. Katya tried to give her a perfectly normal name, and called her Katherine. Everyone wanted to call her Kat, but Katya already used that name, so Little Kat became Kitten became simply Kit, which makes Katya think of that stupid TV show with the talking car.

What would have been wrong with Kate? But one and all, friends and family simply refused to call her that. Like everything else in her life when it came to her children, Katya caved in.

Pick your battles, she'd tell herself, and her friends in her mommy group. Trouble is, she hadn't gotten around to those battles just yet.

She'd wanted Kit to have a normal name because she hated being a white-bread American named Katya Zielinski. As if the clunky, impossible-to-spell Polish surname was not enough, she'd had the misfortune to be conceived during her mother's infatuation with Russian film and literature. In the Cold War, too, thank you, Mom. Thank goodness for the fall of the Berlin Wall.

At least she'd married a sensible Mr. Peterson, and could thus become Kat Peterson, graphic designer and very reasonable woman, thank you.

The other siblings had been victim of Mirabelle's consistency in her naming convention. Anyway, her mother loved talking about their names, when anyone asked, and someone always did.

Katya fires up the skillet for the stir-fry, as Kit winds down her story and flounces from the room, probably to get out her laptop and start instant messaging, or maybe she would just text from her phone. The girl has the most agile thumbs of any grade-schooler she's seen.

The phone rings, and everyone ignores it. The kids all have their own phones, so no one ever calls the house phone looking for them. Charles had already left a message, and Katya doesn't care to talk to him anyway. Clients will have to wait just a bit longer, as she is stir-frying dinner and doesn't want to burn it.

Her answering machine kicks on: "*You've reached Kat's Cradle Design and the home of the Petersons. Please leave a message after the tone.*"

"Katya? It's Mom, listen I just got a strange message here for you. Someone named Tom Petrocelli? Didn't you used to see him in high school? He says, it's the craziest thing, that he thought he saw you drive by his house today . . .”

Katya is cemented to her kitchen floor and burns her baby corn.

The boys are upstairs, supposedly asleep, and probably listening to their iPods under the covers, and Kit is all tucked into her fairy-princess canopy bed with the lavender-dragonfly motif.

Charles said he'd left some files of his at the office, and he's gone off to get them. That leaves Katya alone in the sunken family room with the flat-screen television and a bottle of Shiraz. This night she's watching *Sex and the City,* at turns jealous of these New York single gals, feeling superior because she's already got a husband, thank you, and unnerved by how much Kit already resembles these so-called grown-ups. Just the other day, Katya spotted her pretending to smoke a cigarette, using a colored pencil as a prop. She had walked past her room, and Kit was lounging in her bean bag chair, laughing on the phone with whomever. Her legs were stretched out in front of her, and she was wearing only her little girl underwear and a tank top, sprigged with pink roses. But something about her pose was alarmingly adult, and Katya did not like the practiced way she sucked on the end of that pencil, blowing out imaginary plumes of smoke. Then in a moment, Kit had tossed the pencil away and curled her legs underneath her, and just like that, she was a little girl again.

Katya refills her wineglass, leaving the bottle on the oak end table next to her. She sighs along with that inner unspooling she always feels with the aid of a little wine, or if she hasn't been to the store, some of Charles's beer. Mira probably achieves this state of deep relaxation with meditation or something, but whatever genes she had to help her feel happy and carefree, despite the ugly mess that is life, didn't make it into the Katya zygote.

She hears Charles's heavy feet come in through the front door. He must have had to hunt for those files because he's been gone an hour and a half, and the drive is only twenty minutes. Katya suspects — no, believes with a cold, tomblike certainty — that his long absence has something to do with Tara.

He clumps down into the family room, and Katya notes — but at the moment does not much care — that he has tracked in leaves and grass clippings onto her ivory carpet.

"Hitting the wine already?" he asks, not

looking at her, as he pages through the Caller ID on their home phone.

"I'm not *hitting* it. I'm having a glass to relax. I had a hard day."

"Every day is a hard day," he answers, without emotion, and walks back up the three steps to the main floor of the house. "I'm going to bed," he calls over his shoulder.

Katya gives herself another refill as the credits roll on *Sex and the City*. Every day *is* a hard day. What of it?

CHAPTER 3
IVAN

Ivan lies naked and spread-eagled on his sour-smelling, threadbare sheets — sadly, unfortunately, and pathetically alone. He suffered a critical loss of energy midway through his getting-dressed routine — a core meltdown, even — and thus he finds himself staring at the ceiling, thinking of the Elephant People who live upstairs.

The upstairs neighbors on a several-times-daily basis create a mysterious havoc on their floor, his ceiling, and when Van finds himself too burdened by the tedium of his lonely life, he tries to puzzle out the source of the aural emanations.

Jogging? How heavy would they have to be, to rattle the massive change jar on his dresser, which is half-filled with pennies and must weigh a metric ton by now? And who jogs at 4 A.M.? Likewise went his theory that they dropped free weights on the floor every day. Also, the thuds sometimes come in clusters: *thudthudthudBAM.* How many weights could they be dropping?

Sex? What kind of sex could they be having to cause such non-rhythmic, galumphing wallops on the floor?

Sex makes Van think of Barbara, and the sex she's probably having with someone else, someone hipper and more fun, someone who might cheat on her or ruin her credit, but still is mysteriously preferable to Van.

All men, it seems, are mysteriously preferable to Van.

He finally grows disgusted enough with the stench of his sheets to roll himself up and resume getting dressed for a day listening to high-school freshmen butcher Sousa marches on rented or borrowed trumpets.

Then he will have the distinct pleasure of coaxing his rattly VW three hours up the highway to his mother's place in Charlevoix, where he'll sleep in his childhood room, where he never got laid either, and attend the anniversary party, where he'll endure his older sister's varnished domesticity and his younger sister's bragging about her parties and her dates. Oh, and give a toast, which Van can't believe he agreed to do. But refusing Katya is like holding back a tidal wave with the flat of your hand. "You write songs," she'd said. "You're good with words."

It would have been grand to squire Barbara around at the party. She's far and away the most beautiful woman he's ever dated, with her cascading auburn hair — the lyricist inside him berates him for the cliché, but hell, it *does* cascade — and eyes so verdant green they're like a . . . All Van can think of is "golf course." No wonder no one wants to record his songs.

Van pulls on his boxer shorts, which have a stain of mysterious origin, but he doesn't care, because no one will see them, except maybe paramedics if he gets run over by a semi on the way to school, but even then he can't muster enough concern to find a different pair.

His phone rings, and Van doesn't even flick his eyes toward the Caller ID. No one worth speaking to would call him on his way to Death March High, as he's taken to thinking of his place of employment. It's actually named Dexter Milford High, after some illustrious graduate of generations before who isolated some kind of chemical. It was probably Agent Orange, thinks Van ruefully, and the thought brings a twisted smile to his lips.

He'll get his enjoyment where he can.

The answering machine kicks on at last, and rather than the robotic faux-human voice offering him a lower interest rate, he hears Jenny. "Hi, Van. Wondering what you're doing tonight, if you wanted to watch a movie or get a pizza. Anyway, call me if you're free."

Van knots his tie. Making fun of an action flick with Jenny and a Pizza Hut Cheese Lover's sounds infinitely more fun, but family obligations beckon. A year ago, he would have high-fived Jenny as she whizzed to the staff lounge between her classes of high-school French, but then she'd gotten a new job at a fancy magnet school with an emphasis on liberal education and college prep.

Van dearly missed those times they graded papers together in the school lounge on their brief lunch breaks, cracking up at his students' freshman essays, and her students' mangled French.

Ah well, he thinks to himself, grabbing his blazer with patches on the elbows — not to look professorial, but out of an actual need to cover worn sleeves — as Jenny would say: *C'est la vie.*

Chapter 4
Irina

"Shit."

Irina yanks on her pants zipper and yanks again. The third yank rips the zipper right off her pants, the momentum sending her backward onto the Vegas hotel bedspread.

"Shit!" she cries, clenching her teeth. She whips the zipper overhand across the room like a major league pitcher.

"It's just a zipper." Darius props her back up and starts rubbing her shoulders from behind, sitting next to her on the bed. He leans in and flicks her earlobe with his tongue.

Irina shoves him hard over. "Not now." She adds to herself, *We've gotten ourselves in enough trouble already.*

Darius sits himself back up. "Why don't you take a nap and rest a bit. I'll take a shower and maybe we'll both be feeling" — he raises his eyebrows — "refreshed."

Irina rolls over and burrows into the

sheets, which still smell like sex and sweat. She wiggles out of the jeans and kicks them onto the floor. Could she be showing already? It can't be from overeating. Ever since her wedding — if you could call it that — she hasn't eaten a thing.

Her cell phone chimes for a new message. It's a picture from C. J., flashing her midriff, a guy's puckering lips in the frame near her navel, his face out of frame. The message says, "at aftershock, miss u, r.u. havin fun."

Aftershock, the club back home where all her friends are dancing and hooking up and enjoying the fact they don't have a care in the world.

Is she having fun? Oh, yeah. A freakin' blast.

She puts a hand over her belly. She shouldn't have waited so long to get to a clinic, she thinks. She shouldn't have dithered and pondered, she shouldn't have fondled those tiny pink socks at Baby Gap. In her indecision, along comes Darius and like Newton's Laws, he goes to work on her. An object at rest tends to stay at rest until an overeager wannabe daddy rushes you to some cheesy Vegas chapel.

Out the expansive picture window, she can see down to the pool, where svelte, nonpregnant honeymooners are roasting themselves in fine form.

Weeks ago, before her missed period, she would have loved this vacation, Irina thinks: a week of eating, drinking, gambling, and sex? Sign me up. But Darius had been so hot and cold before now. She'd never have pegged him for the daddy type, or she wouldn't have slept with him in the first place. She once watched an old boyfriend change his nephew's diaper, and she could never bring herself to have sex with him again.

Irina turns away from the pool. She didn't even have champagne at her own wedding. She'd gone to take a sip, and Darius snatched the glass right out of her hand. "Not for my little baby," he declared, grinning a little, but Irina knew he was serious.

So they kissed instead, and the justice of the peace or whateverthehell took the picture himself, but Irina opened her eyes too soon, so it looks like she's giving Darius mouth-to-mouth. Not exactly your typical soft-focus romantic wedding-day photo. Instead of a gauzy gown and veil, she wore a tacky white beaded dress from a consignment shop, which some teenager probably wore to the prom, and a fake white rose pinned in her short black hair. Darius sported a bolo tie and carnation stuck in his sport-coat lapel.

Irina believes that she will remember what she was thinking in that photo for the rest of her life.

What the hell did I just do?

Darius wakes her from a doze. The sun is lower in the sky. He's wearing his glasses with the tortoiseshell frames, a textbook in one hand. The glasses remind her of her father.

"Hungry?" he asks her, and she's relieved to see that he really means food this time.

"A little," Irina ventures weakly, laying the groundwork for her after-dinner bout of faked queasiness so she can have one night's peaceful sleep. Darius's romantic intentions have been undeterred by her delicate state.

"We could order in?" he suggests. He puts down the book and folds his glasses on the nightstand.

"No . . . I'd like to get up and around a bit."

"Sure, baby. Whatever you like." Darius is pulling on a fresh knit shirt over his muscled chest. "So, have you called your parents yet?"

Irina pulls the covers over her head. "I can't tell them all this over the phone."

"So you're going to spring me on them?"

"It's going to be 'springing' no matter how

or when I do it. They've never heard of you, and suddenly you're not only a son-in-law, but I'm having your baby? There's no good way to do it. So I'll do it in person."

"If you say so."

"Yes, I say so," Irina snaps. She's heard Katya say that to her a zillion times in their lives, and from her big sister it means, *You're an idiot, but whatever.* Now she thinks, *I better not have married my sister. I might have to kill myself.*

Darius says, "Are you at least going to tell them I'm black?"

"Trust me, it will be perfectly obvious."

"Have you ever dated a black man before?"

"Course I have. All kinds."

"OK, let me ask that another way. You ever brought a black man home before?"

"No, but don't worry about it. My mother is the original flower child who will probably be thrilled to death. My dad is so out of it that you'll be lucky he even follows the conversation."

"What's the matter with him?"

"He's a writer."

"Oh? What does he write?'

Irina rolls out of bed, having had this conversation six hundred times before. "Nothing you've read, I guarantee it. I'm getting dressed." *That is,* she thought, *if I can find pants that fit.*

It won't be Mom or Dad who care about Darius being black, and in fact no one in her carefully PC family would dare mention it. It will be Katya and her snooty-ass husband, she predicts, who will find subtle ways to broadcast disapproval, at least until they learn that Darius makes an excellent salary selling high-end new cars, and is taking classes at night toward an MBA. Then he'll pass muster. Barely.

In any case, she knows they'll find fault with him somewhere. The very fact he married her may be enough of a flaw.

Irina digs a loose-waisted sundress out of her suitcase. She'll have to get Darius to take her shopping.

CHAPTER 5
MIRA

I push my breasts into my wedding dress, stubborn things seem to be bigger than they were when I got married thirty-five years ago. How is that possible?

I squint into the oval standing mirror and realize my breasts are just as they always were, but there's rather more flesh underneath and around them. Looking at my reflection, for a moment — quick as a flicker of déjà vu — my left breast disappears, my gown sagging in. I blink and it's back, bulging just like the innocent right one.

Am I still high? I don't think so.

I smile at myself in the mirror, and why not? To even be able to slip into — all right, squish into — my bridal gown after all those years and three babies is a rare feat indeed.

It helps that empire-waisted gowns were in fashion, which are forgiving in having the narrow part up underneath the boobs. This might have caused a whisper in the church that I was pregnant, and that's why I needed a loose waist. After all, I had already been brazenly living with Max, with a child already, dear little Katya.

Not that my university colleagues or Max's writer friends gave a good goddamn, being leftist children of the late sixties and seventies. To them, the scandal was that we bothered getting married after all those years. We had a real minister, even, as a grudging concession to Max's parents.

It was our parents' generation that sat with gargoyle faces locked in grimace, or so I had imagined, while we faced the benevolent minister, who wore a beard and a small gold hoop earring along with his frock and rainbow stole.

Max's wild curly hair would not be tamed, even for our wedding day, and his ears stuck out like dessert plates on his head. He'd forgotten to take off his glasses, and they were perched on top of his head throughout the entire, blessedly brief, fifteen-minute ceremony.

And the door behind me opens, and poof! there appears Max now, hair still curly, though it's retreating up his scalp. He's still not dressed for the day. He's got manuscript pages clutched in his fist.

"Oh!" he gasps. "Oh, you look lovely. Just

like the day we married."

I do look nice enough in this, though not at all like the day we married. Instead of brown hair like espresso, it's gone bright silver, and I have pronounced laugh lines, and smile lines, and yes, worry lines, too. Three children will produce plenty of those, to be sure.

The sight of me in wedding garb seems to have arrested Max from whatever he was going to say. He simply stares.

Finally, I ask him, "What did you need?"

He gulps hard and asks me, quavering, "When are we going to tell them? The kids?"

I reach back and undo the zipper, which slides gratefully down, released from its duty. I step out of the dress, which I may wear tomorrow night instead of the suitable matronly frock that Katya picked out. I shake out my silk slip, feeling the air on my skin.

"Tomorrow, after the party, I think. Or maybe Sunday morning, before they all leave."

"Are you going to tell them . . . all of it?"

Max means, am I going to tell them that I won't go back there, to that doctor with her scalpel and her anesthesia, and her chemicals and radiation.

"I think I'd better, don't you?"

"They won't like it." He grips the pages tighter. I expect he's right about the kids. But it's not their choice to make. Nor is it his, no matter what he seems to think. Max continues, "You shouldn't tell them that part. You might change your mind. Why upset them?"

"I'm not going to change my mind."

"Mira, it's only been a few days, give yourself time . . ."

"Leave me alone, I'm trying to get dressed."

Max shrinks out of the room, and I feel a sinking in my chest. Because I have a finite number of words left — who can say how many? — and each one that's less than loving is a squandered opportunity.

The burden of this impending end makes me gasp for air for just a moment, then I shake it off by closing my eyes and brushing my hand across the mess and the dirt and the pain, wiping it all away.

CHAPTER 6
KATYA

Katya clucks her tongue at the sight of her mother's yard, as it comes into view of her Escalade's front windshield. Viny, creeping weeds smother the grass, and chunks of tall fescue stab up through the mess to announce, Look! No one has mowed here for a week!

She feels reassured in her argument against having the anniversary party under a tent in the yard. It's a double lot, it would have been big enough — the carriage house was long ago torn down by some previous owner, so the Victorian home stands alone, with plenty of lawn — but really, for such a lovely event to be held over the top of all those weeds seemed so wrong. Like a Tiffany diamond wrapped in cellophane.

Katya frowns at the clouds on the horizon. They look benign enough so far, puffy and light. But the weather forecasts have been showing ominously increasing chances for rain tomorrow.

"Charles, you missed the house."

"Mmm? Oh. I'll go around the block."

"Dad! I've gotta pee!"

"For Christ's sake, Taylor, you can hold it two more minutes. I've had enough out of you."

Katya winces at his tone with their younger son. Charles remains eternally disappointed that neither of his sons seems appropriate as heir apparent to Peterson Enterprises. Hope is not lost for Kit, but Katya has to allow that she doesn't seem a likely prospect, given her current trajectory on the apprentice-bimbo track.

Anyway, Katya thinks bitterly as the SUV pulls into the long drive up to the house, their daughter could be the next Madeleine Albright and it would never cross Charles's mind to appoint a woman as his successor.

Mira appears on the screened-in back porch. Through the haze of the screen she looks exactly like her youthful self, with the same Rapunzel waves of hair. She never did cut her hair short and resort to a curly perm like her contemporaries. Mira opens the door and the effect is gone like the wink of a firefly. Now she is just her postmenopausal self, wrinkles and silver hair intact. Bangles rattle on her wrist as she glides down the stairs to greet the family.

"Oh, I've missed you," she whispers into Katya's hair as she squishes her into a hug.

Katya steps back. "Mom, you should wear shoes out here; you'll cut yourself on these rocks."

"Oh, for pity's sake, I'm barefoot so often my feet are tough as any old sandals." To demonstrate, she picks up a foot and shows Katya the sole: darkened by dirt and worn as the cover of an old book.

"Maybe tomorrow we should get you a pedicure," Katya muses, half to herself, as she grabs some bags of kid-friendly food out of the car. Chip and Tay each give a barely audible "hi" to their grandmother as they stomp through the porch, heading for the kitchen. No doubt they will be disappointed to see Mira's usual assortment of transfat-free brown-flour sugarless fare. Kit hops out, those damn white iPod cords trailing from her ears. She pops an air-kiss in Mira's direction and bops off to find a comfy chair for her texting. Katya had only asked her to take out the earbuds, just long enough to say hello. Such a simple request.

"A pedicure? Those boys should have carried those bags for you."

"I can handle the bags. I mean tomorrow morning, when we get your hair done. You remember, I mentioned it yesterday?"

Mira chews on her lip and looks Katya in the eye. "No, can't say that I do. Well, a hairdo is fine, then. No sense bothering with the feet, though, those shoes you picked out will cover up my nasty old paws anyhow."

Katya slams the Escalade door with her hip as Charles comes around and takes the bags from her hands, a mere nod in Mira's direction.

"He's tired," she says to her mother. She takes Mira's elbow, and they go up the stairs together, through the back porch, and into the kitchen. Charles is already on his cell phone, and the boys have turned on the television upstairs in the guest room; Katya can hear an abrasive commercial through the floorboards. Mira never watches television herself; the small one in the guest room is a concession for her grandchildren, but even that doesn't have cable. She can see Kit's feet over the arm of an overstuffed violet-leather chair in the front room, tapping to some beat throbbing into her ears.

The kids consider it near purgatory to visit their grandmother these days.

"Your siblings should be here shortly," announces Mira, walking to a cutting board with vegetables and a big knife. She starts going at a piece of celery. "Dad will be down when he finishes his paragraph."

"Or his chapter, or his whole damn book," Katya says with a sigh. She catches Charles's eye and sends him a glance, which after fifteen years of marriage he should very well know means *Get off the damn phone and be sociable.*

He pretends not to see her, though his eyes are trained squarely on her forehead. Katya might as well be a fax machine for all the emotion in his gaze.

Katya glances at her watch. Nearly 5 P.M., almost her self-permitted wine time.

"Did you hear that Van isn't bringing a date after all?" Katya gets up to go rummaging for a Diet Coke. Mira usually has lemonade and mineral water, but to humor guests she keeps some soda around.

"No, he didn't say that. That's too bad."

"Not exactly surprising, though is it? I have yet to see him bring a girl to any family function."

Chop, chop, chop, goes Mira's blade, now on a red pepper. "Not everyone meets the man of their dreams at college freshman orientation." She shoots Katya a look through a lock of silvery hair that's fallen over the side of her face.

"I didn't start dating him right away. I had my share of duds, believe me." Kat jumps up from the table and takes the knife from her mother. "Here, let me do the salad."

Katya doesn't have to ask what's for dinner. Spaghetti, as always when they come to visit. The only Mirabelle meal the kids will tolerate. Mira says, "Did he call you? Did he say what happened?"

"No. But it'll be yet another instance of picking a girl completely wrong for him, same as the last dozen."

"Katya."

"Well, I'm sorry. But look at the girls he tries to date. They're too old, or too young, or dating three other guys at once, or they can barely spell. He's so . . ." Katya waves the knife in the air, searching for the word. "Self-sabotaging."

Mira leans against the kitchen counter, having put the water on to boil. She absentmindedly braids a strand of her hair. "He's not the most savvy of men, that's for sure."

Katya snorts. "Oh, and if he does happen to find a nice girl, he comes on so strong she makes a break for the exit. Remember the time he invited a girl he barely knew to a wedding, then bought her a necklace? She spooked like a show horse."

"As I said" — Mira continues to twine and untwine that strand of hair — "we don't all have your luck, dear."

Footsteps on the stairs interrupt them, just as Katya finishes with the vegetables. She turns to see her father, in brown-corduroy pants and a god-awful salmon pink polo shirt, hair like he lost a fight with a live wire. "Katya!" he cries theatrically, and runs down the rest of the stairs. He reaches the kitchen and sweeps her into a hug, barely giving her time to put down the knife to avoid impaling him.

Katya tries to pull back no less than three times before her dad releases her, and even then he looks into her eyes with a penetrating gaze. He looks up at Mira, still holding one of Katya's hands, and the two of them trade a look that makes Katya shiver, despite the heat from the stove.

Charles walks back in, clicking shut his cell phone. "Damn work, I might have to go back into the office tomorrow."

Lucky me, thinks Katya, as she turns from her father and sweeps the vegetables into the bowl with the side of the knife. *Lucky, lucky me.*

Chapter 7
Ivan

Ivan sits in his VW, listening to the engine tick and hiss, two blocks from his parents' home, where his older sister has no doubt already arrived and taken over everything. Ivan turns his cell phone over in his hand. His gaze rests on a group of children playing jump rope in a yard. But he's thinking about Barbara.

He could call her. Maybe she's had a change of heart.

And what to tell the family? It was ill-advised, but he'd bragged ahead of time about her beauty. He shouldn't say anything at all, let them think what they will. But what to say when they asked about his life?

The job? He'll say, "Great, terrific." One of his students obviously forged his parents' signature on his practice record sheet, and Ivan graded him a "zero" for that week, thereafter getting called on the carpet because his parents swore up and down that they'd signed it, and Jason had indeed practiced his sax the required thirty minutes a day. Sure, and his father just happens to have identical handwriting, right down to the flattened top of the cursive "J" with which Jason signs his own name. And with all this alleged practice, how is it possible not to show even one speck of improvement? If anything, he's gotten worse as one of the busty flute girls has been flirting with him during her sixteen-measure rest, squelching what little musicality he ever had.

Ivan smelled defeat on the wind and gave in.

The songwriting? He could talk about the close personal relationship he has with several rock acts in town, if by "close" he means "running from me like a crazed stalker with a machete" and "personal" means "using my demos as coasters for their drinks."

He notices that the children have stopped jumping rope and are staring at him like rabbits before bolting into the underbrush. He starts the car, leaving the cell phone in the cup holder.

Van knows he can't dodge the Barbara question. Someone will mention it. Someone always does.

The house peeks out from behind the big maple tree, redolent in all its showy Victorian embellishment. Van's eyes go first to his dad's office in the second-floor spire. He pictures Max at his computer, writing his latest novel, with a complicated mix of pride and envy that sits like a stone on his heart. Next, as always, he looks up at his own bedroom window: upper story, far right, above his mother's den. Ivan feels like he's never left that room, and that his apartment near the high school is merely a satellite of his boyhood home, not having the benefit of gravitational pull of his own family to anchor him somewhere else.

Ivan pulls the VW next to Katya's huge yuppiemobile and thinks of writing a song called "Gravitational Pull."

Seeing the house reminds him he hasn't written the toast yet. How is the dull middle child of a hippie and a famous writer supposed to toast his parents' anniversary? "Congratulations, and I apologize for squandering your genetic bounty by teaching freshmen how to bleat scales on the trumpet."

The sun is settling toward Round Lake, which he glimpses between the garage and the house, before opening the door into the screened-in porch. Van wonders if the sax player's parents have a yacht docked out there. It's not unlikely.

His phone buzzes in his pocket, and without thinking he snatches it up and looks at the screen. Before his brain could even form the word "Barbara" in his thoughts, the Caller ID says JENNY and he lets it go to voice mail.

He stumbles up the porch step as he puts the phone away, following sounds of cutlery on plates and the booming baritone of Katya's husband toward the dining room.

"You made it!" exclaims his mother, as she pushes back from the table and rushes to greet him, her long dress rippling behind her. Ivan tries not to pull her hair as he hugs her, having to bend down a significant distance, wishing he wasn't so tall because then he wouldn't have to feel like a grown-up. His entrance and Mira's exclamation have interrupted some story Charles was telling. Ivan slaps his dad on the shoulder, and Max gives him a wink, crinkling up his face like Santa Claus. He always used to wink at Ivan, his only son. To Van it meant, "Just you and me kid, bobbing in a sea of estrogen."

"We've got a plate for you right here," says his mother, leading him to her right. There's an empty chair for Irina, but no food yet at her place, as no one ever knows when she'll pop through the door.

"Where are the kids?" Van sees no sign of his nephews and niece.

"Upstairs." Katya waves her hand toward the stairwell, then adjusts her napkin on her lap. Ivan understands they bolted down their food as fast as they could and scurried away to the television and their cell phones.

Katya changes the subject from his parents' inquiries about the drive up north, cutting right to the chase. She would have made a terrific prosecuting attorney.

"So, Van, I was so sorry to hear Barbara couldn't make it."

"Yes, that was too bad," Mirabelle interjects, and starts a monologue on the virtues of wheat-flour pasta as she loads Van's plate with more than he would possibly eat.

But Katya will not be distracted. Ivan meets her gaze with the same weighty defeat as when he faced the angry sax player's parents and Barbara's indifference.

"We had a falling-out, and that's all anyone needs to know." He attacks his spaghetti, and Katya gives up the chase for the moment, turning instead to wondering aloud where Irina could possibly be.

Ivan realizes as he watches his older sister talk, that Barbara looks a great deal like

Katya. They both have this thick hair that falls wavy, just like Mirabelle's, though Barbara's hair is that reddish color and Katya's is sandy brown, like their father's. And the shape of their eyes is somewhat narrowed, with eyebrows like slashes, which can glare with devastating effect.

Just as well Barbara didn't come then.

"Dad, how's the new book coming along?"

"Hmm?"

Max always seems to be writing his novels on the opposite wall of whatever room he's in, staring into that space with penetrating intensity. Seeing his father in this state of suspended animation makes Ivan think that he himself lacks that level of concentration, and maybe if he could only shut out the rest of the world, he could write a song worth listening to.

"The new book."

"Oh, that. Yes, fine. I'm probably halfway through. Thinking of killing off the confidante."

"Oh, not Augustus Cheever!" Ivan always liked that character, a fussy old Brit.

"Killed him off three books ago," Max says through a mouthful of salad. "New sidekick now, Nicky Pauls. From Brooklyn."

Ivan snags his wineglass, which Mirabelle filled when he wasn't looking. He's embarrassed to be caught not reading his own dad's books, but frankly he can't get excited about the exploits of Dash Hammond, international spy. When he was younger, he liked the car chases and explosions, and there was something so decadent and yet unnerving about reading sex scenes penned by one's own father, even the mild, PG-rated versions in his dad's books, with lots of vague references to "warm places" and "dampness."

But as Ivan's own tastes grew toward the literary and high-flown modern fiction, his dad's potboiling page-turners just didn't boil his pot anymore.

"What's the fate of unfortunate Nicky?" asks Ivan.

"I dunno. Cement boots are a bit cliché. Maybe I'll dangle him over a vat of acid." Max winks, and Ivan smiles. It was their old joke about the ever-more-ridiculous hero-in-peril situations that a long-running series tended to create.

Max asks, "How about you? Any news on your songs?"

"Oh, you know." Van tugs on his ear, thinking his dad probably doesn't know, having had his books in print for so long he hadn't been rejected since Van was in diapers. "It's all subjective, you know. One of the bands said to bring them something else sometime."

"Oh, well that's good. I remember when Jane told me . . ." And Max launches into a "struggling writer" story, which Van tunes out immediately. He's heard most of his dad's repertoire, anyway.

It is not strictly true about the band, and Van feels both guilty and foolish for exaggerating — lying — to his father. His fondest wish — aside from becoming the next Bob Dylan — would be to turn back time and never, ever mention his songwriting ambition. To anyone. If no one knows you're trying, no one can ever know you've failed.

Max's story is winding down, and Van feels his family's eyes on him, waiting for him to respond.

He pushes his face into a smile. "Anyway, you all just wait. I'll win a Grammy yet. You'll see."

Max looks up from his dish into his wife's eyes, with a squinting, earnest gaze. The silence falls heavily.

Chapter 8
Irina

"So, you want me to wait in the car? or what?"

"Why would I want that?" Irina twirls her wedding ring, still unable to believe she had a wedding. She's stalling, openly stalling, and Darius is smart enough to know that. On the flight back from Vegas, she imagined just walking in and introducing Darius as "my new husband, and the father of my baby" but her plan fell apart when they pulled up the drive behind Katya's Escalade and her brother's rusty VW. To her right, the enormous spire on the front of the house looms above her, and Irina feels twelve years old again, when she used to scare herself witless imagining ghosts and ghouls up there.

"If I wait in the car, you can shock them first with just our wedding, then I can walk in and shock them again by being black."

"I told you about that; it won't bother them."

"And I told you, I've dated white girls before. I don't care how liberal your parents are, no one expects it. This one dude was president of the ACLU in his county, and his jaw still fell open. I thought his wife would pass out."

Irina shakes off an unexpected pang of jealousy at the mention of other white girls. "I don't care. I need you with me."

Darius nods and straightens up tall. Irina knows he's glad to be called on for strength and support. He was always courteous before, but the pregnancy brought out a whole new level of deference. She starts to open the car door, but Darius puts a hand on her arm, gives it a gentle squeeze, then hops out to open it for her.

Irina steps out slowly, not from any physical need but to stall again, just a little longer, before getting into that old soup of family issues. She stands at last, fluffing out her loose, flowing blouse.

She bites back the urge to shake off Darius's hand on her elbow as she steps up the porch stairs and ambushes her family, who are sitting on the wicker furniture just inside the porch door, having an after-dinner cocktail.

She spots Mira first, who gets to her feet quicker than reasonable for a sixtyish woman. Mira lights up, and her wrinkles only make her look happier. For a moment, Irina wonders if her own face will radiate like that, at the sight of the baby she carries. But she has no time to linger on that thought because voices are all going at once.

"Irina!" This from her mother and father, not quite in unison.

"Glad you made it! Who's this?" From Katya, getting the well-wishing out of the way quick and getting down to business.

"Hi, Reenie," from her brother, using the nickname she's hated for the last fifteen of her twenty-one years of life. Ivan remains slouched in the chair, while the others close in on her like something from *Night of the Living Family.*

Darius remains quiet, though he's smiling and nodding to each one in turn. His hands are clasped loosely behind his back, and Irina tries to imagine how they see him, if they think he's handsome, if they have any inkling about what she's going to say.

She clears her throat, and Darius puts one arm around her waist. What waist she has left, that is. This action changes the air in the room, and even Ivan sits up out of his dolorous slouch.

"Sorry to be springing this on you all," Irina begins, and already she sees Katya fold her arms and her back go even more rigid. "But it was sprung on me, too, in a way. I've been seeing Darius for a couple of months" — and in this instant Irina decides to parcel out her shocking news one bit at a time, and she has to concentrate on not touching her belly — "and we really fell in love" — and there might have been a gasp at this, but she leaves no time, rushing on to say — "and Darius swept me off to Vegas and married me three days ago."

The most unexpected thing happens. Mira runs from the room, and in that fraction of a second as she turns, Irina could swear she sees her eyes shining with tears. Max just gapes, slumped like a marionette limp on its strings.

"Congratulations," mumbles Ivan, as he hauls himself out of the chair with a great show of effort.

Katya beams at Darius, and it makes Irina want to retch, and not for fake morning sickness, but actually she wants to vomit watching her sister pretend not to be upset in all her soccer-mom sensibilities by Darius. She shakes his hand and offers congratulations in that same syrupy voice she probably uses at PTA meetings or whatever the hell she does with her time.

Katya then hugs Irina, and whispers in her ear, "Come to the kitchen with me."

Irina ignores her and goes to her father, the only member of her family not yet to react. "Dad?" Irina considers waving a hand in front of his nose. It's like he has gone into what she calls "zombie face" where he's writing in his head.

"Sweetheart," he says, coming around at last, and folding her into a hug. His hair gets in her nose and makes her want to sneeze. "Oh, honey, congratulations. I love you so much."

He holds on too long, and for some reason Irina can't articulate, she feels a cold rock sink into her stomach.

She pulls back and meets his eyes — his, too, are watering — just before Katya takes her wrist and pulls her into the adjacent kitchen.

Chapter 9
Ivan

With Katya and Irina in the kitchen, and their mother dashed off crying to somewhere in the house, probably her office, the men fidget in silence.

Darius remains where he started, hands clasped loosely, gaze somewhere in the far corner of the room. Max's hands hang down at his sides like a couple of dead fish on a line, as he remains nailed to the spot where Irina hugged him before getting dragged off by her older sister.

The quiet gets to be too much for Van, who blurts out something with all the best intentions.

"Please don't think we're bigots."

Darius turns to him quizzically. His voice has a studied calm to it as he replies, "Now, why would I think that?"

The speaking seems to have snapped Max out of his stunned trance, and he says, "I'm going to check on my wife. Excuse me."

Halfway to the door, he stops, turns around, and goes back to Darius, shaking his hand quickly but not looking directly at him. "Congratulations. Welcome to the family. Excuse me." And he heads for the door again.

Now Van and his new brother-in-law are alone, and Van starts to sweat like a pro wrestler, which he worries will be further evidence to Darius of their racist tendencies, seeing as how he can't get comfortable with a minority in the room.

A minority, thinks Van, what a rotten way to refer to a human being.

"I just mean," he stammers, "just because they're a little shocked, I don't want you to think we're some kind of racists. We just, I mean, we didn't expect . . . We didn't even know Irina was dating a black guy. Any guy! I mean, she'd never even said . . ."

Darius stares back at him, and Van thinks he might pass out. He lets his gibbering trail off, and that's when he sees one side of the man's mouth twitch up slightly. Van sinks back into his chair. "I need a drink. Can I get you a drink?"

"No, thanks. I'll wait until the ladies get back. I'm sorry I upset your mother."

"Yeah," Van muses, half to himself. "That was strange. My mom is a total hippie, it can't be because you're black."

On this, the screen door bangs into the wall as Katya barges through with Irina in tow. Irina tries to turn right back around but Katya takes her wrist and pulls her back in.

Irina lets herself be pulled in, and puts her other hand to her forehead. "Oh God, Ivan, what have you been saying?"

"My usual drivel," Ivan replies, staring gloomily at the floor.

Darius joins her, and gives her a squeeze and a peck on her forehead. Ivan notes they make an attractive pair. Irina is so fair, with her dark black hair cut short she looks elfin. Darius is tall, broad-shouldered, and not all that dark, really, but the contrast with Irina is striking, even so. Ivan muses that they will make exotic-looking babies, and feels immediately ashamed of himself for thinking so.

As the formal introductions begin, Ivan wipes his sweaty hand on his pants and prepares to formally meet his new brother-in-law. Ivan realizes he might suffer permanent damage from the exertion of not sounding like a bigot — or a self-conscious asshole — for the rest of his life. Or rather, the duration of Irina's marriage. Given the brief history of this blessed event, reflects Ivan, that might not be long at all.

CHAPTER 10
MIRA

Oh, this is so unfair.

I clutch my chest, and I'm drowning in emotion, only I don't know which one, just that it's too much for me at once and I can't breathe.

I throw open the window of my study and suck in the outside air, though it's muggy, and that's not much relief. It's something to do, at least.

My consolation is that someday Irina might have a child of her own, who might do something like this to her, who will just drop in with a husband the same year she can legally drink a glass of wine.

Not that I'll be around to see it.

I lower myself to the floor and, with concentration, sit cross-legged, then lift one heel onto the opposite knee. The second heel takes a great deal more effort.

I place my hands in *chin mudra* and rest them on my knees. The breath is slow. The universe is breathing *me.* The universal life force breathes into my lungs, and back out to the world, and in my mind's eye it looks like a mist of gold.

"Mira!"

Oh, shit and bollocks.

It takes even more effort to unfold, and my wincing alarms Max.

"Are you all right? Are you sick?"

"I thought I might meditate. I mean, she got married?"

The effort of unwinding wore me out, so Max joins me on the floor. We both lean on an old scruffy couch across from my rolltop desk. He puts his head on my shoulder, and I put my cheek on the top of his head. Sitting down, we're the same height. He's all legs, my Max.

"Yeah, that's something. I mean, with all that's going on . . ."

"Not that she knew. But still. I would have flown to Vegas for a shotgun wedding to a stranger, at least I would have been there."

"Shotgun? You don't think . . ."

I wave my hand. "No, I don't. All the birth control available today? Anyway, that's no reason to get married these days. Heck, we didn't think so, and that was thirty-seven years ago."

"I guess you're right." Max sinks back to

his position, nestled next to me.

"Aren't I always?"

Something in Max goes wire-taut. There are all these trip wires in our conversations. Any reference to the future — like Ivan mentioning the Grammys — or anything permanent at all, reverberates in us like the mournful clang of an enormous church bell.

Now that my heart has slowed down from the fifty-yard dash, I can sort out my mosaic of feelings. Shock, certainly. We'd never even heard of this guy, and Irina? I would expect Ivan to up and marry someone out of nowhere, out of desperation. Irina got married. Makes no sense at all, unless she was trying to shock us.

"Mira, honey?"

"Can we just sit, please? I need some quiet."

Max falls instantly silent. He's so deferential lately that I know he would sit there, immobile and silent, all night if I asked him to. Maybe he thinks that if he's sweet enough to me now, he can erase that awful fight and dispel the bitter hangover that tinges our moments.

Trying to shock us by marrying a black man makes no sense, however. We're as liberal as they come, and the last people to give a fig about an interracial marriage.

Maybe Katya would have her conventional feathers ruffled, but tight-ass though she may be, she's no bigot.

Now, I feel robbed. It's not enough that this disease — now I feel like Max, I can't even think the word right now — could steal so much life away from me, Christmases I might never see, great-grandchildren I might never hold. But for Irina to get married and steal away my chance to be there for her . . .

She didn't know. Maybe Max was right, and we should have told them right away. But day after day when I tried to pick up the phone, I could not. They would call me, and still I could not find the words. And I didn't yet have the answers to the questions I knew they would ask. Like, what are you going to do?

Max has suggested that we lie and tell them that there is nothing to be done whatsoever, so they won't know that I've decided, consciously decided, to do nothing. I know he thinks I'll change my mind, and the children could then believe there's been some miracle of medicine to spare me.

I'm emotional, I'll tell her. I'll tell Irina that I overreacted because of the anniversary party and the passage of time, which has gotten me all weepy. I can't tell her the truth yet. Let my children live in happy ignorance — the same happy ignorance I swam around in like amniotic fluid for years as I blew off mammograms and pap smears — let my children have at least the anniversary party to themselves, before I lower the boom.

CHAPTER 11
KATYA

Galloping feet pound down the stairs, and Katya cocks an ear to listen: Yes, it seems to be all three of the kids barreling down the steps. Darius is answering her questions politely, though he does seem a bit guarded. Was that a slight edge in his voice describing his job? Is there maybe a tinge of defensiveness when talking about his MBA studies?

Or she could be imagining things. Katya hides a smile behind her wineglass as she steals a look at Van. He still looks ashen, like he fears he has a burning cross on his head. Irina stares past them all out to the harbor beyond.

"Mom!" bellows Chip as he crashes through the door, nearly destroying a lamp on an end table where her father had been sitting. "Taylor won't let me play his Game Boy!" Taylor appears behind Chip's shoulder, shouting, "It's mine! I don't have to share!"

Kit whines, "They were fighting, Mom! They almost kicked me in the head!"

"What's wrong with yours?" Katya demands, trying to send her best Glare of Death, but the kids have long ago built up immunity to it.

"The battery's dead."

"I told you to charge it before we left home."

"Isn't it about time we left anyway?"

Kat's blood burns in her veins at the imperious way Chip spoke to her, sounding all too much like Charles.

Katya stands up and stares hard at her son from across the room. He's big — bigger than she could imagine from his tiny newborn self — and he's leaning against the doorway to the kitchen. He has the temerity to yawn.

"You will not tell *me* when it is time to leave. I don't give a damn about your lousy stinking battery, and if you can't play nice up there, I'll take Taylor's away, too, and Kit's iPod, and you'll sit up there in silence and, horror of horrors, maybe you'd have to read a book or, heaven forbid, actually talk to each other. But we won't leave this house one second before I'm ready. Are we clear?"

Kit emits a high-pitched sound somewhere between a whine and a disgusted snort. "What did I —"

"Nothing, shut up, I don't care, get out!" Kat digs the fingernails of her left hand into the palm to keep herself from throwing her now-empty wineglass against the door-frame, where Chip lounges. He finally peels himself away from the door and leaves without comment. Kit turns back to roll her eyes, and it's only the presence of Darius the outsider that keeps Katya from flying across the room and slapping her impudent little face.

Katya hasn't even sat down, smoothed her hair, or regained her composure when her husband comes in, clicking his cell phone closed as he goes. "Oh, I just told the kids to get their stuff. We need to get back to the hotel."

"Why." She throws the word like a dagger. Charles doesn't even flinch.

"I need to upload some files to Tara, and we need the Wi-Fi connection at the hotel."

Mira files in quietly behind Charles, followed by Max. Despite her earlier outburst, she looks serene, floating into the room, in sharp relief to the homicidal rage Katya feels roiling in her own gut. She swallows down a primal scream. "I'm staying here."

Charles finally looks directly at her for the first time all night. He says nothing, merely raising his eyebrows slightly.

"You take the kids to the hotel, but I feel like staying with my family now. We've just had quite an announcement here, which you've missed all this time on the phone. Irina has gotten married to Darius, here. He's a sales manager at a BMW dealership, and he's studying for his MBA."

"Congratulations," Charles said, but he hasn't looked at his sister-in-law and her groom. He turns the phone over in his large hand. "How am I going to get any work done around the kids?"

Tend to them yourself for the first time in your life, you lousy selfish motherfucker.

"Give Chip his Game Boy battery, and they'll leave you alone. It's not rocket science, as you've mentioned to me more than once."

This finally provokes a reaction in Charles. He had turned away, but he looks back at her through lowered eyelids. Katya is sure that only she notices the tiny lift on one side of his lips, a sneer meant for her eyes only. "Fine. I'll bring your bag in from the car."

He strides out to the car, and behind him in a blur are the children, spitting out, "Bye Mom," as they run past, giddy to be getting out of their grandmother's house. Katya knows without her there, they will empty the minibar of all the twelve-dollar cashews and five-dollar cans of pop, and probably order room service, since Charles won't notice once he boots up his laptop.

Katya knows that a better mother would care about this, and further, would do something about it.

Charles opens the back door and deposits Katya's Louis Vuitton bag next to the couch where Darius sits with Irina. Only his arm actually makes it through the door, just enough distance to drop her bag and disappear outside again.

The grinding of gravel under the Escalade's tires is the only good-bye she gets.

An hour later, Katya sucks down more wine in a lawn chair on the back lawn, which overlooks the harbor. With Charles and the kids absent, and the fuzzy warmth of wine wrapped around her, she feels liquid in the chair. Virtually mellow.

She holds the goblet of Pinot Grigio up and peers through it at the sailboats. They look wavery and yellowed. The sun has fallen below the buildings across the harbor, leaving behind a vapor trail of bright orange clouds and a halo of pink that brushes everything with a pastel glow. A mosquito lands on her linen pants and stabs through to suck at her. *What's one more parasite,* Katya thinks. *Go ahead, suck me dry along with everyone else.* The reflexive shame kicks in at thinking of her family this way.

So Charles is imperious and high-handed. She knew that when she married him; in fact, she considered it one of his charms.

Katya tips her head back in her chair and closes her eyes to the dusk, remembering when she met Charles at a fraternity party. She'd just rushed Gamma Phi Beta. In those days, the girls took to calling her Kitty Z. He never was physically imposing; it was his personality that made people abandon their own wills to him. He had his hair rakishly long and wore neatly ironed shirts in a sea of frat boys with their T-shirts with vulgar slogans. There was a guy at the Sigma Nu house causing trouble, the loudest lout of the bunch, who was groping the wrong girls too often. The girls stayed away from him in ever-wider orbit, but he never got the hint — more likely, didn't care — and he was nearly chasing them around the room in the space of an hour. Katya herself had been tit-squeezed near the keg.

The other frat guys had been cracking their knuckles and exchanging glances, but thus far no one had done a thing about it. Perhaps it was the lovely furnishings in the room that no one wanted to bust up, maybe they were waiting to build up their liquid courage, or maybe the knuckle-cracking was just a show, and they never intended to do a thing about it. They were probably cheering him on, silently.

Charles, who as far as Katya knew was not attached to any one particular girl at that party and thus had no real stake in anything, suddenly slapped his arm around that guy and started talking to him loudly and forcefully, like a tourist in a foreign country wanting to be understood. Katya couldn't hear what he was saying from the kitchen, where she was hiding out with her sloe gin fizz. But she could see the man's face turn red, then pale, then he was out the door and down the steps and into a cab. It was either a stroke of incredible luck, or Charles had thought ahead long enough to call him a taxi, whether to see him home safely or just make sure he wouldn't stumble back in, was anyone's guess. As the door closed behind the drunken loser, applause erupted around Charles, who smiled in a satisfied, feline way. Katya wouldn't formally meet him for another two weeks, but right then she was awestruck by the force of his personality.

She watched him through their courtship build his reputation on campus and in the fraternity as a smart young man with a future in power. She watched him maneuver his way into the best internships by befriending the professors with the best connections. She witnessed that same finagling into a job, and by the time they were married, stood in awe of his wooing venture capitalists to start his firm, wooing them again to start her design business, then that relentless push forward led him to take his company public at a tidy profit.

Barring some unimaginable disaster, they will retire in comfort with all their children's college educations paid for in full. Which is exactly what Katya wanted, along with the beautiful home, two new cars, and happy, conventional stability.

So, who is she to complain?

"Aren't you cold?" Irina has appeared next to her and settles into the lawn chair at her side. "It's pretty out here."

Katya looks over. She's wearing one of Darius's suit jackets; it's tremendous on her. She also looks about twelve years old.

"Congratulations," says Katya, trying to screen for bitterness, but feeling impaired in that goal by all the wine.

"Thanks. I didn't mean to upset Mom like that."

"What did you think she would do?"

"She normally rolls with things. Ivan freaking out, sure. But I didn't expect that from Mom."

"Wait 'til you have kids someday. You'll understand."

Irina shifts in her chair. "I guess. Anyway, I apologized. Seems like something's wrong, though."

"You heard her. She's just emotional because of tomorrow. Thirty-five years married, wow."

"Yeah. Wow."

"Aren't you happy? You're a newlywed." Katya studies Irina and detects not an ounce of marital glow.

"I am, I'm just overwhelmed is all. Tired by the flight."

"Where are you going to live?"

"Darius has a condo in Bloomfield Hills."

"He seems very nice." Katya can't help herself, and says, "But he's so much older than you are."

Irina sinks lower in the chair and pulls the jacket tighter. "And?"

"Isn't that a problem?"

"It's my business if it is, and no, it's not," she snaps. Katya could have anticipated her answer. Always on the defensive.

"Does he have other kids?"

"Oh, why? Because a black guy has to have three other baby-mamas in the 'hood?"

"I don't even know what you just said. A guy doesn't usually get to be forty years old or whatever without an ex-wife and kids behind him in the dust."

"Go to hell, Kat."

"So I'm right?"

"He has an ex-wife. No kids, by her or anyone else. Happy?"

"If you say so." Katya sips again. The sky is bluing above her, the pink fading away. It is getting chilly, and Katya is relieved, because that means maybe the weather predictions are wrong, and the storms predicted for tomorrow night will miss Charlevoix. Though she'd just checked her phone before coming outside, and the forecast hadn't changed, Katya reaches into her pocket to look again. But she must have left the phone in the kitchen.

The boats are coming in from Lake Charlevoix to one side, Lake Michigan from the other, gathering in Round Lake, a man-made harbor between the two. They're tying up at docks, mooring out in the water if the boat's draft is too deep. Charles wants a boat, says he'd name it *Katya,* or *Kitty Z,* if she'd prefer.

"How did you meet?" If Irina is going to remain sitting, Katya might as well get her out of sulking.

"At the dealership."

"You bought a BMW? Never pegged you for the type."

"Har de har. No, I was applying for a job as a receptionist."

"Did you get the job?"

"Actually, I never even took an application. Darius came out to help me, and I left him my phone number. Forgot all about the job until I got home."

"He is a handsome man."

"That he is."

"He looks a little like Denzel Washington, doesn't he?"

"I guess."

"Or maybe a young Sidney Poitier."

"Yes, I get it, Kat. You think black men are handsome. Fine."

"What is up with you? I'm not prejudiced against your boyfriend. Husband. Nobody is, it's all in your head."

"So stop trying to prove it to me. And anyway, you certainly asked him lots of questions about his job, didn't you?"

"I do that with everybody. It's just interesting to know what people do."

"Hmmph."

Katya and Irina both turn at the sound of shoes gliding over grass. It's Ivan, carrying a bottle of beer limply between his fingers, hanging his head. As he reaches them, he looks around briefly for a spare lawn chair, then plops down on the grass, folding his spidery limbs.

"Hi, girls," he says, head curved down toward his lap. "Where's your husband?"

Irina pulls Darius's jacket tighter around her. "Studying. He's taking a class over the summer to finish his MBA faster."

Katya notices Van's shoulders slump and decides to needle him. "So you can relax, Bubba. The big scary black man has gone."

Irina whips her head around. "Shut up, Kat! Jesus."

"I'm just teasing. Relax already."

"Oh, you're one to talk about that," Irina spits back. "Did you check the weather again in the last thirty seconds? How about your voice mail?"

Katya scowls at Irina. So she's keeping tabs on things, so what? "I have a business to run, thank you very much. That means I have responsibilities, unlike some people."

"I have responsibilities!" Irina wheels around in her lawn chair so fast it leans to one side, and Van sticks out his arm in case she falls. "You don't know everything about me."

Katya bites back a retort. She wants to ask, what responsibilities? Are you raising three kids? Running your own business? Keeping a house? She didn't even know if Irina was working anywhere, if she was, it was yet another punch-clock job involving a counter and hairnets, or maybe rudimentary typing skills.

Irina sits back in her chair, sinking lower and scowling at the beautiful harbor.

"Can I get you a drink, Reenie?" offers Van, taking a pull from his beer.

"No," she barks.

Irina never wants anything when she pouts. Katya is as sure as her name is Mrs. Peterson that Irina wants a drink, for the same reason Katya herself is enjoying her wine. A little booze files off the rough edges. Already her annoyance is falling away.

A gull caws in the distance, and Van startles at the sound of the Beaver Island ferry blowing its horn for the bridge.

Van says, "Barbara dumped me."

"We know," responds Katya, then regrets sounding so hard. She really is too tough on her brother. "Sorry."

"What happened?" asks Irina, most likely by rote. She fiddles with the buttons on

Darius's jacket sleeve. They've been down this road many times before.

"I dunno," he says, pulling on his ear with his non–beer hand. "She said she needed space. I think she wants enough space for another guy. I would have given her that. I wasn't trying to marry her or anything."

Katya slides her eyes over to Irina, who smirks at her behind Darius's sleeve. They've heard that tune before, too. Van falls early and hard, and never, ever wants to share.

Katya finishes her wine and decides to go inside. It's getting cold out, and too dark to see her siblings. She has a big day tomorrow, having to get her mother up and around first thing in the morning for a hairdo, and maybe a pedicure if she can talk her into it. She'll have to get on the phone to confirm with the florists, the caterer, have to get over to the inn to supervise the setup. As she stands up, she has a sudden thought.

"G'night, guys. Reenie, let me ask you, do you love him?"

" 'Course I do. I married him."

"Just asking."

Katya walks back to the house, casting a glance over her shoulder, half-expecting Irina to be sticking out her tongue, making a *nyah nyah* face.

CHAPTER 12
IVAN

Ivan rests back on his childhood twin bed and checks his cell-phone voice mail. Three messages, all from Jenny.

One: "This is an EX PARROT!" into the phone in a perfect Brit accent.

Two: "Not much of a cheese shop then, is it?" in the accent again.

Three: "You bloody well better call me back, you lousy wanker," her accent finally breaking up over "wanker." She recovered after her giggles and said in her usual Midwestern voice, "Just wondering how your drive was, and I had a funny story to tell you about my class today. *Au revoir, mon frère.*"

Ivan smiles at her Monty Python references but can't summon the energy to call her back. Anyway, it's late. Though he knows she'll be awake on Friday, reading or watching an old movie.

Much as he likes hearing Jenny's voice, he

was hoping for Barbara. Ivan has been somehow thinking by shutting his cell phone off he would get messages, like a variation of Murphy's Law. *The call you are waiting for will not come in if your phone is on.* But he knows by now you can't fool Murphy's Law. Doing something specifically to tempt Murphy means you will get the exact opposite result.

Ivan thinks of writing a song called "Tempting Murphy."

He hears a low voice through the wall, apparently Darius. Irina and her groom ended up in the guest room just behind Ivan's room, since Irina still has a twin bed in her old childhood room. No one was expecting an extra guest, so Max had to put sheets on the bed at the last minute, before retreating back to his office in the tower.

Ivan just hoped they wouldn't start having sex right next to him, or he might fling himself out of the spire. He never expected to be the last one to find a mate. He has eleven years on Irina, and as ill-fated as this quickie marriage might be, at least she has somebody.

And Katya, with those three beautiful children in her fantastic brick house and a husband who provides her with every comfort. She fairly glows with self-satisfaction, and it's almost too much for Ivan to stomach. He is happy for her, though. Academically, anyway. In theory.

A soft knock at the door tells Ivan his mother is out there. He walks to the door and opens it up. Mira is in a terry bathrobe over a nightgown, and without all her sparkly jewelry she suddenly looks like anyone's grandmother. Ivan turns away from her sudden age as she follows in.

"You have everything you need?"

"Sure," he says, answering only in reference to towels and soap and such.

"You want to talk about Barbara?"

"Not much to say. Ivan the Terrible strikes again."

Mira laughs, a sound like a short burst of jingle bells. "Oh, honey."

Ivan flops himself down on the bed, facing Mira again. "What is with these women? Don't they want a guy who's dedicated, who listens to them and wants to be there for them?"

"Sometimes I think you were born too late, like your soul was meant for the turn of the previous century."

Mira crosses the room to him and rumples his hair, just like she used to when he was a little boy and only as high as her waist. "The right girl will know how wonderful you are.

Just make sure you keep your eyes open."

"Oh, they're open, Mom. Wide open."

Mira hugs him to her chest suddenly, as he sits on the bed, and she stands above him. Her clutch is tight, there's a fervent quality to it that Ivan doesn't understand. And just like that, she straightens up, blows a kiss, and walks out.

Ivan hears her in the next room with Irina and Darius. He rests back on his bed again and follows a crack in the plaster ceiling as it wanders across the room like a river on a map. Mira said the right girl would recognize his wonderfulness. Maybe, but Ivan's tired of waiting for that mythical girl who will appreciate his quirks.

Against his better judgment — Ivan knows he has judgment, he just ignores it routinely — he speed dials Barbara's number on his phone. As predicted, and to his great relief, voice mail picks up.

"Hi, it's me. Look, I'm really going to be lonely at this party tomorrow without you. Maybe you've already made other plans, in fact you probably have, but anyway . . . I was really looking forward to seeing you." The words "I love you" are in Ivan's throat, but he chokes them back down, instead leaving his mother's address, knowing Barbara could enter it in MapQuest and get directions in a matter of seconds if she were so inclined.

First order of business, Van tells himself. Stop saying "I love you" so quickly.

Chapter 13
Irina

"That went all right, I think." Irina peels off her dress and slips a cotton nightgown over her head, sneaking a peek at her belly. Her waist might be a little thicker. Maybe.

"Sure, I guess so." Darius hangs his clothes up in the standing wardrobe.

"Don't worry about Mom. She's just emotional today."

Darius turns to her, his brow puckered and his mouth hard. "Why didn't you tell them about the baby?"

Irina shushes him reflexively, remembering all too well from their youth how well sound carries in the old house. Darius turns away, throwing his shaving kit hard into the suitcase. "You're ashamed of me."

"I am not!" Tears spring into Irina's eyes, surprising her. "I swear I'm not, I'm sorry, I just got scared."

"Scared of what? You said they're hippies, and they won't care the child is biracial, so what's the problem? They were perfectly pleasant to me when they came back to the room and talked to us. I kept waiting for you to tell them about their grandbaby."

Darius has finished hanging his clothes, and he stands still in front of her. Irina sinks down to the edge of the bed, unable to coalesce her emotion into words.

"You're thinking of an abortion."

"No!" she stage-whispers. "Of course not, I wouldn't do that to you."

Darius drops his head and walks with a heavy step to the bed. He sits down, elbows on knees, and puts his head in his hands. "You don't want the baby anymore. You're going to have it, but you don't want to."

"That's not it, I'm just nervous is all. Don't forget I'm only twenty-one. You've wanted this your whole adult life, and I've just started my adult life. I guess I want to get used to being a . . . mom, before I let my whole family in on this. I have to sort this out in my own head without hearing Katya lecturing me about pacifiers or something."

Darius sits back up, but Irina can see in the furrows of his brow that he's unconvinced. "Yeah, she is a piece of work."

"Sorry she grilled you."

"I'm just glad I had the right answers.

Though I thought about telling her I worked in 'pharmaceutical sales' just to get a rise out of her."

In spite of herself, Irina laughs. "Oh God, don't do that. Katya gets enough rises on her own without any help, really."

"Your dad seems nice."

"Sure, he is. He's just always distracted when writing a new book."

"What does he write again? Really, tell me."

Irina sighs. She can't remember ever running into a reader of her dad's work, though supposedly they sell very well. Or used to. "He writes thrillers, you know, spies and international intrigue and stuff. His hero is" — she swallows a giggle — "this is so corny, his hero is Dash Hammond. He's got a villainess named Savoir Faire."

"Oh, like Dashiell Hammett. A tribute, maybe."

"Who?"

Darius brightens. "You know, I think I've seen his stuff. I remember picking up a book at an airport once about a Savoir Faire."

"Yep, he's big in airports."

"But I don't think the name was Zielinski."

"It's not. They always thought Max Zielinski sounded too ethnic. His pseudonym is Maxwell Playfair."

Darius laughs. "Of course! Now I remember. Huh. Your dad, the famous writer."

Irina shakes her head, looking at the floor. "Oh, I don't know. Not hardly famous. But he does seem to be good at it." Irina flops back onto the bed. "I wonder if I'll ever find something I'm good at, like Dad. Something I enjoy so much I can't stop doing it."

Irina feels the bedsprings compress as Darius stretches out next to her. His low voice rumbles in her ear. "I can think of one thing that qualifies."

In spite of herself and her faked morning sickness, Irina feels a delicious chill race over her skin, and she turns to him with a smile, eyes closed.

CHAPTER 14
KATYA

Katya tosses herself around on the lumpy twin bed in Irina's old room, where Irina would have been sleeping if not for her surprise new husband. The room was years ago adapted into a studio of sorts for their mother, because its view of the harbor is apparently just the thing for doing yoga or chanting or whatever the hell.

She gives up on sleep again, her head fuzzy with insomnia, repressed rage, and too much Pinot. She flicks on a lamp and flicks open her cell phone. She'd surreptitiously added Tom's phone number to her cell, under an entry called GYNO.

His message for her left at her mother's house was perfectly bland and innocent. He told Mira "it's the craziest thing, I could have sworn that was Kat driving by, though it's been years, so it probably wasn't." And then he left his number and Mira couldn't remember his exact wording that went with it, which is driving Katya insane in the wee hours of Saturday morning when she should be sleeping next to her husband in the hotel.

Did he say, "Please call?" Or "She can call if she wants to" or "I'd love to hear from her"? Her mother has no idea which and doesn't understand why it matters.

It shouldn't matter, Katya reminds herself. He's an old boyfriend and you're married with children and you've been driving by his house. She wonders if that's considered stalking.

Katya walks to the window and looks out over the yard behind the house — just a dark expanse now, the night has gone cloudy — and the lights sprinkled around the harbor at piers and on back porches, and city lights in the park. A necklace of lights along the bridge connects the north and south ends of Charlevoix. She entertains a pleasant memory of making out with Tom in the grass, after the Venetian Festival fireworks, when he was supposed to have walked home, but instead hid out in the daylilies until everyone else went to bed.

Katya refuses to think, allowing her thumb to flip the phone open and hit buttons until a phone is ringing.

A baritone voice thick with sleep mumbles, "Hello"?

Katya snaps the phone shut and throws it on the bed, regarding it like a venomous snake.

Her face grows hot. So many people have Caller ID that his phone probably lit up with KAT'S KRADLE DESIGN OR WORSE, KATYA PETERSON, and he'll put that together with her drive by his house and run to the court for a restraining order.

Unless he would be glad to hear from her, assuming he can look past that whole stalker thing. She conjures him in memory, that athletic, wide-shouldered frame, blond hair that would never lie flat no matter how much he combed it, hazel eyes flecked with gold in the right light. She places her own arm across her chest and imagines his strong arms ringed around her waist on prom night.

Katya's body is seized by wanting, a desperate wanting she hasn't felt since . . . She walks to the door, double-checks the lock, and lowers herself to the futon, where she reaches down to her panties and pretends that she's not pathetic at all.

■ ■ ■ ■

Part 2
Celebration

■ ■ ■ ■

CHAPTER 15
MIRA

I stretch under the covers, rolling from one side to another trying to trick my brain into thinking it's comfortable, wooing sleep. I'm almost in a cocoon with the sheets tangled all around me. Max is moving more tonight in his sleep than he does on a typical day when he writes in front of his computer. He keeps raking his hand over his face. In a slight glow from the hallway night-light, I can see his nose wrinkle up. He may be grinding his teeth.

I'm struck with a sudden vision: Max alone in this bed. Will he still sleep on the left side? Will he move to the middle? Will he remember to change the sheets?

Dr. Graham comes to mind, talking to me with her carefully modulated voice, a smile meant to be reassuring, but not so big as to be inappropriate during a diagnosis of a dread disease. I noticed she was about my age, her silver hair cut short in a fringe just over her icy blue eyes. She'd been sketching a breast, and a tumor, and lymph nodes as she talked. Those eyes followed me, as I rose from my chair and backed out of the room. She held her card out to me, then to Max, when I didn't take it, telling me to come back and talk next week. I was shaking my head, and she stared back at me, the smile gone, her face calm but serious, those eyes holding mine, right out the door.

I've never been a very good patient. I eschewed drugs for my labor before hospitals had birthing pools and whatnot. I rarely take an aspirin, and seldom do I darken my doctor's doorstep. I don't trust medical breakthroughs. One only has to look at a year's worth of headlines to know why.

Then, of course, there was Ivan, that time he was so sick, and I said to the doctor that it doesn't seem right, there's something wrong, and my natural remedies aren't helping like they usually do . . . Maybe that's when they pegged me as a whacko and shut down. In any case, whatever remaining trust I had for industrial medicine fell away when I later had to carry my little boy to the ER, erupting with fever, wanting to scream, *See! I told you!*

Give me Ayurvedic medicine any day, which has stood the test of centuries in

India, whose cures are translated from ancient tongues like Sanskrit. Acupuncture. Meditation.

I watch Max's chest rise and fall and wince with the memory of that day: the diagnosis, silent car ride home, what happened when we crossed the threshold into the kitchen, and I finally let him speak to me.

What they don't understand is that I can't control my death, I can only have a small influence over the timing. And really, not much of an influence at that. A drunk driver could plow into me tomorrow and render the whole thing moot. I'm going to die. Anyone can say that because it's true for every last one of us. I don't see why I should have to endure surgery and procedures that will sicken me, sap me, disfigure me, all when the final result is the same.

It's my damn body, and I'll let it go when I please.

Who am I arguing with? It's dark, and I'm alone, and after that first morning, Max has assumed a deferential, almost reverent attitude toward me.

I feel something like grief well up in my chest. No matter what happens with the cancer eating my insides, I have lost the joyous simplicity that comes with life stretching up to the horizon, with an undetermined end.

I roll myself out of bed to go find my Sleepytime tea.

The morning sun finds me somehow. Our room faces west, but I sense the lightening of black night to the soft orange of dawn. Last night's anxiety of loss and fear prods at my edges, but I shove it back: not today. Today is our anniversary; thirty-five years of marriage to my Max, and 120 people are coming to celebrate with us.

Can't use my yoga room, Katya is in there on the twin bed, avoiding her husband and probably her children. I wonder if she knows how obvious it is, the distress she's in. I see new lines on her forehead, and her hair is coming out, sandy brown threads on the shoulders of her pressed blouse. I used to rush in with advice and ministrations and fussing over her. When the boys were little and she didn't stop their sassy mouths right then, and she was so brittle with stress I thought she'd break in two, I tried to help her see how a little discipline would bring some peace, at least in the long run. I may have hippie credentials, but being at peace with the universe doesn't mean allowing children to treat their parents as galley slaves. But then, an icy wall sprang up between us. Now I know better than to try.

A mother feels pulled like taffy between the impulse to protect, coddle, and intervene, and the higher plane of knowledge that one's children must experience some failure in order to grow. And then they get old enough to ignore you with conviction, and it all becomes pointless.

But then, it's all pointless, isn't it? I throw back the covers and swing my feet down to my wood floor, searching the floorboards with my toes for my fuzzy leopard-print slippers. I get off the bed slowly, partly because I'm stiff with nighttime, and partly not to wake Max. I peek behind the window shade to the harbor outside. The sun sparkles in the windows of the fancy condos across the water, and some fishermen are revving up their boats already, probably trying to beat the tourists and the Jet Skis out to the deep, still water of Lake Michigan. I try to slide the window open gently, but it comes open herky-jerky and loud.

Max doesn't stir, and for a moment I stare at his chest to make sure it's rising and falling. How would that be for irony, if he dropped dead first? But no, he's breathing.

The window's only open a few inches. I feel the heat already streaming in through the screen, rushing inside my old house, which was wearing the cool of night like a cotton nightgown. I push the window back down, knowing that when the sun gets high, it will steam up in here. Still, I'm not tearing apart my plaster walls to run ugly ductwork for central air.

My neighbor Patty says that's only because I haven't had her killer hot flashes. I credit all the herbal tea, then Patty calls me a lucky bitch and slaps me on the shoulder.

I peel off my nightgown and pull a sports bra out of my dresser. That's all I'll need for now.

Chapter 16
Ivan

Ivan blinks against the morning light and holds his breath for a moment. He hears no sounds of romance from next door and relaxes. He tries to put out of his mind all the noises he heard last night, how long they carried on, and the fact that it's his baby sister over there.

Ivan pulls on his jeans and doesn't bother with a shirt. Coffee. A desperate need for coffee pulls him up off the bed and out into the quiet house.

Baby sister. Ivan thought he'd be much older before his life compressed so dramatically, but it really does feel like yesterday that tiny newborn Irina dropped into their lives like a penny in a fountain.

Katya was a teenager then, at turns enthralled and resentful, especially when she got stuck babysitting because Mira was teaching a night class, or grading essays and needed some quiet. Ivan was a preteen, just noticing girls.

He remembered only holding her when he was seated on the couch and she was sleeping; otherwise, he was too afraid to drop or break her. By then, Max was old hat at this, and he'd sling her around like a sack of sugar. But Ivan could hardly believe his eyes. Irina didn't even look real, so limp and pliable she was, but the warm lump on his arms filled him with something warm that swelled his chest. He would later call that brotherly love and protectiveness.

Then it seemed his teen years flew by, and he was always busy at guitar lessons, or at his after-school job, and went off to college. His student-teaching year he did live at home, but he was working so hard he barely noticed the passage of time. By then he was well into a long string of disastrous girlfriends, who thought Irina was precious.

As Ivan comes down to the main floor of the house, off the staircase, he realizes that some of those girlfriends probably stuck around longer just to keep smiling at Irina. And she was easy to smile at, with those huge round eyes and that tumble of black hair that was never combed neatly because who had the time to do it?

Ivan is brought up short by the sight of present-day Irina, hair uncombed, in a nightgown, leaning on the kitchen counter, shoulders slumped and her head dropped. He hears something like a gulp and realizes she's sobbing. He runs over to turn her around in a hug and she jumps a foot off the ground, then hits him in the chest.

"Damn it, Van! Don't sneak up on me!"

Her nose is running, her eyelashes are wet with tears, and Van's heart stops for a moment, because he remembers seeing her face like this before. He sets her arm's length so he can peer into her face, thinking of Darius.

"What's the matter?"

"Nothing, I'm fine. Just a little emotional, is all. It's been crazy." Irina shrugs away from him and wipes her tears and snot with the back of her hand.

"Nothing? I come down here to find you sobbing in the kitchen, and you say nothing? What did he do?"

Irina turns away and starts to make coffee, continuing to sniff. "Who?"

"Who? Your husband?"

"Oh, heh. I'm a little spaced, I guess. No, he's fine. Never better. He's sweet as could be."

Irina flips on the coffee, and Van pulls her shoulder until she turns back around. "What's the problem?"

"I . . . I can't tell you. I'm sorry, but you

wouldn't . . . I mean, it's private."

Van fills in the rest of her sentence. *You wouldn't understand.* Because it's about marriage, and God knows Ivan couldn't possibly understand anything connected to a relationship. He reaches past her to grab a coffee mug. "Well, I'm glad it's not your husband because I'd have to punch him, which means I'd end up in the ICU and miss the party."

Irina laughs, and she sounds like Mira, that same tinkly sound, like glassware clinking in a merry toast. "Oh, Van. You're so funny."

"A regular laugh riot. I know my students think so. I mean, I think they're laughing *with* me."

She smiles, and Van relaxes a bit. He decides to write this off as travel exhaustion and "female issues." Doesn't appear to be anything like with that Alex creep last year.

They both fill their mugs and take seats at the kitchen table, a piece of fifties kitsch rescued from a soon-to-be-demolished diner, one of Mira's more whimsical decorating touches in this old Victorian house.

"So," Van begins, as Irina wipes her face again and shakes her mop of hair off her face. "What's it like to be married?"

She gulps hard and shifts in her chair. "I

don't know yet, really. We just got back from Vegas, after all. It just feels like I'm on an extended vacation with a boyfriend."

"How long have you known him?"

"Long enough. Look, don't start in like Katya and grill me. I've had enough of that for the rest of my life."

"Enough of what?" Katya has come down the steps and shuffles across the kitchen, zombie fashion, her voice gravelly with sleep.

"Forget it," Reenie says, sulking into her cup, though no one has said anything insulting to her yet as far as Van can tell. She always used to get angry about what you might do before you'd even done it. About the only thing she planned ahead in her life.

"Where's Mom?" Katya plunks down on a chair, resting her head in a hand, wincing at the coffee. "Lord, Van, you made this strong enough."

"Reenie made it. Mom's off doing yoga somewhere I think, since you were in her usual place."

Katya gets up. "I want to flip the radio on and listen for the weather." She searches the kitchen counters, and Van trades a smirk with Irina.

They all turn at the sound of footsteps on the stairs.

Darius appears, wearing a white T-shirt and baggy flannel pants. Van shivers at the memory of all the romantic noises last night. Darius walks to Irina, takes the back of her head in one massive hand, and bends to kiss her, lingering far too long for a quick "good morning" peck, in Van's estimation. Then he straightens, looks at her cup, and says, "That caffeinated?"

"Yeah," she answers. "What of it?"

He cocks one eyebrow and says, "Go easy on the caffeine. It's not *good for you.*" He nods to Ivan. "Good morning. I have to run out to the car a minute."

Katya flips on the radio and pauses in fiddling with the dial long enough to cast a look back at Van. She cocks one eyebrow and shakes her head.

Van tries to meet Irina's eyes to ask, *What the hell was that,* but he's interrupted in that effort by a shout, and Darius blurs past them, running.

"I'm sorry, Mrs. Zielinski!" he yells, as he trots up the stairs.

Irina and Van turn to peer through the door leading to the back porch. They see their mother, upside down on her yoga mat, in her underwear.

"What's his problem?" grunts Mira, looking back at them from between her legs. She folds herself down to the floor, legs flat, arms straight and upper body curled up toward the ceiling. "You'd think he'd never seen 'downward-facing dog' before."

CHAPTER 17
KATYA

Katya's cell phone blasts hip-hop in her ear, and she would like to ignore it, like she's ignoring the bright morning sun and a bladder so full she feels like a cow in need of milking. It stops and the silence is like a balm on her aching head, but it starts up again right away. *It's getting hot in here, so take off —*

She snatches it up. The clock on it reads "7:58" and the Caller ID says CHARLES. Katya wants to reprogram it to say THE BASTARD.

"What."

"I can't find the kids' toothbrushes."

"Why is that my problem?"

"Where are the toothbrushes, Katya?"

"Don't take that tone with me, I'm not a child. The kids were responsible for their own packing."

"Well, none of them have toothbrushes." The reproach in his voice is unmistakable.

"Well then, you'll have to go out to the toothbrush fields and harvest some new ones!" She snaps her phone closed, then slaps it down on the bed. Cell phones, you just can't satisfactorily slam them, she thinks.

"It's getting hot in here . . ." Katya decides to ask Irina to fix her phone.

"What."

"What's the matter with you today?" Still Charles. Who else?

"It's early, and the first thing I hear from you isn't: Good morning, sweetheart, how did you sleep? Or even a hello, simply a demand to find some toothbrushes that are not my responsibility."

He sighs roughly into the phone, and says in a voice both acidic and sickeningly sweet: "Good morning, sweetheart. How did you sleep? Now, the kids seem to have misplaced their toothbrushes. Do you have a suggestion for me?"

"Oh, I have a suggestion all right . . ."

When she hangs up a few seconds later, she imagines Charles gaping at the phone, surrounded by whining kids. And despite the hangover, and her desperate need to pee, Katya smiles.

She descends the stairs, her body feeling so heavy she leans against one wall the whole way down.

A shower does little to ease Katya's headache, and nothing at all to ease her own sense of embarrassment at being hungover on such an important day. She thought she had only had three glasses of wine, which is not so bad over several hours and dinner, but she must have miscounted. The coffee Irina made looked like used motor oil, so she just dumped it in the sink.

What was up with Darius and getting on her about caffeine? Odd for her to hook up with someone so bossy, but then, he is almost twice her age.

For the getting-ready portion of the day, Katya selects a pair of cropped pants and a silk sleeveless blouse. She blow-dries her hair in front of the oval standing mirror in the corner.

With each pull of the brush, more hair comes away on the bristles, until the whole thing looks like a rodent with a purple handle. Katya tips her head forward toward the mirror and pulls along the side part in her hair, trying to detect thinness. It would be just her luck to inherit Max's baldness gene instead of Mira's lush, thick hair that's gone a gorgeous shade of silver.

Mine will probably go all gray and snarly,

thinks Katya, scowling at her face. She dots on her makeup with practiced precision, picking up different compacts for different areas of her face: lightening for her dark circles, bronzer for her cheeks, cover-up for a blemish or two.

Someone knocks, and Katya says "Come in," because that's what one is supposed to say.

Mira comes in, wearing one of Max's old shirts and apparently nothing else. Katya looks away from her back into the mirror. Just like her mother to run around half-dressed with company in the house, like it's still 1966.

"Oh, I forgot, Irina's next door. Well, I'll just say 'Good morning' to you, then. How did you sleep?"

"Grand." Katya gets out the blush stick and tries to sweep color across the apples of her cheeks. For this, she affects a wide smile that reflects the exact opposite of her emotional state. "Think Darius has recovered from his accidental peep show?"

"He'll live."

Katya pauses in her making up to look at her mother in the mirror. "If you need some proper yoga clothes, I'm happy to take you shopping."

"I don't need some yoga clothes. Underwear works just fine on a warm day. Anyway, the sooner Darius gets to know us, the better. Get those blinders off right away."

"If he sticks around much longer."

"Katya."

"I can't say I'll be shocked if they split up. Can you?" Mira doesn't answer, and Katya knows it's because she's right. Reenie's closest brush with monogamy before getting suddenly married was a six-week boyfriend she heard about named Alex, whom no one ever got to meet.

Katya continues making up: eyeliner, lipliner, powder, and she notices her mother is still standing there. She stops in midpuff with the powder and turns to face Mira. "What?"

"Nothing. Just waiting for you to finish so I can get a proper hug."

Katya puts down her puff, checks her face, and crosses the room. She squeezes her mother's shoulders and goes back to the mirror. "You got any Aleve around here? I'm not feeling well this morning."

"Indeed not," Mira says, calling over her shoulder. "But I can make you some willow-bark tea. Excellent for headaches."

Katya grimaces into the mirror. Bark? No thanks.

CHAPTER 18
IRINA

Irina shoves open the door to find Darius shaking in the corner of the room, curled up, fetal style.

"Are you all right?"

That's when she notices his face, contorted with the effort of holding in laughter. He finally lets loose a guffaw, which turns to chuckles. Irina leans in the doorway and waits for him to collect himself. "You got it together now?"

"I'm sorry, baby. But . . . damn. I may never get over the sight of that ass in the granny panties."

"Hey!" Irina whips a pillow across the room, and Darius ducks into the fetal crouch again. "That's my mom, it's not funny."

"Then why's she hanging out her ass on the porch?"

Irina shakes her head, feeling a headache pressing its way to the front of her head. "I don't know, but don't laugh at her. I hate that."

Darius rubs his hand over his face and breathes deep. "You're right, I'm sorry. I'm not good with embarrassment."

Irina's limbs feel heavy with sudden exhaustion. "You know, I'm feeling pretty tired. I think I'm going to rest for a while."

Darius is at her side in two beats of her pulse. "Are you OK?" His hand hovers over her stomach. She stretches out on the bed.

"Fine, just tired is all. They say that happens in the first trimester."

Darius curls himself down to plant a kiss over her belly button. "Good to know. That means our baby there is doing her thing."

"I'm sorry, I feel like I should entertain you here, in a houseful of my relatives. But I'm just . . ."

"No, it's all right. I can study. Or if I get sick of that, I'll dig up one of your dad's books and read it. There must be one around here somewhere."

"Sure. Just don't expect Tolstoy if you get ahold of a Dash Hammond book."

"Got it." He plants another kiss on her forehead after she burrows under the thin cotton sheet.

Irina turns over to face the window, which opens up to Patty's house to the north. She sees a figure moving behind the house's gossamer curtains as they're tossed around by the wind. The air swirling around the room already feels heavy with summer, though it's not even midmorning.

Irina is not sleepy in the least. Exhausted, physically, but not sleepy. She simply wanted privacy, space to think, something that's become a premium with Darius around.

Thirty-five years her parents have been married, and together over forty years, dating back before Katya's birth. Almost twice the span of her life. Irina can't grasp it, and it makes her heart hammer to think about it. She feels more sure at that moment than she's ever been about anything, that she can't stay with Darius that long. She won't even last five years with him.

Irina remembers her best friend in school, Dawn. Dawn's parents were split up, something she bore pretty well, all things considered. For one thing, it was as common as catching a cold to have divorced parents. So she didn't have to worry about a stigma. But, Dawn was always missing out on something because she was at her dad's house every other weekend. She even missed Irina's sixteenth birthday party — a slumber party, with all the girls giggling on the second-floor sleeping porch — and Irina had told her just to switch weekends or have her dad drive her over.

"No," Dawn had responded solemnly. "Everything goes through the courts. We do exactly what the paper says."

Then there was the drinking. Dawn always was a drinker.

Irina shifts, trying to get comfortable, despite a strange pulling sensation in her side.

I can't do it, she thinks, the silent admission bringing both fear and relief. Fear because of what she's gotten into, relief that she could finally admit what she realized the moment of their kiss at the cheesy Vegas chapel. She hasn't lied to Darius. She won't abort his child. In her own mind the thing inside her is shifting from a cluster of cells to something resembling a person, and she can't just throw it away at this point, even if she's legally allowed to.

He wants the baby. She can see it in the ardent smile on his face when she walks into a room. It's not for her, she knows. It's for the child.

Before that missed period, he was nice enough, but he didn't call consistently, and he canceled plans on her once with almost no notice, and Irina suspected that he was seeing another girl.

She almost didn't tell him about the baby, but her conscience prevailed upon her at the last moment, and she never expected him to start campaigning for marriage. The most she expected was cash toward an abortion.

She still wasn't going to marry him when he started wooing her so actively, with flowers and jewelry, and heartfelt if corny "I love you" cards that made everyone at the office jealous. The breaking point was that night when he formally proposed, on one knee, in front of the entire restaurant. He had the Vegas plane tickets already in his pocket.

No, earlier than that, Irina corrects herself. It really started the previous week, when he told her that he and his first wife had lost a baby, and they just couldn't keep their marriage together after that.

Irina never stood a chance after seeing a single tear skim a laugh line on its way down his face.

She resolves to give him the baby and a divorce. Annulment maybe, if that's possible. He will likely hate her forever for leaving him. But Darius doesn't understand he's not getting a mother for his child and a life companion.

No. He's getting a girl barely out of

adolescence who doesn't know jack shit about anything, and who would never be able to finish the marathon of motherhood. Darius will marry another girl who is smarter and older and wiser, who will raise the baby just like her own, and they will all be happy together. She pats her belly. *Sorry kid, but you'll be better off without me right from the start.*

Irina hears two quick knocks and buries her head. What could Darius want now?

But it's Katya's voice. "Irina? Are you in there? I need some help with my cell phone."

CHAPTER 19
KATYA

Katya stomps through the house, searching for her mother. Her cell phone buzzes — thank God Irina knows about this crap, it's finally just a buzz — and she flips it open, still striding down the hall. "Kat's Cradle Design."

"Kat Peterson? This is Angelica from the caterer. Just confirming your guest list of two hundred twenty people —"

Kat stops in midstride and growls into the phone. "One hundred twenty. Not two hundred twenty."

"Hmm, right here in my notes it says —"

"Well, that's why they have these confirmation calls. We have confirmation for one hundred twenty only."

"What am I going to do with shrimp cocktail for an extra hundred people?"

"Not my problem." Kat snaps the phone shut and bellows through the house. "Mom!

Come on! We're late for your hair appointment!"

Mira shows up, nearly floating out of her study, a goofy smile plastered across her face. If she didn't know better, Kat would think she'd gotten laid.

"Let's go, Mom, those people are waiting for us. Oh God, what's that smell?" Katya sneezes at the scent of something woodsy and musky assaulting her nostrils.

"It's just a little patchouli oil. I think it smells nice."

"Whatever, let's go. Are you wearing that?"

Mira looks down at her raggedy patterned skirt with the hem falling down, Birkenstock sandals, and threadbare white button-up shirt. "What of it?"

"Nothing, I guess it doesn't matter right now."

On the way to the driveway, the cell phone buzzes again. "Kat's Cradle."

"Hi, Mrs. Peterson, we're just confirming delivery of the flowers to . . ." Kat barely listens as she strides ahead, glancing back to make sure Mira hasn't gotten distracted by something. In doing so, she comes down the porch steps and nearly has a head-on collision with Patty, her mother's next-door neighbor.

"Oh!" she gasps, and the voice on the

phone says "What?" at the same time as Patty says, "Holy shit!"

"I'm sorry, I almost crashed into someone. You. I'm sorry I almost crashed into you," she says.

"Oh, Patty McFadyen, my darling!" Mira sings out, skipping down the steps.

The two women launch into an animated discussion on either side of Katya, who can no longer hear what the florist is saying. "Yes, thank you, that's fine," she says, hanging up. She looks longingly at the harbor and imagines flinging her phone into it. Or herself.

Patty climbs into the backseat of Van's VW, which they're borrowing because Charles still has the Escalade at the hotel. Patty shoves papers and files out of her way as she goes. "What are you doing?" Katya asks, more sharply than she means to.

Mira says, just before closing the front passenger door, "Oh, I asked her to come along. No harm in that, right?"

Katya sighs. "Of course not. Let's just go, please."

The car maneuvers slowly through the streets like a ship at sea, trying to avoid the tourists and locals out for their morning walks, or trinket-shopping trips. Banks of petunias line the streets in candy pink, white, and rich purple. Baskets spill over with petunias hanging from business awnings and lightposts. It's the local garden club's contribution to keeping the town motto ringing true: Charlevoix the Beautiful. Nice enough. But surely, a lot of trouble to keep the weeds pulled.

At the Diamonique Salon, Mira immediately embarrasses Katya by refusing to get her hair washed. "I washed it this morning, and it's not gotten dirty in the last hour. Just do something with it to make my daughter happy, so I can get on with my day."

"But ma'am, it's really no trouble . . ."

"Do I look like I haven't bathed? Honestly. My hair is clean, I promise."

The salon girls trade looks over the top of her mother's head, arching their almost nonexistent eyebrows. Katya had chosen the most expensive-sounding salon in Charlevoix, based on the name and their refusal to list prices on their Web site. She didn't want some cut-rate beauty-school ninny working on their hair, and she knew Mira would have just run a brush through it and called it good enough.

"I can vouch that she's a regular bather," pipes up Patty from the waiting area, where she's leafing through *People* magazine. "Her bathroom window faces my kitchen."

The salon girls now titter and shrug. "Whatever you say, ma'am." The taller of the two ushers her mother toward a chair. "And what can we do for you today?"

Mira smiles, but Katya recognizes the tightness in it. She's barely tolerating this experience. "Why don't you and my daughter discuss it? I'm hopeless with hairstyles, as you might have guessed."

Katya steps forward. "It's her thirty-fifth wedding anniversary today, and she'll be wearing an ivory sleeveless dress with a fitted jacket. It's really gorgeous."

The taller girl — Katya sees her name tag, she's Fatima, of all things — taps her comb into her palm. "Hmmm, I'm thinking a chignon would be very nice. Unless you want some of it left loose."

"No," Katya interjects. "I think having it up would be gorgeous."

"Sounds nice." Mira smiles into the mirror at herself, and Katya's just glad she's not complaining. "And how about that pedicure?"

Katya stops rummaging in her purse for her phone to gape. "Well, sure! That sounds great." Katya suddenly feels generous. "Patty? You game for that?"

"If these young gals can stand my gnarly

old feet, I'm game."

Fatima and her partner give each looks of studied passivity. "That will be fine," Fatima says, patting Mira on the shoulder as she pumps with her foot to move her chair up.

Katya accepts the hair wash, and in no time at all, her own rusty brown hair is pulled up into a bun that's designed to look loose and careless, but takes more than a dozen hairpins and enough hair spray to shellac a sailboat. She accepts three phone calls from various vendors associated with the party, two from clients, and one from her middle son, whining about his father making him eat breakfast.

"But *you* never make me eggs! Why do I have to eat eggs? Why aren't you here?"

That last sentence sounds so like her own voice that she almost drops the phone. She casts a glance at Mira in case she can hear both sides of the conversation. The other salon girl keeps pulling Katya's head up straight so she can futz with the locks of hair left loose from the bun.

Katya ignores Taylor's accusatory question. "Your father's in charge, so do what he says. I'll see you at lunchtime at Grandma's house."

She cuts off his next whine by hanging up.

Katya looks sideways over at Mira, who chats with Patty via her reflection in the mirror. Patty has taken up residence in one of the empty salon seats. The two are into high-volume reminiscing about other neighbors, and kids growing up. Patty's white hair is teased up like a cloud of cotton candy over her face, with its sharp little nose and eyes that look tiny until she pulls her glasses up onto her face from their chain around her neck. Then those eyes get huge and always seem to be following you.

In Katya's memory, those two were peas in a pod, their unconventional attitudes sometimes rankling their staid neighborhood with its grand houses and lake views afforded by the well-to-do. Patty was a truck-stop waitress who inherited the house, free and clear, from her late husband. Legend has it they met in the box seats of Tiger Stadium, right behind home plate, when she sneaked down from the bleachers in the fifth inning to get a better view. She got a better view, all right.

"Isn't that right, Katya?" asks Patty now, with that cackly laugh that betrays her age.

"Sure enough," Katya responds, the same way she always does when caught lost in herself. She catches Mira's look, before Fatima firmly puts Mira's face back toward the mirror. Her silvery locks are being wound up and fastened in a complicated array of swirls. Too much hair to be swept all together at once.

Katya knows that if her mother heard Taylor whining through the phone, she'll think of the same incident that came to her own mind.

Why aren't you here, Taylor had said.

Because when Katya was twelve, and Mira was with her father on a research trip to Paris and Nana Zielinski was staying with them, she'd said those very same words.

The phone buzzes, and Katya groans, feeling like Pavlov's dog as her hand snatches it up almost before she registers the noise.

She sends an apologetic look up to the salon girl, who stops spritzing and rolls her eyes.

"Kat Peterson."

"Katya? Is that you?"

This time she does drop the phone, and it crashes against the chair before hitting the tile floor with a loud thwack. She stares in horror, and everyone in the salon can hear a baritone voice saying, "Hello? Katya? Are you there?"

CHAPTER 20
MIRA

"Well, Mrs. Zielinski? What do you think?"

My hair is all wrapped, bound, pulled, and sprayed away behind me. There's a little height at the crown, but really, all I'd need is a pair of wire-rimmed reading glasses and a Peter Pan collar, and I could be anyone's librarian.

A chorus of platitudes zips through my head, like, *Goodness, you really worked hard on that, didn't you?* But, I go instead for the outright lie.

"I love it. Really, thanks so much."

My neck feels like it's full of marbles, it's so stiff. In the mirror, I can see Katya, pacing the sidewalk outside with her phone. I know that's not her husband on the phone, so I can only assume it's Tom, who called the house the other day. Interesting that he has her cell phone number. I know I didn't give it to him.

"It'll be a short wait for your pedicures,

ladies," says this Fatima girl, nudging me out of the chair.

"How short is short?"

"Ummm . . ."

"We got time for a drink down the street?"

"Sure, you do," says Fatima, brightening. Maybe she's hoping we'll never come back.

"Come on, Peppermint Patty." I pull her up by her hands, acting playful, but knowing that these days she really needs the assistance in standing. "I'll buy you a drink."

"It's the morning, isn't it?"

"It's happy hour somewhere."

As we approach the door, I see that Katya has stopped pacing and is staring at me quizzically. I arch an eyebrow right back at her. She murmurs into the phone and stops to look at me.

"I'm taking Patty down the street. They're not ready for the pedicure yet. If you don't want to wait, drive home without us, and we'll walk back."

The sun on the back of my neck feels strange and oppressive, like the hand of a teacher pushing me toward the principal's office. The weight of my hair all yanked up on my head pulls on my scalp. I scratch just above my right ear, and already a lock of hair has come loose. Jiminy Christmas, I can't even touch my own head without messing this up.

I have to slow down my step when I notice Patty has dropped behind me. We swing into a pizza joint, and she walks away from a booth to a table with chairs, which must be easier on her hips. I'm thinking that I hate to see my friend showing her age, and it hits me with a *thunk* to my chest that I may not see her that much longer.

"What's wrong with you?" she asks after we plop down, dispense with small talk, and give the young waiter our order for a draft beer each.

"What do you mean?" I trace the knot in the wooden tabletop with a long, wrinkly finger. The first part of me that's looking like an old crone's.

"What are you not telling me?"

"You can keep a secret, right, Pat?"

She squints those milky blue eyes at me, bunches up her little nose, and says, "You know it."

Now the moment comes. I'm going to speak this aloud to someone outside the family. Our beers arrive, which delays the moment, and I fortify myself with a swig.

I press my voice into a low whisper, because this town is small and ears are everywhere. "Cancer."

"Oh, Lord in heaven, not you, Mirabelle."

"Like it should be someone else?"

"I just mean . . . Shit, it isn't supposed to be fun people that get sick."

"Oh, you're a sweetie." I haven't looked her in the eye yet.

"Well, they'll cut it out, right? Where is it? Not in your brain or something, I hope."

My whisper is even lower, such that I have to repeat myself when Patty squints at me. "Breast cancer."

Damned if she doesn't light up when I say that. "Oh, babe! Hell, I've had three cousins and an aunt get that. They can just cut it right out, or even lop off a tit or two. You'll be right as rain."

I can't answer her. Nor can I look at her. I have another decision to make about how much to tell.

"Mira? Honey?"

That weight rests on my chest again, it's like something pressing down, a vice, pushing, pushing. I put my hand over my heart to remind myself it's still beating. "It's worse than that," I finally choke out.

"No." Patty grabs my hand across the table. "How much worse?"

I put my forehead in my other hand. It's so much harder to say this out loud than it is to smile and ignore it. I'm so right not to have told my children yet. Patty takes this gesture as her answer. "How could that be, in just a year?"

"A year?" I finally pick my head up, and pull my hand back from hers. I need both hands to steady my beer for another drink.

"Since your last mammogram." Realization grows in Patty's face, and her countenance darkens. Her eyebrows droop, and everything about her slumps a little lower. "You hate going to the doctor. Bet you haven't gotten one of those things in years."

As with most best friends, I don't have to speak. She can read my answer in my face, just like she knew already that I was sick though I'm putting on a pretty good act where everyone else is concerned. Though I've known her for more than twenty years, I'm not sure whether she'll be angry, or crying, when I meet her eyes again.

I look up, and I see neither. Her face is soft, expression mild. She's a vision of compassion and openness, ready for whatever comes next.

I put my head down on the table and weep, much to the horror of the college student waiter, who has come by with lunch menus. I don't deserve such friendship.

CHAPTER 21
IVAN

The boards of the dock creak under Ivan's feet as he walks out to its end. As a boy, he used to get a touch of vertigo out there, seeing the sandy lake bottom appear to undulate under the clear, cold water.

The fishing boats normally docked here are already out. It's a perfect day for boating: hot and steamy on land, but out on the water, the lake breeze would be a welcome gift. Mira and Max never owned a boat, though. They were always so busy with their careers that they wouldn't have used one, anyway.

Ivan sits on the edge of the dock, dropping his bare feet into the bracing cold of the lake. He can still remember the summer his feet could first reach the water. He was twelve, and his girlfriend at the time was Kimmie Addison. Well, not so much girlfriend as object of distant affection, Ivan clarifies to himself. So little has changed.

He could write a song called "Distant Affection."

Across the way are the condominiums, which seem to be winking at him with reflected sunlight. Ivan knows he'll never live in a condo, because that's what beautiful people do. Katya has a condo in Florida. Though, "beautiful" strikes him as the wrong word when he remembers Alex and what he did to Irina that day in his fancy condominium.

Van pulls out his phone. He knows there are no more messages because he's had the phone in his pocket all morning, and it vibrates so hard when it rings that it rattles the change in his pocket. Even so, he checks the voice mail. No new messages.

He dials a number so familiar under his fingers it's easier to dial it manually than page through the menus to select it from the programmed list. She picks up after two rings.

"Hi, Van."

"Hey, Jenny. Got your message about the parrots. We're fresh out, I'm afraid."

She heaves a great, dramatic sigh. "Alas. How are you fixed for parakeets?"

Van can't keep up the palaver today, though he appreciates the vicarious buzz he gets from being around someone so impossibly happy all the time. “Not so well on parakeets, either. So anyway, I’m up here at my mom’s for the party tonight.”

“Oh, right. Did Barbara come up with you, or is she driving separate?”

“I have no idea what she’s doing today, but it doesn’t involve me.”

“I thought . . . ? Oh. Sorry.”

“Eh. Ivan the Terrible strikes again.”

“You’re a lot of things, but terrible doesn’t even make the top ten. Say, I’m not busy today. You want me to come keep you company?”

Ivan chews his lip, and buys some time. “What? Sorry, didn’t catch that. Damn cell phone.”

Jenny repeats her question too quickly, and he has to answer before he’s ready. “Sure. That would be nice.”

“Are you sure? I don’t have to, it was just an idea. If you’d rather not . . .”

“Sure I’m sure. Come on up, it’ll be fun. You can meet all these crazy people.”

As Ivan gives directions, he wants to wind back time and not call Jenny. Now he’ll have to deal with all the questioning: Is this Barbara? No? Who’s this? Oh, she’s not your girlfriend? It also means he’ll have to entertain her, so slinking off into a corner won’t be allowed.

At his best, with Jenny, he's witty in his self-deprecation, and he floats along on her borrowed confidence. With his family, he's boiled down to the essential nugget of his pathetic failure. He's not ready for those worlds to collide.

They exchange details about the time of the party and the style of dress required for the occasion. Ivan reports he'll be wearing a sport coat over his shirt and tie, but not a full-on suit.

"Van? I'm really sorry about Barbara."

"Thanks. But let's not talk about her today, OK?"

"You got it."

After they hang up, Van pulls his feet out of the water and sits cross-legged on the rough wood. He remembers he forgot to ask her about Irina, crying in the kitchen. If that's something a woman really is prone to do out of just being "tired."

The boards bounce beneath Van as someone approaches from behind. He turns to see his father, striding along with his hands clasped behind him, peering out over the harbor.

"Good morning, son. How's the speech coming?"

Van bites back a groan. The speech. In his Barbara-wallowing, he'd neglected it.

"Katya should have done this. She's the married one."

"You really want Katya in charge of every single thing? Anyway, you're the lyricist. Maybe you could write us a song and just read the words." His dad could be joking, but he's not laughing. Nor smiling, even. Van squints up at him, taking in anew his dad's gingery hair, going gray in odd threads here and there, his freckly scalp exposed more each time Van comes home. His eyes framed by deep wrinkles; too much squinting, maybe. Too much reading. Van catches himself pulling on his ear, so he takes his hand down and stands up from the dock. There's something else going on. He seems slumped or sad.

Van doesn't know what to ask, exactly, so he says, "You OK?"

"Sure." He smiles, and it seems like his usual one, crinkling his round face into a grin.

Van wonders if he's become hypervigilant of his family's emotions, like his sister monitoring the slightest change in the barometric pressure. He turns his thoughts to the speech he must deliver this evening. All the time that Van's been ruminating, Max has been staring at the water. Van knows the feeling well; one could lose whole chunks of an hour just watching the sunlight dance on the lake.

"Can I ask you something, Dad?"

"Mmmm."

"How did you find Mom?"

Max looks away from the horizon. "Huh? She's at the salon with your sister."

"No, I mean, the first time. When you first met."

"I never told you that story? I found her at the library."

Ivan chuckles. "What, did you look for her under 'D' for Delouvois? No, that's not what I mean. I've heard that story before. How did you *find* her, though? Someone you could stay married to for thirty-five years?"

That something returns again, something like sadness, a slumping. Maybe that's what old age looks like. Maybe you lose the ability to stand as tall as you once did. "Dumb luck." Max reaches up and ruffles Ivan's hair, just like Mira had done the night before. "I know what you're talking about. And my advice to you is: Stop looking so hard."

"You weren't looking when you met Mom?"

"I was only looking for a book."

Chapter 22
Katya

"I'm sorry I dropped the phone." Katya mumbles this, as if any of the tourists going by on the sidewalk can hear her, or care that she's on the phone with an old boyfriend.

"What? I'm sorry, I didn't catch that. We must have a bad connection."

You don't know the half of it, Katya thinks. "I was just apologizing for dropping the phone."

"So, that really was you who called last night? My caller ID said K. PETERSON, so I took a chance that it was you and dialed back."

Katya is distracted by her mother and Patty saying something about pedicures and walking back, and she waves them off, settling onto a wrought-iron bench at the next storefront. *Took a chance it was you . . .* He wanted to hear from her.

She clears her throat, aware the silence on her end has stretched too long. "I, uh, didn't realize it was so late. I was just, I got to talking with my parents, and . . . Anyway, sorry about that. I realized it was so late just at the same time as you picked up, and I ended up hanging up on you. I didn't mean it, but it hardly seemed right to call back and bother you again to explain."

Tom chuckles, and that sound fills Katya with a ticklish warmth. "That's my Katya, always with an explanation. I wish I had a better one, myself, for why I called you to begin with."

Katya grips the arm of the bench to remind herself where she is. She looks down at the platinum band on her left hand, with a three-diamond anniversary ring above it. "Oh?" is the only reply she gives.

"I mean, it must sound pretty strange, for me to be calling you based on a mirage of you driving by my house."

"Oh, I don't know." Her voice feels tight, like her windpipe is closing. She coughs and takes a breath. "Maybe you've just got old times on the brain, you know?"

"Sure, must be. So, how are you? Married? Kids?"

Katya feels a heavy connection again with the real world, the iron bench pressing into her thighs, leaving red imprints of filigree. The hot sun scorches her feet, which are outside the shade of the awning. The tourists flocking by seem louder, more bustling, their shouted conversations reminding her of squawking birds at the zoo.

"Yes, I'm married to a man I met in college. Charles. He's a businessman. I have my own business, too. Kat's Cradle Design; I do graphic design."

"Ah!" Katya can hear the smile in his voice, and she pictures his dimpled chin. "I remember those little cartoons you used to do. You used to draw the cutest little sketches of all our friends."

"And I have three children, now. Chip — that's Charles Jr., — Taylor and my youngest is Katherine, but we call her Kit."

"Sounds like a full life."

"Yes, it's busy all right." Katya wonders if that's what he meant by "full." "And you?"

"I've got a daughter, she'll be thirteen next month."

"Oh, how nice. I'll bet she's excited." Katya digs her fingernails into her thigh, trying to stop herself, but she asks anyway. "And your wife?"

"Not married anymore. Emily lives with my ex in Chicago."

"Oh, so far away." Katya cringes for him. Much as her kids drive her insane, she'd sooner rip off her arm than live in another state.

A silence falls. Something beeps somewhere in Tom's house, like a microwave or oven timer. Katya can't stand conversational silence, it makes her ears ring. "I'm up here celebrating my parents' anniversary. Here in Charlevoix, that is."

"Say hello to the lake for me, and don't forget to trip a fudgie."

Katya laughs. "Trip a fudgie" was their inside joke about the tourists who flock north and buy fudge, along with T-shirts that proclaim Charlevoix as the home of "Boats, Bars, and a Few Weirdos."

"I could do that right now, there's a whole parade stomping by. Though really, I guess I'm a fudgie myself. I live down in Grosse Point."

Tom gasps. "So do I! Say, maybe I really did see you that day. You ever have cause to drive down Oak Tree Lane?"

She shifts uncomfortably on the bench, then stands up so quickly she nearly whacks her head on a hanging planter filled with petunias. "Oh, I don't know, I run the kids so many places. It's possible, I guess."

"You'd think it was fate, or something."

"What brought you downstate, anyway?"

He goes into a small-talk spiel about a

new job and more money luring him away from God's country up north, and Katya sees something ahead of her on the sidewalk that makes her body go into fight-or-flight, complete with sweat and hammering heart. Her hands buzz with adrenaline.

Charles is bearing down on her, forging a path through the fudgies, who part with a mixture of irritation and awe. His mouth is so hard it looks forged from iron. The kids trail behind, hands jammed in their pockets or arms folded. It has clearly not been a good morning.

Though a part of her cries out against it, she snaps the phone shut at his approach. She pushes the button on the side to shut off the ringer.

"Oh. There you are." Charles pulls up in front of her and the kids all jam into a cluster around him. Katya feels the presence of the building behind her, awning above, and this ring of family closing in, and she would like to bellow like a wounded bear and shove Charles with what little strength she has, right in his chest.

"Good morning," she says instead, because that's what one says.

"Your sister told me where to find you. If I'm going to this thing tonight, I have a lot more work to do, so you need to take charge of the kids."

"The kids can take charge of themselves, back at the house, with Aunt Irina and Uncle Van, and Grandpa Max, and plenty of other people who are perfectly capable of *taking charge,* because I'm a little bit busy right now organizing an event."

"So you don't want to deal with them?"

Katya steals a glance behind Charles. Chip is ogling some girls in skimpy shorts passing by on the sidewalk, Taylor is crossing his eyes at his reflection in the store window behind her, but Kit appears to be taking in every word. Her hands jam deep into her pockets, elbows locked straight. Shadows darken her eyes, as she tilts her head down.

"Children are not problems to *deal with,* Charles. They're not a conference call, or a meeting with investors. They are supposed to be important."

"So why don't you want to take them?"

"I didn't say . . . Why do you have to turn things around on me?"

"I had a simple request, for you to take over for me on minding the kids because there's freakin' crisis at work, and I'm trying not to burden you with it, and I'm trying to get it taken care of before the party so I don't have to spend the whole thing on my cell phone having you glare daggers at me all night."

"What crisis?"

"Nothing to worry about, unless you want to keep paying the mortgage."

"Charles . . ."

"It might be nothing, but it might be important, so please, Kat, instead of having a fight right here on the sidewalk in front of every tourist in northern Michigan, just keep track of the kids while I go try to get my ass out of the fire."

Charles doesn't wait for an answer but turns on his heel and strides away, so fast that Katya feels his presence sucked away from her. The kids stand on the sidewalk in that same semicircle, as if he's still there.

Chip and Tay are paying attention now, too. The mention of money snapped them out of their daydreams. "Mom?" Tay's voice cracks a bit, whether from anxiety or puberty Kat can't tell.

Katya comes forward to give them all a quick group hug. It takes them a moment to move close to her, after all, people are watching, and they're too cool for that kind of thing. But they relent for a quick squeeze. "Your dad is stressed out, and you know how he gets. Listen, what should we do now? How about we go get some lunch back at the house?"

They all make a face, and Katya's surge of irritation rises up at their automatic rejection of everything associated with Mirabelle. Then she closes her eyes and wills it back down again. After all, she herself gets sick of wheat-flour pasta and pita bread. "Let's eat out, then. Where would you all like to go?"

"Pizza!" shouts Kit, coming to life, dark circles now gone, her face bright again.

She lets them lead the way down the street. They thread between the fudgies clogging the sidewalk. How like Charles, in a way, that they just forge ahead without an "excuse me" or without even slowing their steps. She almost loses sight of them, but catches Chip's short crew cut shining in the sun and Kit's pink poufy ponytail holder, and she latches onto those cues to pull her toward her children. Yet they are not like Charles at all. His path through the crowd was arrow-straight, and people flowed around him like the river around an upstream steamboat. Katya finds it oddly heartening that the children at least seem aware of other people.

In the dim restaurant, they bump into Mira and Patty, who are just leaving. A lock of Mira's hair has already drooped from her hairdo. Katya resolves not to say anything about it, and instead knows she will pin it back up herself, later. Patty gives her an extralong hug, just like Max had done the night before. Katya pulls away quickly, wanting to sit with the kids, feeling suddenly very attached to them. Mira and Patty announce they're not interested in a pedicure, and instead they're going back home to spend time with Irina and her new husband because Patty is dying to meet the Denzel look-alike, she says, and finally Katya is released from their small talk. Though she does notice an oddly distracted air about her mother, and she smelled beer on her breath, and for heaven's sake, it's not even noon. Honestly.

The kids bicker good-naturedly about pizza toppings, and Katya finally rewinds herself to the moment when Charles mentioned the mortgage. He's always left her out of the business because she wasn't especially interested, and he's never been a forthcoming man on such things. His tales from the office are typically in miniature: which assistant is screwing up, a boorish salesman. He studiously avoids mentioning his own assistant, Tara, which is one more dead leaf on the compost pile of her suspicion about the two of them.

Katya couldn't even say for sure what

Peterson Enterprises did, though it had to do with investing and various esoteric technological advances, on the order of robots who would wash your dishes or brush the cat. Or, rather, the tiny components inside such robots.

Charles continues to bring home more than enough money to pay the mortgage (two mortgages, counting the Key Largo place), or so Katya assumes. Though, truthfully, he's the one who pays the bills through online banking; in fact, Katya doesn't even know the password to the account. She only knows her ATM pin number.

"Mom? Can we get ham and pineapple?"

"Sure, whatever."

"Your hair looks like a football." This is Kit, who already enjoys a nasty feminine pleasure in deriding Katya's looks.

"Glad you think so," she says, choosing to pretend she'd been paid a compliment.

Katya pretends to root in her bag for a compact or a tissue or some such thing, and surreptitiously glances at her cell-phone screen, which shows two voice mails recorded in the last fifteen minutes.

CHAPTER 23
IRINA

In the mirror on the back of the bedroom door, Irina tries to imagine her belly swollen with child. Instead of this sunny yellow dress fluttering smoothly from her bosom to her knees, there would be a huge . . . mass. A growth.

She flops down on the end of the bed. Her bare feet just skim the wood floor. She swings her legs, brushing her toes across the varnished surface, picking up grains of sand that may have been brought in by her own siblings years before, after a trip to Ferry Avenue Beach.

What kind of mother refers to her unborn child as a growth? That's one step shy of tumor. Irina nods; she's right to give this baby over to Darius completely. She's still a child herself and doesn't even own a cat because it's too much responsibility.

Irina hears a knock, and she can tell it's Ivan. The knock is soft, hesitating, as if the knock itself is asking, *Can I come in, if it's not too much trouble? I'm sorry to bother you . . .* Sometimes Irina thinks that Katya got the balls in the family.

"Come in."

Indeed it is Van, wearing khaki slacks with a ballpoint pen smudge on the thigh, and an unbuttoned shirt that looks yellowed from too many bleachings. His tie is loose around his neck. His black hair sticks up spiky, not in the current fashionable way; just because it does that. Irina would like to smooth it down, but she's too comfortable on the bed, and anyway, Van is too tall for her to reach his head.

"Hey, Reenie."

"Hey."

"You look pretty."

Irina smiles down at herself. Big brothers are good for the ego even if they are blinded to flaws like chicken legs and limp, flat hair. "Thanks. What's up? Need me to tie your tie?"

"Nah. I'll figure that out eventually for myself. It's just too damn muggy to get fully dressed yet. Have you seen those clouds? Kat's having a seizure over the weather report."

"What does she care? The party's inside."

"There's a balcony, though, and she

wanted the sunset to backdrop the toast."

"Well, she can pass around a petition against God for making it rain. Jesus."

Any two Zielinski children's favorite pastime is gossiping about the third. Irina has no doubt this includes her when the older two are together.

"What's up? I should finish getting dressed."

"Are you OK?" Van chews his lip and pulls on his earlobe, a habit that's persisted ever since Irina can remember, and from years before her birth, according to family lore. Mira likes to joke that his right earlobe is longer than his left from all the nervous tugging.

"I'm fine. I'm just worn-out from my whirlwind wedding."

Van sits gingerly down next to Irina, as if he's afraid of jostling her too roughly. "Are you really?" He squints at her on the "really," and Irina almost laughs. But she knows he's in earnest. Van always is.

"Yes, really. What's your problem?"

"I'm just worried about Darius. He seems so . . . bossy."

Irina frowns, trying to remember when Darius has even been around Van except for their first meeting. Then she recalls the incident with the coffee and Darius concerned about the caffeine.

"Oh, that. He's just concerned about me. I don't take care of myself very well, you know."

"Seems to me you're doing OK." Now Van folds his arms, and Irina knows what he's thinking about. So unfair; Alex was an aberration.

"Look, I would think you'd be pleased that I have a decent guy who wants to look out for me."

"I just don't like his controlling behavior." His voice drops to a theatrically low register. "Has he ever . . . pushed you? Or anything?"

Irina jumps up. "For fuck's sake! Leave it to Ivan to take one tiny thing and turn into battered-woman syndrome. If this is the way you act around girls, no wonder they freak out and bail on you."

"I'm not going to apologize for worrying about you! Speaking of romantic pasts, you don't exactly have a sparkling record yourself."

"How dare you bring that up!"

"You started it!"

"Oh, very mature. Get the hell out."

"You never did answer my question."

Irina's heart flips over when she hears a low voice say, "Answer what?"

Darius stands in the doorway, his textbook

dangling from his hand, his thumb marking a page. His body is angled forward and taut.

"Nothing," Van says. "Forget it. Minor sibling squabble. You'll get used to it if you hang around here long enough."

Van hurries past Darius, but there's not much room in the doorway, and the effort of squeezing by makes his loose tie fall from his shoulders. He keeps going down the hall.

"*If* I hang around here?" Darius shouts after him. "What is that supposed to mean?"

CHAPTER 24
MIRA

Max's hand presses against the small of my back. He wants to urge me forward, through the double doors into the dining room at the Lighthouse Inn, where 120 of our family and friends await our entrance, to celebrate thirty-five years of marriage.

Through the frosted glass on the doors, I can see the indistinct forms of the guests. The buzz of party chat rises and falls like the humming of a lullaby.

I can't explain my hesitation. I glance at Max, and he's knitted up his eyebrows, probably wondering if I'm having some sort of attack.

"I have to go to the bathroom," I say, and duck away from his hand and into the ladies' room to my left.

I lean against the row of sinks and meet my own eyes in the mirror. I had to wash that ridiculous style out of my hair. All those pins and twists hurt my head, and anyway, when I sneaked off to have a joint before getting dressed, the smell was trapped in my hair, so I needed a shampoo.

Are those age spots in my décolletage? Or maybe they are tiny skin cancers. That's it, let's have a race to see what kills me first. I'd put my money on the melanoma as a long shot. I always had a soft spot for the underdog.

Katya will have a hissy fit about me washing out my hair. I'll offer to reimburse her for what she spent at the salon, and that will shut her up. I have an excuse about the dress, though. I accidentally (on purpose) spilled tea all over the front of it when I was getting ready.

Because after I slid on that ivory-linen frock, so suitable for my age and the occasion — it looked like something they would choose to bury me in. My knees buckled, and I knocked a hand mirror off my dresser trying to grab for something solid.

I can't explain that to Katya, though, so I spilled on it, then found my old wedding dress, which looks pretty nice, even with a yellowed champagne stain near the hem.. Now, I look like me.

Why should I spend one single minute looking like anyone else? Or worse, like a corpse.

Good thing I had that joint. That vague sense of panic I had this morning has retreated to something like a mild itch in my palms, and I can ignore that readily enough. I have extra provisions in my purse, too.

I better get out there before Max recruits one of the girls to come in and see if I've dropped dead.

And yes, he does look relieved as I step out. He extends his elbow toward me. Max is wearing a sensible dark suit, much like he did the day we got married, except without that god-awful ruffled shirt.

I reach up to his head and gently remove his reading glasses from his balding crown. I fold them up and slip them into his inside pocket, patting his jacket over his glasses and his heart. I give him a quick kiss, then a longer one, before I step back so he can open the door.

And, oh, it is lovely.

Dozens of family and friends turn at once to the music struck up by a trio of musicians. The singer — a brunette with dynamite legs — is talking into the mic and probably announcing us or something, but I can't hear her because my ears are stuffed with congratulations and greetings, and I'm gulping in all the happy smiles and delighted waves.

Over all their heads, past the display of photographs spanning four decades of our lives, beyond the bar, is a huge window that spans nearly the whole west side of the room, framing Lake Michigan, which ripples like an emerald swath of silk. A cottony haze has wrapped itself around the sun, turning its painful midday glow into something like candlelight. Sailboats on the horizon make me think of origami cranes, which mean good luck to the Japanese.

Paul made me one of those, on my first day as a teaching assistant at the university. It was on my desk when I first arrived, perched in a nest of wadded Kleenex, and I almost threw it away in my distraction. That was years before he became department chair, but only minutes before the genesis of our friendship.

It's my night with Max, though. It's with Max that I'm celebrating thirty-five years of marriage, forty years of couplehood. So I grab Max's face and mash my lips against him. He's too surprised for a proper pucker, so it feels like I'm attacking him more than kissing, but he wraps me in his arms anyway, while a tender chorus of "aaaaaah" envelops us.

Chapter 25
Katya

Katya turns with everyone else when she hears the singer announce the arrival of Mirabelle and Max Zielinski, "thirty-five years married and still in love like the day they met!" It was a slight derivation from the script Kat had given her, but nothing worth fighting over.

"Shit."

"Oooooh, Mom said a swear." Taylor had appeared at her elbow, already sporting a mustard stain on his collar.

"Sorry, Tay." She pats him on the shoulder — he's getting too tall already to ruffle his hair like she always used to — and watches him head for the appetizers before turning back to her spectacle of a mother. Of course she would wash out that hairstyle for which Kat paid a ludicrous sum. Of course she wouldn't wear that tasteful suit that Katya spent weeks hunting down in just the right size.

No, instead she's got her hair straggling down her back like she hadn't even bothered to comb it, and she's squeezed herself into her old wedding dress, for the love of God. Extra flesh squishes out of the dress at its edges, around the neckline, and armholes. A large stain mars the front of it, presumably a champagne spill never touched in thirty-five years. Mira probably smells of mothballs, unless she doused herself with her hippie oils like she sometimes does. The dress is floor-length, but Kat wouldn't be surprised if her mother was barefoot underneath it. She can't be wearing heels because the hem is dragging on the floor in front.

Why had she expected anything less? Why did Mira ever pretend to go along with her plans in the first place? *Ha! Fooled you, Katya. Made you think your opinion mattered.*

Har de har, Mom. Katya turns away, examining the sky outside. The haze gathered all day, and now it's right down on the ground, wrapping itself around the building, seeping in each time someone opens the balcony door. The Lighthouse Inn's air conditioner hums nonstop, and still the room gets warmer with each new arrival. At the horizon, Katya detects some darker clouds and bites her lip. The weather forecast had changed throughout the day, each time she checked, the chance of storms grew higher, and the last time she looked, while on Charles's computer, instead of a cartoon sun partly obscured by cloud, there was a storm cloud with a yellow lightning bolt.

That's when she saw that odd e-mail from Tara. She sounded desperate to talk to Charles, and something about the language was overly familiar. Too many slang words, maybe. The way she signed it with only her initial, "T."

Once before there was another girl in Charles's life. They were dating, but temporarily broken up. Over what, she could no longer remember. She was stung by how quickly he took up with another woman, but as he coolly pointed out later, she had dumped him. So that wasn't even technically cheating.

Charles touches the small of her back, and the jolt is electric. A bit of her martini sloshes onto her bosom.

"Nervous?" Charles sips an Amstel Light and smiles at someone across the room, handing Kat a handkerchief from his inside pocket without meeting her eyes. Kat recognizes his business face, all smiles and winks and backslapping, his mind all the while calculating the cost-benefit ratio of each conversation.

"No, just lost in thought, I guess. It's a big night." She can't help herself. "I'm surprised you're not on the phone."

"I didn't plan a crisis for this weekend, and no, I'm not on the phone. I shut it off."

Kat turns to him and raises one brow. "Off?"

"Vibrate, anyway. And look, I have voice mail. I promise not to interrupt any conversations by answering my phone. Instead, how about a dance?"

The question flummoxes her so much that she's briefly stymied about what to do with her drink. Charles takes it from her hand, places it on the nearest table — half-occupied by university types from the English Department — and then pulls her with both his hands toward the dance floor.

Kat tries to read his face, unable to remember the last time he'd asked her to dance, and it's been years, even though they usually attend three weddings every summer, and the Peterson Enterprises Christmas party is always a big affair.

Though he has yet to look her in the eye.

When they reach the dance floor, he pulls her close, closer than she feels comfortable in such a crowd. She feels jittery at such a display and takes her hand off his shoulder to tug at her dress in case it's riding up to show that one prominent vein behind her knee. She tries to conjure a view of herself last time she glanced in a mirror.

As Charles guides her across the floor, her eyes gliss across the crowd.

The sight of her mother demands her attention. She's laughing loudly, hanging on to Max's elbow in that ratty old dress. With only a little more wear and tear, she could be that crazy jilted bride from *Great Expectations.* She lifts her hem to show off her shoes: Birkenstock sandals. Not even new ones. Katya had last seen them on the back porch, exposed to the elements.

Chapter 26
Ivan

Ivan frowns into his beer. The music has all the charm of a buzzing mosquito locked in your bedroom at night; someone had the brilliant idea to get the band to play hits from the years around when his parents were married. That someone no doubt was Katya. He can't imagine his parents enjoying "Close to You," à la The Carpenters.

He shouldn't have borrowed his dad's computer to check his e-mail before the party. He saw an e-mail from one of the local girl bands, Murkwood. Maybe Kelli liked the demo he thrust into her hand during a break in their show two weeks ago?

His hope only lasted as long as it took his finger to click the message.

"hey sorry didnt stop to see u after show song good but not r thing, thx 4 comin out"

Then he'd turned in his father's office chair to face the bookshelves, the top row lined with pristine hardback copies of Max's

Dash Hammond thrillers. The oldest ones were faded in the sun, so that their spines grew brighter and more vibrant from left to right. The "reading copies" were the small paperback versions, the kind you would tuck into your pocket or airport carryon. Those were the ones he brought out if a newcomer asked, "Oh, what do you write?" and showed some desperate curiosity about his work. Some of the oldest books were missing in the paperback version, having been given away or loaned out and never returned. They were out of print these days.

For a time, Van had a poster of his hero taped on his apartment wall. Bob Dylan stared down at him every night and every morning, heavy-lidded, cigarette drooping.

Then Van got drunk on whiskey and self-pity one night and ripped it down, and in the blazing light of morning, through his hangover fog, he'd noticed that the paint had faded all around where it was taped, so he'd been left with its imprint. It was like a chalk outline around the corpse of his ambition.

One thing Barbara had said in their last argument was that he had to stop dragging himself to smoky dives every weekend, paying cover charges to cozy up to local bands, then try to talk them into listening to a demo. Van had tried sending his songs to the big music publishers, but he never heard back, and that seemed like the remotest possible path to hearing his music on the radio. So Plan B was to suck up to those local bands who might make it big, like The Verve Pipe did back in the nineties, when everyone went around singing "The Freshmen."

'Course, like The Verve Pipe, most of them wrote their own music. And the rest regarded him as somewhere between desperately annoying and odd enough to be potentially dangerous.

He's had to dry-clean his leather jacket constantly to keep the bar stench out of it.

He slurps down the rest of his beer and gets up from the table with more effort than necessary for someone only thirty-two years old. Barbara is right, he should hang it up. Let his dream dissipate like fog in the dawn.

Though, "Fog in the Dawn" could be a good refrain.

Van meanders out to the balcony. Boats stream in from the big lake, headed through the channel toward the harbor. The partygoers are waving down to the people in the boats, who wave up with boozy smiles and sunburned faces. The boats have clever-pants names like *Sea You Around* and *Retirement Fund.* Van could silently mock them, but the fact that they have boats while he has a mysterious green mold growing in the corners of his apartment takes some of the zing out of the exercise.

At the other end of the balcony, Van spies Irina and Darius. His hand looks huge and spidery on her bare upper arm. He turns toward the lighthouse to suppress the urge to knock that hand away. How can he help but be protective? Especially after that one night.

Van coughs into his fist. The air has thickened through the day, and breathing seems effortful. A trickle of sweat skims down his spine. He wants to go back in before he starts sweating like a linebacker, but the band is probably playing Peter, Paul and Mary or something else ghastly. A sudden wind races down the channel off the lake, shoving the muggy heat into his face.

Before he goes in, Ivan steals a look at Irina and her groom. Darius is pointing out pieces of scenery, his face open and jovial, that hand still on Irina's arm. She's got her head down, so Van can't see her face behind her hair. She's fiddling with her wedding band, fingering it, loosening it, putting it back on. He can picture her flinging it into the channel. In her teen years, heck, even last year, such an extravagant gesture would not be out of character. Irina now looks pensive, weighted down somehow.

Van escapes the balcony, noting that most of the other guests have done so as well. Besides the heat, that wind persists and blows around hair, dresses, cocktail napkins, cigarette smoke.

The band is on a break, and Van murmurs, "Hallelujah."

"I didn't know you'd found Jesus." Van startles, and looks down to see Jenny at his elbow. She reaches up — way up, she has to get up on tippy toes — to give him a hug around the neck. She says, "Hey there! Hope I dressed OK. I don't have much formal wear."

Jenny at school was always wearing cargo pants and plain T-shirts, with Birkenstock sandals; technically in the teacher's dress code, but only just. Off-hours she favors thrift-store Levi's a size or two bigger than she needs and colorful shirts that are either vintage or secondhand, depending if she bought them downtown or at the mission store.

Today she looks a little like an Eastern European refugee. She's got a loose dress in a pattern that makes Van's eyes hurt, all dark purple and green. She's wearing black flip-flops and a purple kerchief over her hair. She wears her gold hoop in her eyebrow, which she has to take out for school. Van doesn't know the rules for face jewelry at anniversary parties, so he doesn't know if it's appropriate. Katya would say no, Mira would say yes.

Jenny beckons him to follow her to the bar, and as she walks away, he notes that the straps on her dress are narrow enough to reveal her tattoo on the back of her shoulder; some symbol she discovered in yoga class.

Van falls a few steps behind Jenny in the crush of people headed toward the bar and snacks, so she doesn't seem to notice someone calling his name. He hears it, though, and turns to the sound, expecting to see a long-lost cousin.

A slim figure in a white dress with a long tumble of auburn waves slices through the crowd, headed straight for him.

It's Barbara.

"Hey!" she calls out, finally reaching his hand and pecking his cheek. "I decided to come after all. Oops!" With a giggle, she uses her thumb to rub his face where she'd just kissed. "Got lipstick on you. Well, aren't you going to say hello?"

Van has forgotten how to speak.

CHAPTER 27
IRINA

Irina studies the sloshing waters of the channel until she begins to feel the balcony is sloshing, and leans into Darius for stability. He's enjoying Charlevoix so much that she feels sick to her stomach because only she knows that he'll probably never come back here. After she abandons him with their child and divorces him . . . or maybe she can get an annulment. Aren't annulments standard operating procedure in Vegas? Then she would still have left a mistake behind, two mistakes, actually. But she wouldn't be a *divorcee.*

Whatever she is, Darius won't be coming back here for Christmas parties and birthdays and family weddings. He'll be no one's son-in-law.

Though, he could bring the baby here, Irina realizes. The baby is still Mira and Max's grandchild, cousin to Katya's kids, Van's niece or nephew.

Her field of vision collapses to a pinprick of jade-colored light where the lake should be, and Irina feels lighter than she's been in weeks.

Then there's shouting, and she feels the scratch of the wooden balcony under her legs, and Darius holding up her torso.

Irina opens her eyes. Darius's face is so close he blots out the sun like the moon in an eclipse.

"Irina! Is the baby OK?"

There's a gasp behind her, probably Katya.

"Oh, shit," Irina says, and closes her eyes again.

Darius insists on carrying her back inside until she screams at him to "put me the fuck down." Her family zoomed to her side like someone lit the Bat Signal, and now they flutter behind her, murmuring and concerned and she wants to beat them all with her shoe.

"I just want a place to sit and a glass of water and for everyone to please shut up!" she cries. The buzz subsides, but only for a moment.

Irina slumps into a corner chair and wraps her hands around a glass of ice water, already wet with condensation. She looks up from the water and sees her family, pressing in on her from all sides. "Everyone go away! Please!"

Katya walks away first, her lips pursed in that prissy disapproval face Irina has seen so often, saying "If you say so." Ivan walks away pulling his ear, trailed by a pretty girl in white and some other chick. Max and other hangers-on follow behind. Darius hovers by the door to the balcony, probably still scared off by the burst of profanity.

Only Mira remains. She's studiously quiet, staring past Irina at the lake beyond, her hands resting lightly on the back of a chair.

"Mom, could you give me a minute?"

Mira doesn't answer. Instead, she sits down at the table, not right next to Irina. There remains one empty chair between them. Mira still hasn't met her eyes. She clears her throat, and asks, "Do you want to talk about it?"

Irina notes her voice seems more husky than usual and that her mother has clasped her hands in a way that seems loose and casual, but her white knuckles reveal the strain.

"No. I'm going to walk back to the house for a while."

"You nearly fainted on the balcony. It's too hot out there for you to be walking alone to the house. Let Darius drive you."

"We both walked. Most of us did, didn't we?"

"Katya drove."

"I'm not getting in a car with her right now."

"And I don't want you to collapse on the sidewalk halfway there. If you thought there was an embarrassing fuss just now, imagine an ambulance ride. Believe me, I know how tired and sick you can be in a pregnancy. And unexpected pregnancies always seem to be the hardest."

Irina cringes, reminded again that her family was not prepared for her. The huge age gap between her and Ivan always made that obvious. Then there was the tremendous distraction of her parents the whole time she was growing up, both so involved in their careers. Max was pumping out books at a frenetic rate, and Mira was president of the faculty association and forever in meetings, if not grading papers or preparing for class. Irina was routinely passed off on the older siblings, or Patty next door. Mira never said "no" to a sleep-over at someone's house. Irina could detect the relief in her voice as she no doubt thought, "Ahh, one less child around."

"Reenie? Let Katya drive you back. I'll make her promise not to hassle you."

"You'd have to staple her lips shut."

"I've got a sewing kit in my purse. Will that do?"

In spite of herself, Irina smirks. She dreads the trip, no matter how short a drive it is, because she doubts Katya will contain herself. Even the way she sits in the car will betray her disappointment. But the big empty house calls to her. The alternative is remaining at the party, the subject of family gossip, multiplied to include cousins and old friends and Uncle Frank and Aunt Petra. A black surprise husband, a secret pregnancy, then a dramatic fainting episode.

You sure outdid yourself this time, girl.

"Fine. I'll take the ride. But you go ask her."

"Deal."

Irina does a double take as her mother gets up from the table. Mira seems to stumble as she stands, and her hands shake.

Chapter 28
Mira

Irina was grinding her teeth when I helped her into the passenger side of Katya's huge truck, and Katya herself pursed her lips so far they'd disappeared.

But Kat promised to chauffeur only, with no commentary, and at least Irina can lie down in a quiet place for a time.

I need a quiet place now, like a drowning person needs air. It's not to be, though, not at my own party.

Darius is at my elbow, watching them drive off. Droplets of sweat have gathered at his temple. He wears the face of a man standing at the gallows.

"Why doesn't she want me with her?"

"Pregnancy does crazy things to your emotions. Try not to take it personally. In fact, that's a good rule for the next year of your life, at least."

"It's more than that." He turns to face Mira, and says forcefully, "It's more than that, for sure."

I reach up and pat Darius's elbow, where he has it crossed tightly in front of his chest. I don't know what he's talking about, but I suspect he's probably right. Despite their short courtship, he probably knows Reenie better than I do anymore. Until the planning for this party, I hadn't gotten a spontaneous call in months, and when I called, she would never answer, instead returning my call from her cell phone in the car, cutting me off when she arrived wherever she was going.

"Darius, I'm sorry about this weekend."

"What for, Mrs. Zielinski?" He's staring off in the direction of the Escalade's path.

"We haven't exactly been welcoming to you. With the party, and the whole family in the house . . ." I trail off, not sure where I'm going with this. But I remember meeting Max's parents for the first time. I felt lost and heavy with the weight of pretended perfection. I was never any good at that. It makes me sweat to recall it even now. "We'll have you to dinner after this weekend, and meet you properly. For what it's worth, you're making a very good first impression."

I'm not even sure he's heard me. After a moment he smiles down at me, but it's a distant expression of a businessman putting on a face for clients. "Thank you, I'd like that. Excuse me."

Back in the air of the Lighthouse Inn, not cool exactly, but less oppressive, Max greets me in the lobby. His glasses are back on his head and his tie has gone all herky-jerky.

"So she is pregnant! I'm shocked!"

"I know."

"We're going to be grandparents again." This is a phrase that should be joyous. It should be followed by an embrace, some enthusiastic whooping, maybe. But Max reaches for my hand and gives me his beseeching look again. I know what he's asking me by staring at me like that, wrinkling up his face. He clutches my hand tighter than I think he knows, like he's trying to squeeze the right answer out of me.

I can't bear it.

"Max . . ." I pull away and dash into the party, and in doing so, come face to shirt buttons with Paul.

"Congratulations!" he says, and reaches down to peck my cheek.

Oh, I want to tell him. I want to tell him why this is no time for joy. But I can't, here. Not now, and not with Max, who I can tell is staring at me through the door to the ballroom. I have no doubt that he knows, even through that wavery glass on the door, that I'm speaking to Paul.

So I say, "Thank you. It's a surprise, but wonderful, anyway."

"I was talking about thirty-five years married to the same man, actually. But yes, congrats on the grandchild as well."

I just nod. To avoid looking Paul right in the eye, I look past him to take in the party. The room has dimmed as the sun has settled toward the lake and become obscured by some darker clouds that are pushing in from the horizon. These clouds are not the wispy dollops of this morning, nor the smooth grayness of the afternoon. No, these new clouds are roiling and heavy. Could be a soggy dash home.

"Mira? Are you all right?"

"Those clouds look bad."

"That expression on your face has nothing to do with weather." He places his hand on my elbow. Certain people can touch you in a way that's the very soul of innocence — a pat on the shoulder, a simple handshake, maybe — and it will still send a guilty twang right through your gut.

I step slightly to the left, away from his arm. He looks for a second at his hand, like he's wondering what's wrong with it, then places it in his hip pocket.

I still haven't answered, so he tries again.

"This isn't such bad news, is it? Irina has never done things the conventional way. And you and Max didn't wait to have kids."

My mother told me once that I should never cry in public. It's vulgar, she said. She felt the same way about loud laughter, angry words, and hiccups. Belches and farts didn't exist as far as she would admit.

So it was from her that I learned this trick: to stop oneself from crying, look up with your eyes. It's physiologically impossible to cry when looking skyward. Also impossible to cry when swallowing something, so taking a drink will work, too.

Since I don't have a drink right now, I look up.

"No, of course that's not it, Paul. I just can't talk about it."

He steps closer and lowers his voice. "Is it Max?"

He means, is there trouble with Max? Have we been fighting? Yes, and if he only knew why. And it's not just Max, it's the kids, and now this grandchild on the way. It's all of them, Dr. Graham, and probably Paul, too, when he knows. It's all of them, wanting me to do something I can't do.

To take up arms against a sea of troubles, as Shakespeare wrote. Except he was referring to Hamlet, who wanted to put himself out of his misery. Someone else finished him off several scenes later. Lucky bastard.

"No, it's not Max. It's just . . . I'm emotional, change of life shit."

Paul has known me for more than the thirty-five years I've been married. And, in the spirit of Hemingway, he has a shock-proof bullshit detector. So he only says, "We'll talk later, when you feel you can. Can I get you a drink?" But then he looks up, and says, "Oh, here's Max."

"I'll get you a drink, honey, what would you like?" Max wraps his arm around my waist, and pulls me close, the way he might if a car drove by too close as we walked on the side of the road.

"I'll see you two later. Congratulations, Max." Paul nods and strides away. It's only when Max relaxes his arm a little that I realize he was even tense.

"Well?" Max follows Paul with his gaze for a moment before turning to face me fully. "I don't know about you, but I need a drink."

"Sure, babe. See if they've got a Pinot Noir. Otherwise Shiraz. Something red."

Max kisses my cheek and is absorbed into the crowd on the dance floor.

More well-wishers and friends throng around me, faculty friends and parents of my kids' friends, who remained close to me even when the kids moved away and grew up. I suppose my face is probably animated and happy, as my shock is receding, and the tension in my hands unwinding. At least I don't seem to be in danger of crushing the goblet when Max hands me my wine. He stays with me for a few minutes but as the chatter turns to university shop talk, he fades away again.

All this happens on my surface level, but in my own head I'm reviewing my life as Paul's friend, though "friend" is far too simple a word.

We met the day he put that origami crane on my desk. He was a new professor already, having been some kind of grade-school wunderkind. He was my age, but leaps and bounds ahead of me professionally, which turned out to be lucky for me, later.

I had just met Max and was dating him whenever he pulled his head out of his manuscripts, which at the time were earnest stories about young blue-collar kids coming to terms with things. But between Max's job ringing up groceries, his studies, and his writing, I didn't get to see him much. So it was not unusual that on a sunny autumn Thursday, when I had finished my graduate assistant office hours and talked one panicky freshman out of jumping off the clock tower over the grade on his composition, that I had nothing else to do. So of course I said, yes, I'd love to join you for a coffee.

Coffee somehow became a beer or three, at a bar whose name is lost in my memory now, but it had outside seating along the sidewalk. Fabulous for people-watching, and avoiding the eyes of your companion. I found myself doing that quite a lot with Paul.

His hair was a deep, shiny black then, and he had a moustache and sideburns. His eyes were startlingly pale in contrast to his hair, the pastel blue of marbles and Easter eggs. He kept his eyes locked on me in a way I found unnerving, and I hoped Max wouldn't happen by.

I repeatedly assured myself this was only a drink with a colleague. Max did the same from time to time. Perfectly innocent.

Over the years, I came to understand the phrase "perfectly innocent" only applied when the situation was anything but.

That day, with the hot smell of burning leaves in the bright clear air, Paul reached across the table and took my hand. It startled me so much I froze and let my hand lie in his like an artificial limb.

"You're lovely, you know," he said.

I think I gasped, but I can't remember exactly. I reacted with surprise in some physical way before I took my hand back. "I am seeing someone."

Paul simply said, "So? You're still lovely."

To this day, I'm amazed at his composure, after I'd just rejected his bold advance. It was like he was juggling plates, and one of them had just been shot out of the air and he carried on, never losing eye contact with the adoring crowds.

I spent the next several days in the fog of indecision. Max was so affectionate and sweet when I could get time with him. It was easy to laugh with him, easy to cuddle up with him, simply easy to be in his uncomplicated presence.

Paul was something else. I couldn't relax for the maelstrom that brewed whenever he came near. It was a soup of lust and anxiety and Max-provoked guilt plus attraction, but I couldn't sort out whether that attraction was only physical or, perhaps there was something else there . . . Not that I was so hung up on rules and restrictions, but I didn't want to hurt Max, especially for the sake of a simple rutting. If I were to leave wreckage in my wake, I at least wanted to have gotten something worthwhile out of it.

Then I saw Paul with his arm around

another woman at a birthday party, and saw him kiss her neck. I tasted the relief of a decision that had been made for me, tinged with a sinking disappointment that I never had the chance to feel his lips on my neck.

Around this time, Max finished his screed and came out of his torpor, and that's when I started leaving a spare toothbrush in his apartment.

Paul and I remain friends to this day, very good friends in fact, but there is an unanswered question between us that only seems to grow more prominent with time. I have been hoping that with his retirement from the university and my constant proximity, that question would at last recede.

I drift away from the current cluster of party guests to find out if Katya has returned from dropping off Irina at the house.

It seems to me that growing older means a growing collection of paths not taken. More and more "what-ifs" left behind.

As the band strikes up another tune, oh Lord, it's "All Along the Watchtower" done by a wretched wedding band, I'm waylaid by the last person I want to see short of Dick Cheney.

It's Roxanne, the new department head, who happens to be half my age and in her mind, twice as smart.

"Professor Zielinski!" she calls out, striding toward me. Her hair is swept up in a bun and she's wearing glasses with dark, severe frames. She's got a baby face, and I can tell the hairdo and glasses are her attempt to appear managerial and authoritative. Maybe someday she'll learn that authority is intrinsic, not a costume you put on in the wings. Her use of my title is irksome. It's unnecessary, and patronizing, going out of her way to pay me respect, which implies that I don't automatically get her respect. She has to make such a display of it.

Oh hell. I miss my hippie days when I was going to antiwar protests in bare feet and long skirts that got muddy along the hem. Who gave a shit about office politics then? There was only one kind of politics that mattered. At least to me.

"Hi, Dr. Sutton," I answer.

"Lovely party," she says, and I loathe speaking to her now. I want to smack that pink drink right out of her hand and tell her to get the hell out of my party. If she doesn't want me on the faculty anymore, I sure as hell don't want her in my face on the weekend.

"I haven't read that memo yet, but I will," I say, getting it over with because I'm sure she'll find some subtle way to bring it up, as she has every time we've run across each other in the last weeks.

"Oh, this is a party! No need for talk about that," she says, turning her gaze to the collage of family photos along one wall, assembled in a frantic weekend by Katya, who raided my shoe boxes full of old photos. "Though, it would be nice to spend more time doing fun stuff like that." She gestures with her glass toward the pictures. Just like her to use my memories against me.

I should have told Katya not to invite her. To hell with what she thinks. But she insisted. To be polite. For appearance's sake.

"Oh, we'll see. I still like teaching, you know."

"Even though the kids send text messages under their desks? You mean all that doesn't get to you after a while?"

"In my class, that doesn't last longer than the first day. My grades are tough enough that the slackers drop it fast, and only the interested and dedicated students remain."

"Indeed." Roxanne smooths a lock of hair back into her bun. "Your classes are so small, really. That's why it's so problematic for the budget."

"The budget is not my problem. My problem is quality education." This is why

Paul was such a savior for me, because I could mouth off to him, and he would let it slide. He was a buffer between my surly remarks and the administration, the only thing standing between me and forced early retirement.

"It's everyone's problem, Mira. The state is cutting our funding to balance the budget, and we've got to cut costs. The faculty contract isn't up for a few years yet, so we're stuck with that. We've got to shuffle around courses to make the most efficient use of staff. You might be expected to carry a bigger load this fall, and we need some help teaching freshman comp."

She's going to torture me with freshmen until I leave.

"Oh, listen to me! And I said I wouldn't talk about this at your party. I'm sorry, Mira. Look, just read the memo, I think you'll see the deal is fair. And is retirement so bad? I mean, you'll have a new grandchild to spoil!" She throws me a smile and gives me a fingertip wave before gliding back into the throng. How did everyone hear about the grandbaby so fast? Gossip sure flies at a party, especially with booze to grease the wheels.

I've already read the memo, actually, to make sure the retirement deal includes some kind of health coverage, which it thankfully does. But if I take it, what will I do with my time, while I wait around for my body to rot from the inside out?

I check my purse for that joint, as a surging anxiety builds in my chest. Nothing doing, because here comes Max, smiling with arms outstretched.

Chapter 29
Katya

Clambering inside the Escalade is like climbing into a preheated oven. Katya cranks the ignition and turns on the air-conditioning full blast, though at first only hot air belches out of the vents.

Irina winces away from the hot air as she snaps on her seat belt. Katya sees her so differently, now. She sneaks glances at her baby sister's waist to look for signs of a pregnant pooch. Irina's listlessness and lack of appetite make more sense.

Though her shotgun wedding still seems ridiculous because who, in 2007, would be holding the shotgun?

"Are you OK?" she asks, solely out of sisterly concern.

"Shut up."

Kat clenches her jaw to keep from spewing out any number of profanity-laden retorts. Irina has always been this way with her, angry before Kat even has a chance to articulate her own emotions. Convicted before she even commits the crime, half the time she goes ahead and says whatever it is Irina is angry at her about, because well, why not?

Just get through the party, she tells herself. Get through the weekend, send her some baby clothes, and stay out of it.

Katya taps her steering wheel, peering up and down Bridge Street, trying to find a gap in traffic, when a deafening clang starts up. Katya consults her watch. It's exactly on the half hour, which means the bridge is going up. Traffic has already begun to stack up behind the crossing arms as they come down, pedestrians hustling off the sidewalk, tourists lining the channel to watch the sailboats make their stately way from the big lake into the harbor.

She doesn't have to cross the bridge to get back to the house, so in theory, the bridge shouldn't affect her. Trouble is, a pack of jackasses has neglected to leave a space for her to get out of the parking lot.

"Look at these idiots. They're blocking the driveway, so now I have to sit and wait for the goddamn bridge."

"Oh, and your time is so precious you can't sit for ten minutes?"

"It'll be more than that; have you seen

that line of boats waiting to come through? And then traffic has to clear, and . . . Oh, forget it."

Irina stares at her through some strands of black hair that have fallen across her face, dark creases under her eyes.

Now she's also guilty of being frustrated by idiot drivers. And the only reason she's in the car at all is Irina's version of an adolescent tantrum.

Katya stares away from Irina and swallows back a groan at the line of traffic, which stretches all the way past the turnoff to their mother's house. She could walk it faster, even if she had to carry Irina the whole way.

Katya uses a fingernail to scrape at a piece of crud on her steering wheel. Why does Irina try so hard to be the black sheep? It's as if she believes every family needs one; she's only completing the tableau. Nonsense. They were doing just fine on that score, anyway. Van had his own moodiness and determination to fail. And in a way, Katya had so fully rebelled against Mira's hippie-granola sensibility that in a way that counted, too. White sheep in her family, then.

Katya smirks to herself.

"What?" Irina shoots that word from the passenger side.

"Nothing." Kat swallows a sigh, too. She daydreams about a cigarette, something she hadn't thought of in years. It was a bad college habit, picked up in her sorority days because she thought it made her look sophisticated, plus a not thinly veiled attempt to piss off her mother. Mira had never smoked cigarettes, even though back then they weren't the evil, un-PC cancer sticks of today.

Katya is quite sure her mother smoked other things, and who knows what else. And also probably burned various undergarments. She's never asked, because unlike Van, who seemed fascinated by his parents' hippie past, she was only interested in planning out her own future.

Katya remembers practicing married names before she was even dating. She always picked standard WASP-y names, and would try out various signatures. Always using "Mrs." though, never "Ms."

Mrs. John Anderson, Mrs. Kat Anderson, Mrs. Joseph Reynolds, Mrs. Kat Johnson.

She may have even written "Mrs. Charles Peterson" at some point. It would have been in character, anyway.

"You're in such a hurry, then go!" barks Irina from her side. The bridge is down and traffic has started to move, and two cars have stopped before her SUV to let her out.

"Stop yelling at me for God's sake. If this is the way you treat Darius . . ." Katya clamps her lips shut. Too late.

"I knew you couldn't keep your mouth shut about this. I'm getting out to walk."

Katya punches the childproof door locks and takes a bitter satisfaction in Irina's failure to open the Escalade's door. Not that Irina would likely fling herself out, even at the glacial pace they travel in the heavy traffic.

Reenie slams her fist sideways into the door and slumps lower in her seat. "Mom said you promised not to hassle me."

"Technically I only promised not to mention you being knocked up. I didn't say anything about the Insta-Groom."

"Aren't you clever."

Katya drops their argument long enough to negotiate the tricky turn off the main road; tourists and locals out for a stroll are streaming across the side street. Finally, a couple of them pause long enough to let her through.

Irina is a sullen lump in the passenger seat.

"I'm sorry, kiddo."

"For what?"

Katya pauses to think. For what exactly? For her own attitude? Or for the unplanned pregnancy? What exactly is the proper rejoinder to that announcement, anyway? "Congratulations" hardly seems appropriate. It would be a bit insensitive to offer condolences.

"I'm sorry I jumped on your case."

Irina turns to her, slit-eyed, as Katya pulls the SUV in alongside their mother's house. With no one home and all the windows dark, the house looks forlorn. Katya is jolted by a vision of the future when both her parents are dead, and the lights are out for good. The hair stands up on her arms.

"Yes, I'm really sorry. I'm sure you don't need that," on top of everything else, Katya nearly adds. But then Irina would just crawl up her ass about what "everything else" meant.

"Are you going to let me out now?"

Katya releases the childproof setting and pops open the lock.

She hops out of the car and nearly tumbles onto her ass, courtesy of her spiky heels and the gravel. She tiptoes around the Escalade in order to shadow Irina, who doesn't look altogether steady on her own feet. The muggy heat is murder on a pregnant woman, Katya remembers all too well. She's been just-pregnant, enormous, and middling pregnant in the summer, and it's never easy.

When is it easy, though? And Irina barely out of her teens, married to a virtual stranger, and much as the lefty liberals would like to pretend it doesn't matter anymore, Katya knows that Reenie is going to catch hell somewhere, sometime, for marrying a black man. And the kid, too . . .

Reenie doesn't hold the door for Katya, and the screen slaps into her outstretched hand.

Katya's doctor is always telling her to stop grinding her teeth. *My doctor,* she thinks, *doesn't have to live with this family.* Katya consoles herself by thinking that soon she'll be back at the party with the wine.

"Why are you following me?" Irina shouts into the air around her, not turning around.

"I want to make sure you're OK in here before I leave. I'm getting you some ice water. You should stay hydrated."

Katya can see Irina nearly vibrating with indignance, but at the moment she cares more about the niece or nephew in there than Irina's stupid youthful pride. She needs water, after all.

Irina's shoulder blades visibly spike through the back of her dress as she drags herself up the stairs. Katya figures she lives on Chinese food, booze, and sex.

After Irina flops onto the bed, Katya positions two box fans, one on either side of her for maximum coolness, leaves the water glass sweating all over the side table (why doesn't Mira have coasters anywhere?), and ducks out the door without hearing a word of thanks.

Mothers are used to doing without thanks, something Irina will realize soon enough.

Katya is almost out the door and back to the party when she sees Charles's laptop open on the kitchen table. She pauses before the computer. Tiny specks of light zoom across the screen. She brushes the touchpad, and the computer wakes up with a cheery *ding.*

Charles has his spreadsheet open for Peterson Enterprises. It's similar to the one he created for Kat's Kradle Design, but his business has many more columns and rows. She is about to turn away, not sure why she stopped at the computer in the first place, when something about the screen jerks her attention back.

All that red. An awful lot of red, as in negative numbers. Deficit. Broke.

Katya steps back from the computer like it's alive and might go for her throat. She remembers Charles's offhand comment that morning about paying the mortgage. Or was it truly offhand?

The computer reverts to a screen of shooting stars, as Kat stands, locked in place, unable to grasp what her husband has been keeping from her.

Chapter 30
Ivan

Not once in all of Ivan's three decades of life has he ever imagined himself with two women at once.

Well, not fully clothed, anyway.

"Oh, this view is beautiful!" Barbara not only has his hand, but she's walking so close to him he must squint at his own feet to avoid tripping her up. Barbara has been gushing about the view since she arrived and insisted they walk out to the pier despite the sky and lake looking ever more restive and dark.

Jenny ambles along on his other side, her hands clasped loosely behind her, gypsy dress whipping around her knees in the wind.

They have the pier almost to themselves. The tourists have headed off to their condos, or their hotel rooms, or the various restaurants and bars along Bridge Street. Locals know better than to be out on the pier during a storm. And for any other idiots who might remain, the Coast Guard has posted signs the size of billboards, which blare in huge black letters over eye-piercing yellow that it's dangerous to be out on the pier in rough weather.

Whatever the weather, he should be enjoying himself, with all this attention. His best friend on one arm, a gorgeous girl in a clingy dress on his other . . .

But even Van is not so dense that he could miss the way Barbara's behavior has changed. She's more gushy, more animated, and physically she's hanging on him like a burr stuck to his sock. He can't puzzle out the reason for the change. Having an audience in his family? Possessive in Jenny's presence? She was perfectly friendly when Van had introduced them, at the bar after Jenny ordered a Guinness. Van remembers that Jenny had a line of foam on her upper lip, and he wanted to wipe it away for her. Meanwhile, Barbara was all shimmering and giggles as she extended a hand and exclaimed over the pendant on Jenny's neck.

Jenny fingered her pendant as if she hadn't remembered it was there.

Now they are on the pier. Barbara made the suggestion to take a walk, and though Van wasn't entirely sure the "we" in her sentence included Jenny, he wasn't about to leave her bobbing in a sea of his relatives, unattended.

And why did Barbara come at all? What made her change her mind about him? He'd never expected his desperate, clingy message to actually work.

Van changes the subject away from the view.

"Barbara, how's your writing coming?"

"Oh, I don't know. I haven't had much time lately, I've been working a lot of hours. Though, there is this one story I've been working on." She slides her eyes over to him and smiles. "I thought maybe your dad would read it. Maybe give me some advice."

"Well, he's going to be pretty busy this weekend, this being his anniversary and all . . ." Van tugs his ear and keeps his eyes down on the concrete pier, which is pockmarked by gull shit.

"You're a writer?" asks Jenny from Van's other side. She doesn't look at Barbara. Her face is still pointed toward the horizon, where the sun should be but now is only sheets of cloud.

"I write a little, here and there. For my day job I'm in marketing, I work for Lakeland Crossings."

The local shopping mall. Van has seen

some of her handiwork during the Christmas season. Giveaways, promotional events like fashion shows. She has a hand in the Santa Claus display every year.

"That's cool," Jenny says. She takes the scarf off her hair and shakes it loose. Its normal mousy brown is shot through with bright orange. Her hair is short and cut into chunks of varying lengths, so she looks a bit like a bird with ruffled feathers. Jenny faces into the wind to let it blow her hair back, then she fastens the scarf back in place.

Jenny seems different, too. Normally she'd be brimming with sarcastic remarks and asides in French, or she'd randomly quote Monty Python sketches which might or might not be appropriate to the context. She has barely said six words since they went out to the pier.

Van wants to ask her what's wrong, but he doesn't see much chance of shaking off Barbara for any length of time.

Barbara releases his hand and wraps her arm around his waist. He drapes an arm around her shoulders and a burst of her scent — something spicy that made him think of the Far East — reminds him that he really doesn't want to shake off Barbara. She is his date. Jenny invited herself, come to think of it. He can't be held responsible if she's not having a good time.

"How about you? Any luck yet?" Barbara says this, resting her head lightly on his shoulder, making it even more difficult to walk without tumbling onto the cement of the pier. They near the lighthouse. In better weather, people often fish off the end, and walkers make a loop around the lighthouse and head back to shore.

"You know how rough it is," Van answers loudly, over the wind and waves crashing on the breakwater. Though he can't remember Barbara's actually submitting any of her short stories and poems for publication. Her writing is competent, and can be really good, but she seems more interested in starting new drafts than in revising what she's got. Van admits he can understand the impulse of something new all the time. He has stacks of unfinished songs scrawled on manuscript paper in his closet.

Jenny chimes in. "You can do it, Van. You've got some great songs. You've just gotta keep at it, is all."

Van's answer is eclipsed by a bright flash and a building roar of thunder that ends with a crack like that from a whip. The clouds start to spit and Barbara shrieks like a 1950s cartoon housewife who has spotted a mouse. She runs tiptoe, her hands up in the air, back down the pier.

Jenny laughs out loud, and though she speeds up her pace a bit, she continues walking. Van frowns at her laughter and runs to catch up. He doesn't blame Barbara for running. That white dress will be transparent if a downpour starts, and though he'd enjoy the sight, he wouldn't enjoy everyone else getting a look at her panties.

Once inside — and only moderately damp — he sees that the partygoers are being seated for dinner. Katya had arranged for a fully catered affair. Van is certain his mother would have been content with vegan burgers and roasted corn grilled in the backyard.

Ivan starts making his way to their table, already pointed out to him earlier in the evening by Katya as she was still in her final flurry of organizing.

Katya didn't seat all the siblings together, explaining to Van — though he hadn't asked — that it would be more fun for them to see other family and friends. Van arrives at the round table for eight noting that he'd been seated with his cousin Fancy and her husband; one of Mira's favorite grad students, Mark, and his partner, Samir; and neighbor Patty with Patty's daughter, Vicky.

Vicky is already there, and they nod hello. He shakes Samir's hand as Mark introduces him, and turns to explain to Barbara why Fancy is called that (her name is actually Fantine) when he feels a tight knot of anxiety curl up in his gut.

Next to his place at the table is a marker that reads, "Guest." As in, only one guest. And he has brought two.

Barbara pulls out the chair and plops herself down. "I can't wait, I'll bet the food here is fantastic. Hi, I'm Barbara," she says to Samir, fixing him with a smile.

Van turns to Jenny with his mouth open, and his voice box in complete seizure.

He has never been so grateful to see Katya appear at his side.

"Oh, Van, that's right, you have two guests. Hi, you must be Jenny? I'm so sorry about the seating, I just didn't know. But as luck would have it, Irina isn't back from the house yet, so you could sit by Darius. I'm sure he could use the company."

"Of course," Jenny replies and gives Van a brief smile. "Guess I'll catch you after dinner." She hoists her bag higher on her shoulder and strides off.

"I'm sorry . . ." Van starts to say, but his voice is drowned out by the band singer, encouraging people to find their seats for dinner.

Max and Mira are suddenly in the spotlight, having been outfitted with their very own table, a brainstorm of Katya's, to avoid having to decide who gets the privilege of sitting there.

Someone starts tapping silverware to glass, and others start hooting and hollering for a kiss. Van's parents stare at each other in the yellow light. Max grips Mira's hand, and she breaks his gaze, looking down like a blushing girl of twelve.

To Van, something about her looks brittle, and he's relieved when she finally looks up and Max kisses her firmly on the mouth.

He can't quite believe it when Barbara grabs his face and smashes his own lips with a kiss, right there in front of the gay couple, just as his cousin and her husband are pulling out a chair to sit. His ears are still ringing from all the tapping on glassware when Patty lets out a loud hoot, whether for his parents or himself, Van can't be sure. He's still working out whether his breath was rancid, when she breaks off the kiss and sits back in her chair with a quick exhale, like she'd just completed a satisfactory task. Like a crossword puzzle or a knitted sweater.

"Wow," is all Van can muster, with a quick glance around the table. Samir and Mark smirk at each other. Patty has already launched into a good-natured interrogation of Barbara while Vicky rummages in her purse, and Van's cousin Fancy is standing agog. Her mouth hangs open so long, it's all Van can do to keep from reaching up and nudging her lower jaw back in place. She always was a pain in the ass.

"Fancy, this is Barbara, my . . ." here Van pauses for the briefest moment and hopes no one notices, ". . . date. This is my cousin, Fantine, and her husband, Tom." And so go the introductions around the table. In one way, it's just like Van had hoped, back when he first invited Barbara, before she dumped him, requesting "space." Back then he imagined everyone staring with great admiration, and even wonderment, that dumpy old Van managed to land himself such a great catch.

The politically correct synapses fire off to remind him that Barbara is not a fish to be landed. Van blames his unfortunate analogy on the nautical setting and the presence of Darius, who still makes him unaccountably nervous.

He turns to glance over his shoulder at Jenny and, in doing so, notes that Barbara has turned to look as well. She casts a fluttery wave back over her shoulder and faces the center of their table again, where Samir and Mark are arguing good-naturedly about the last film they saw.

Jenny is talking to someone else since Darius seems to be absent. Jenny glances up at Van, and he shrugs, hands up, apologetically. She turns back to the other guest without acknowledging the gesture.

"Congratulations, dear heart," says Patty, standing up to reach across Fancy and her rotund husband — whose round face has gone red with the heat, so that he looks like an apple — to slap Van in the arm. "You're going to be an uncle."

"I'm already an uncle," is his first response, because he is, though Katya's kids have never really taken to him. Probably because he used to buy them children's adaptations of great works of literature, complete with drawings and big print. It's not like he could compete with their own parents, gift-wise. Katya has never denied them anything. Then he remembers that a new niece or nephew should be a happy occasion, and he says finally, "Thank you."

"Reenie will be just fine," she says, though no one has suggested otherwise. Not out loud, anyway. "That Afro-American she married seems nice, and it's good that he's so much older. She'll need that, now. And she'll have help, won't she? Especially if she lives somewhere near Katya, or maybe they could even move in with your mother . . ."

Patty had been tearing apart a dinner roll like a lion with its kill, but as her sentence trails off, she drops a piece of it into her salad. Her hand remains, pincerlike, over her plate. "Oh," she says. "I've got to . . . um . . ." She pushes back her chair and almost falls backward out of it.

"Mom?" Vicky gets up and tries to follow, but Patty assures her she just needs "the loo."

Van feels the skin on the top of his head crawling around with the sensation that something critically important is just outside his comprehension.

Then he remembers with a jolt that he has to give a speech in a few moments. With the shock of Barbara's arrival, he had forgotten, and his hastily scribbled notes don't yet amount to much.

He takes out the old grocery receipt he was using and a nearly exhausted ballpoint pen and sets to writing.

Chapter 31
Irina

Irina luxuriates in the solitude like it's a down bed wrapped in silk sheets.

It's too hot and muggy for comfort, and her stomach still quivers with a seasick kind of nausea, but she's alone.

Outside the open windows of the house, she hears the *chug-chug* of boats motoring to their docks, the merry braying of the gulls. The hum of tourist chatter melds with the traffic on Bridge Street into a white-noise hum that's not unpleasant. The slicing light of midday has been blunted with dusk and clouds. Everything feels candlelit.

Thunder cracks and even that, though startling, is a welcome sound, because it brings the promise of change — cool air, refreshing breeze.

Then a baby cries.

On the sidewalk, a family must be walking by. Irina can't see them, but she hears the shrieks of an inconsolable child pierce the evening. The baby screams like it's being scraped with sandpaper. At first the wheels of the stroller, or carriage, or whatever it is, stop, and she hears some murmurs from the parents. Then they apparently decide to just keep moving, and the stroller wheels roll more quickly. The keening and wailing recede into the evening. Rain has begun to slap the windowpanes in the wake of the thunder.

As the screaming child fades out of the range of her hearing, Irina notices her heart slamming into her breastbone. She's clenched her fists, and her fingernails have dug creases into her palms.

She pulls herself up off the bed and sips some of the water Katya left on the side table, steadying the glass with both hands. She'll have to get back to the party and face Darius. She feels a pang of guilt that she abandoned him there without knowing anyone. Van is probably reciting the "I Have a Dream" speech to convince Darius they're not bigots.

Also, she's probably missing dinner, and her hunger is overpowering her nausea.

She hears the downstairs screen door *whap* shut and footsteps coming across the screened-in porch.

Now her heart pounds for a new reason.

She doesn't recognize the footfalls. No one is calling out to announce themselves, like her family would. The steps are tentative and unfamiliar in the house, cautious, rather than deliberate.

Fear seizes up her throat, and she freezes with her hands on the glass. She could climb out the window, but she's on the second floor. She would survive the drop, but what about the baby? The footsteps are coming up the stairs now, slow and halting. It's the sound of sneaking.

Irina moves off the bed and winces as the springs creak. Still holding the glass — fearing she won't be able to put it down soundlessly — she fumbles with the knob on the old wardrobe in the room. She could fit into it. The door flings open and Irina screams, letting the glass fall and shatter on the hardwood.

"Irina! It's just me!"

"Goddamn it, you asshole, why are you sneaking up on me?"

Darius grasps the doorframe with both hands, his eyes wide. "I didn't want to wake you up. I just wanted to check on you."

"All I hear is someone creeping through the house, and you're not supposed to be here . . . For fuck's sake."

Darius finally comes into the room, stepping around the glass. He folds Irina in his arms, but the adrenaline won't let her relax, and she stands stiff as a coatrack in his embrace. "Baby, it's OK. I'm sorry I scared you. I shouldn't have let you come back to the house alone."

"I didn't want you to come. I wanted to be alone."

"You don't always know what's best, do you?"

Irina wants to slap him for that. Instead she slumps into his chest. It's true; she doesn't know. She hasn't ever known.

They decide to wait out the cloudburst together, hoping the rain will let up — or at least slow down — long enough to walk back to the party. Irina had been starting to feel guilty about ditching her parents on their big night. Also, she's still hungry and all Mira has in the house is muesli and a whole lot of flavor-sapped hippie food.

So, they lie down on the bed, with Irina curled in the crook of Darius's arm, to wait for the storm to end.

Irina watches the white filmy curtains in the storm breeze. They look like dancers twisting their way around the room. Darius's heart thrums reassuringly under her hand.

"Irina? Do you want to be with me?"

"Of course," she answers quickly.

"I don't mean 'of course,' I mean, do you really?"

"I married you. And I didn't have to do that."

"Hmmmm."

Irina can feel his muscles taut under her arm. He doesn't believe her, and why should he? She hasn't exactly been brimming with joy since their honeymoon.

Irina pulls herself up on one elbow so she can look Darius full in the face. She studies the slight creases near his eyes, and that close she can see slivers of gray among the curls of his hair. It makes her feel tender and caretaking toward him.

She is jarred by a sudden image of elderly Darius bedridden, mouth slack, with a vacant stare, and she's at his side, old beyond her years.

Why didn't she ever think of that? How he'll be old while she's still in her prime? Who is she kidding? She never even thinks more than a week ahead, obviously, which is why she hadn't refilled her birth-control prescription. Katya pops up in her head now, wagging her finger and yammering about safe sex. Not that Irina has ever known her to wag an actual finger. Still, it would be just like her.

Sex is never safe, though. Irina knows that better than anyone.

Darius hasn't relaxed. The tension in his body spreads through the room like vapor, until she can no longer stand it. She breaks off staring at his hair and face and closes her eyes. At her first kisses, he doesn't respond right away — not frozen exactly, but not active, either. She ignores the frisson of anxiety at this change in him and carries on. Finally, he yields and returns her kiss. His arms wrap more tightly around her and in a smooth movement, he hoists her body on top of his. She feels like a hood ornament; she's so small compared to him.

"Is this OK?" he asks in his voice that only goes husky like this when they're about to make love.

"Oh yes." She moves over his body to demonstrate how "OK" it is. He is a beautiful man.

"No, I mean for you, with the baby. Are you comfortable?"

At "baby," it's Irina's turn to freeze. The baby can't be bigger than a field mouse, and it's already invading their most private spaces.

"It's fine. I feel fine."

Irina kisses him deeply again, but she can

only think of that screeching baby on the sidewalk, as if it was right there in the room with them.

Irina switches on her inner porn star, moaning when she should, moving as if someone stood in the wings to direct her. "Push here, touch there, arch your back just so . . ."

It's enough for Darius. Irina fakes a good loud orgasm in sync with him, and they fall back to the bed. They're both slicked with sweat.

She never would have guessed that she'd have to fake it with Darius.

When she walked into the BMW dealership, her breath caught in her chest. He cut an impressive figure in a light tan suit, and he was standing behind the main reception area, on the phone. His face lit up when he saw her, as if he knew her. In fact, Irina looked behind her to see who he was smiling at. He finished his conversation with his eyes trained right on her, that smile never leaving him.

"Well," he said, hanging up. "What can I do for you?" He put the emphasis on *you.*

Irina tucked one piece of hair behind her ear and shifted her weight to one hip, one of her most coquettish gestures. "I'm here about the receptionist job."

"Let me get you an application," he said, still smiling. Irina was pleased to note that he continued his warm gaze, even after realizing she wasn't there to buy a car and thus not worth a commission to him.

She left him with her phone number, and she left the blank application sitting on the counter.

They met for sushi the following Saturday. Irina had a few too many Sapporos and couldn't stop giggling at her failed attempts with the chopsticks. She was also entranced by the grace of Darius's hands as he deftly clicked his chopsticks around the platter, even picking up the smallest bit of rice he might have left behind.

He didn't call every weekend, and it was three more weeks before they slept together, after a night at a club. Irina was having fun, but Darius had looked bored until he finally suggested they head back to his place for a nightcap.

Irina had never had such an attentive lover, and she thought that night that she'd be spoiled for sex with anyone else.

She never imagined she'd end up married to him, without a chance to test that theory.

Darius stirs next to her and strokes her belly, which still lies flat when she's on her back. Irina starts to push his hand away, realizing at the last moment how that will look. Instead she clasps his fingers.

She wants to say "I love you," because that's what a wife would say. It's what a mother should say to the father of her child. She takes a breath in, preparing to say it, feeling like she's bouncing on the highest diving board, moments from springing into the insubstantial air.

"Oh look," Darius says. "The rain stopped."

"Huh," Irina says, propping up on one elbow and searching for her crumpled yellow dress. "So it did."

Chapter 32
Mira

The clinking of glasses and merry cheers of the crowd still ring in my ears as Max breaks off the kiss. I can hear his thoughts broadcast by the scrunched-up forehead, the way he bites his lip.

After that one terrible argument, he hasn't breathed a word about it. He hasn't pressed, suggested, guilted, or pushed me toward getting my breast sliced off. Which saint was that? Oh yes. Poor martyred St. Agatha, walking around in medieval paintings with her tits on a plate.

I'm no saint, nor am I Catholic or any particular religion. I was raised in a general Christian way, but to *Maman,* church was social convention, a place to wear pretty hats on Sundays. Papa didn't care for it, and never attended, though my mother still asked him every single Sunday for the whole of his life, as if it were really an open question. Was that optimism? That would be unlike her. Or just her way of needling him?

"How is your meal?" asks Max.

I have barely tasted it. I suppose it's exquisite, because everything Katya does is exquisitely perfect. She looks perfect tonight, truly. She probably thinks I don't give her any credit, and maybe I don't say it enough out loud, but she always was a beauty. No, I wouldn't choose those same clothes, or hairdo. But I'm not blind.

Now Ivan, he is the blind one. From my vantage point I can see nearly every table, and this Barbara girl is stuck to him like lint. When just yesterday she wanted nothing to do with him? Something is rotten, as the bard said.

But Jenny. A girl after my own heart. Anyone with eyes could see she loves him. And she ends up relegated to a rear table next to Darius's empty chair.

Darius could be good for Irina. He seems stable. "Unflappable," is the word that comes to mind. Just the right person to take care of my youngest baby. Irina has always seemed so loosely moored. One wave will rip her away and toss her into the open water.

I'd almost feel good about leaving the world if I knew Darius would stay, watching over my Reenie.

Ivan stands up to give his toast, pulling on his ear. I look down at my plate and push it away. I try to listen, I should concentrate on the speech he's crafted just for us, likely agonizing over every phrase.

But . . . A new grandchild. Just when I'd marshaled my defenses against Max and the anticipated arguments of my children, as I'm holding off the doctor and her knife.

The knowledge of this new life causes the sand to shift underneath my stone-carved resolve.

I smile at the memory of cradling baby Charles Jr., tiny Chip. I felt none of that new-parent panic, none of that trepidation and coronary over every little pimple and whimper. It was like joy shot right through my veins. There's no love like the easy rapture of grandparent love, at least in those early days.

Later, as the grandchildren grew more remote and frustrated with my lifestyle and boring, no-cable-TV house, the love became tinged with sadness. They wouldn't sit still for me scooping them up for hugs anymore. And they're all too big for that, anyway.

Now Irina brings me another chance.

Laughter ripples through the crowd as thunder claps behind us. Rain, which had been sputtering through the evening, is again rapping at the windows in earnest. I catch a glimpse of canary yellow at the back of the room, and see that Darius and Irina are coming back in. She's smiling, and much more rumpled than when she left. Maybe that's just from her nap. Or, maybe not.

The crowd applauds, and they all raise their glasses to us, beaming like little candle flames in the room now dimmed by the outside dusk and the inside ambient lighting.

I think of those who aren't here, not because they RSVP'd with a decline, but because they're dead. My parents, some aunts and uncles. Max's brother Stephen, dead of liver disease. Patty had a melanoma removed last year and casually mentioned another appointment to get a funny mole checked.

Control is an illusion. I may not have religion, but I do believe our time is up when it's up. We can't choose when to go, but some of us are lucky enough to choose how.

The toast is over. I should have listened. It was probably beautiful.

Chapter 33
Katya

Katya misses most of Van's toast to her parents because she's hissing orders at her children, sotto voce.

"Chip, put that phone away, so help me God."

"Tay, get the spoon off your nose."

"Kit! Sit up!" She'd slouched so far under the table Katya thought she would slide completely out of sight. It was disrespectful, plus, her dress was riding up on her thighs.

She looks away from Kit as the toast winds up. She'll assume Van did well enough because people laughed, and the laughter didn't sound mean.

She exhales and gulps more of her martini, feeling its sting all the way down her throat. She'd never been good at hard liquor, but tonight seemed to be as good a time as any. Charles would drive them all home, as he always did, and now that the toast was done, all the official parts of the party were behind her. It was up to the band to play for a couple of more hours.

"I love this song!" Kit jumps up from her torpor and skips to the dance floor. How she knows "Mustang Sally" is beyond Katya's comprehension.

Her daughter rolls her hips in rhythm, and lifts her thin wrists skyward. This also hoists up her dress, which was far too short, but still better than some of the others she campaigned for. Katya had exclaimed, "Who makes such slutty clothes in little kids' sizes!"

Kit had dropped a handful of clothing to the floor and dashed into the mall, forcing Katya to run after her, an awkward proposition in her heels. They were shopping between the Rotary Club luncheon and a client meeting. In the red-faced screaming battle that followed, Kit ran down a litany of suffering under her mother, the recent being calling her a slut — her protestation that she was talking about the clothes, not Kit herself, fell on deaf ears like those only a preteen girl can have — and then referring to her as "a little kid."

Katya had burst out crying right then, adding another tick to Kit's list of mortifying mother moments.

You *are* a little kid, she'd wanted to say,

but couldn't articulate, because she was too busy trying to pull herself together in front of the gawking shoppers. *You are my little girl, my last baby, and you're in such a hurry to grow up and leave me.*

Then she went home and called the doctor about perimenopause. She needed hormones, stat. She couldn't afford to be having meltdowns because she had a business to run, thank you very much.

Irina has no idea what she's in for, and that's probably just as well, Katya reflects. If anyone really knew what they were in for, there would be a run on vasectomies and tubal ligations.

"Kat, you've hardly talked to me." This from Charles, to her left. She looks up, hardly more shocked than if he'd jumped on the table to sing a show tune.

"What?"

"You insisted I put away my phone, insisted I drop everything to be here, and now you will barely look at me. You've been bossing everyone around and now we're at dinner and you're staring at your drink. How many of those have you had, anyway? Point is, am I your husband or am I a prop?"

"A prop?" Katya tries to shake off the sense that her brain is wrapped in wool. She can't make out what Charles is trying to tell her.

Charles shakes his head and takes a long pull from his beer. "I don't know what you needed me for."

"It's my parents' anniversary."

"I know the date on the calendar. As I said, you've barely said two words to me. Even when I asked you to dance, you were so busy studying the crowd you didn't look me in the eye."

Katya slaps her martini glass down on the table. "I can't believe you're talking to me about feeling neglected. When was the last time you and I spoke three sentences that didn't have to do with the house, kids, or logistics? You've been ignoring me for years now, and suddenly I'm a little distracted at a party I spent months organizing, and you're the one who's wounded? Give me a fucking break." At this she seizes her glass again and sucks the rest of her drink down, though her throat tries to fight her on that effort by giving her a few hearty chokes.

She probably went too far with that "fucking break" part.

Charles sets his beer slowly back down on the table, with exaggerated care. He uses his cloth napkin to dab at his mouth, places that back on the table, and pushes his chair away.

"I don't know why I'm here."

He strides off across the dance floor and disappears into the men's room.

Katya looks up at the table. Kit is still on the dance floor, jumping up and down to "Shout," and Chip has wandered off somewhere, maybe texting on his phone, though she told them all to leave their phones at the hotel. But Taylor is gaping at her, his eyes rounded and mouth opened in a little "O."

"I'm sorry, Tay . . ."

"Are you and Dad getting a divorce?"

"What? No! We just had an argument. We've had arguments before."

"You never swore at him before."

Not that you heard, Katya thinks. "I've had a long day, honey. That's all. Honest, it's just fine." Kat comes around the table to hug Taylor, but he ducks her arm and says he wants to get another piece of cake.

Katya heads off for the bar. Taylor doesn't need to worry. She's not going to be a Mrs. Peterson with a tan line where her diamond ring used to be, schlepping the children to and from visitations and splitting up which holidays she gets to spend with her babies. Going out to noisy bars dressed like a harlot half her age, trying to hook a new man.

Katya remembers her own cell phone, which she set to vibrate this morning after the hair appointment and after Tom's surprise call. The bartender makes her another drink, winking as he says, "You must like the way I make these, ma'am," and she spirits her drink away to a corner table, where no one is sitting. Suit coats are resting on the backs of chairs, half-consumed drinks dot the surface, and wine spills have marred the linen tablecloth. A digital camera and a handbag have been abandoned, but no sign of the partiers. They're probably up there dancing to "Old Time Rock and Roll," now that the male singer has taken over the band.

A muted rumble of thunder crescendos into a sound that cracks the air, and somewhere, a girl screeches, then laughs.

She listens to her voice mail and she indeed has one new message, from Tom: "Kat, our call must have been dropped. I hope you get a chance to call me back. It will be fun catching up with you."

Katya checks her watch. Not late at all. She wishes she could go out on the patio.

She opens her phone and scrolls through the messages to where she's hidden Tom's number under GYNO.

"Nothing wrong, I hope?"

Kat snaps her phone shut. "Hi, Mom. No, I'm fine. Are you enjoying yourself?" Katya turns to face her mother, whose silvery hair glows in the candlelight like something out of an oil portrait. If Kat overlooks the age spots across her mother's chest and her saggy neck, Mira looks radiant in her old wedding gown.

"Yes. Thank you for the party. It's really beautiful. Much nicer than anything I would have done for myself."

"Oh, it's no trouble." Katya realizes she's told two of her most popular lies, right in a row.

"It certainly was a lot of trouble, but it's beautiful."

"I just hope it's memorable."

Mira glances down at her lap, then surprises Katya by taking her hand, and squeezing it. Katya fights an urge to pull away.

"I wanted to tell you that I think you're beautiful. And I'm really proud of you. You're so competent, and capable, and smarter than I ever was. You work so hard for your family. I just wanted you to hear that."

"Um. Wow. Uh." Katya sips her drink, having been reduced to monosyllables.

Mira releases her hand, then pats it,

awkwardly, as if she's not sure what to do now. "I just thought I should tell you. I'm going to find your father now."

Mira hoists herself out of the chair and drifts off through the crowd, the short train of her gown winding behind her.

Katya searches through the crowd herself until she finds Ivan, looking typically miserable and fraught, half-hidden behind a large potted plant covered in twinkle lights.

He startles as she seizes his wrist.

"Hey, Kat."

"What's wrong with Mom?" she asks him.

Van frowns at her and shrugs. "What do you mean?"

"She's just being weird."

"I'd worry if she were normal. Are you drunk?"

"Why does everyone keep asking me that? And why are you hiding in a plant?"

"I'm not in the plant. I'm behind it, sort of. It's the two girls. I started out not having any date, and now I have two, and it's killing me to divide my time between them, but it's like driving toothpicks under my thumbnails to talk to both of them at once."

Katya laughs and sloshes her drink. "A bit dramatic, aren't we?"

"They have nothing in common. I talk to Jenny, and Barbara starts sighing and fidgeting. She even started filing her nails and checking her e-mail on her phone. I talk to Barbara, and Jenny goes silent and eventually wanders off, until I find her again because I feel guilty for leaving her alone. But Barbara sticks right with me, so it's three of us again."

"Vicious cycle."

"Then I bumped into Darius, and I can't think of anything to say to him. Geez, Kat, does that make me a racist?"

"Of course not." Katya pats his arm, giving it a little squeeze. "But it does make you a moron. So how'd you shake the girls and end up behind the plant?"

"They both had to go to the bathroom."

"Keep the faith. Less than two hours and the band will wrap up and we can all get on with our lives."

"You might want to consider wrapping up early. I haven't seen the weather or anything, but it's looking bad out there. Maybe people should get out before we have to build an ark."

Katya turns from Ivan to face the window. To get a better view, she stands close to the glass and cups her hands around her eyes to block out the light from the room. In the struggling red light from the lighthouse, she can discern waves crashing into spray.

Lightning flashes brighten the scene to daylight for just a moment, then it's black again, except for the weak lights along the channel and the red glow of the lighthouse. This time, the thunder cracks so loud Katya gasps and jumps back from the glass.

A voice from her memory says, "It's just noise, Katya. Noise can't hurt you." Her mother. The memory is blurry, but she must have been very young, because she can't remember Ivan's being there. Max was out somewhere, and there was a storm. It must have been serious because they were in the basement, a spooky, cobwebby place that Katya never liked at the best of times.

She blinks and now sees only her reflection in the glass. Her chignon has started to come undone. Katya looks down at herself. All else seems in order.

But she sips her drink again because an uncomfortable feeling has started to creep up her spine, and she can't find the words to explain it.

She flips open her phone to check the weather.

Chapter 34
Ivan

Van twirls a tiny bit of napkin between his fingers until it resembles a tiny Tootsie Roll, then he drops it onto the bar, where it joins a dozen other tiny napkin rolls. He's hating himself for hiding from the girls in the hotel bar but doing nothing else about it. It's a familiar position, and thus is not entirely uncomfortable. Like an ugly sweater that fits and always seems to be at the front of the closet.

At least the toast went well. He'd started with a bit about how his parents had met at the library, so appropriate for two people in love with the written word. Then he told the story of how in the heat of an argument that had cropped up while Mira was watering flowers, she squirted Max with a hose. They both started laughing and forgot what they were mad about. That got a laugh, and so did his closing line: "Maybe that's the secret to a long, happy marriage. Never take yourself too seriously and always have a garden hose at the ready."

So. That seemed to go okay. He'd been trying to seek out Jenny's eyes in the crowd, but the light was too bright on him, and everyone around him looked like dark lumps.

"Another one?" the bartender asks.

Van nods. Paying cash at the hotel bar rather than drink the free beer up at the shindig is stupid, on top of cowardly and rude. But his nerves are shot from the anxiety of trying to keep both Jenny and Barbara happy. He needs a rest.

He glances up at the small television in the corner. A map of their bit of Michigan appears in the lower left hand corner, obscuring part of the Stanley Cup playoffs. Charlevoix County is in red. Severe thunderstorm warning.

The lights flicker as a thunderclap booms.

No shit, thinks Ivan.

Katya had hurried off — as much as she could hurry, given that she was weaving around the room — to confer with their mother about aborting the party early. That left Ivan with the uncomfortable question of what to do with Jenny and Barbara. It was never really discussed where either of them would stay, to say nothing of both of them.

Would Barbara want to stay in his room?

Mira wouldn't mind. She's always been rather relaxed about her adult children's sleeping arrangements, based on Irina getting to share a bed with the boyfriend-du-jour anytime she visited. Ivan hadn't brought anyone home to stay the night in . . . never, actually.

Then, where would Jenny end up? Though Barbara is a quasi girlfriend, it seems wrong to relegate Jenny to second place since he's known her for years.

But Barbara is the only one expressing much interest in him at the party. Jenny has been distant all evening.

Van's head hurts. He drinks more beer and knows that it's counterproductive to drink more when his head aches.

But it's all he can think of to do.

"Ah. So here you are, *mon frère.*"

Van cringes in his seat and catches the bartender smirking at him.

Jenny hops up in the seat next to him.

"Sorry," Van mumbles.

"Don't apologize to me. Your girlfriend is the one in there prowling the place like a lioness on the hunt."

"She's not my girlfriend."

Jenny turns on her barstool to face Van. He looks at her out of the corner of his eye, too embarrassed to look her straight in the face. She wears an ironic smirk, leans on the bar with her elbow, and says, "So what is she, then? First you were done for. Remember, you told me you were Ivan the Terrible? Now she's here and going all moony-eyed over you, but she's not your girlfriend? What brought about this miraculous change of heart, anyway?"

"I guess she changed her mind about coming at the last minute." Van recalls Barbara's mention of his famous author-dad, and her manuscript.

"And she didn't tell you? She just — poof! Appeared?"

"Something like that."

Barbara told him at the dinner that she felt rude dumping him just before the party when she'd agreed to go, and, really, he was very sweet, and she was rethinking this whole "needing space" thing. Maybe they could go away together next weekend? She batted her eyes at that. Literally.

When she said this, Van nearly plopped himself face-first in his salmon. She was damn gorgeous and giving him another chance. So what if his famous father tipped the balance in his favor? So what if she'd steered the dinner conversation to the identity of his father's agent and whether he ever put in a "good word" for new writers?

"So, why are you hiding out here, then, if your ladylove is in there looking for you?"

Van straightens up and looks Jenny full in the face. She's smirking in that way she reserves for school-administration debacles and "idiot parent" stories, the way she sneers when she talks about her stepsister's latest dramatic caper.

"What have you got against Barbara?"

"What have *you* got against her? You're the one hiding from her."

"I've got nothing against her. I think she's stunning, she's beautiful, and . . ."

"And . . . ?"

"She makes me feel like I'm not a loser."

Jenny laughs, just once: "Ha." She turns back and puts both elbows on the bar. "You mean the adoration of your best friend doesn't do a thing for you?"

"That's not what I mean."

"Ah, I'm just busting your balls. I know what you mean. So go back in there and get her."

"Huh?"

"Go back in and get your ladylove, *mon ami.*"

"Aren't you coming?"

"Nah. I'm going to finish this up and I think I'll take off. If I get going now, I'll make it home before midnight."

Van stands up, and puts his hand on Jenny's shoulder, nearly bare in her hippie sundress. "Are you sure you're OK to drive? And in this?"

"Hey, I'm fine. I've only had two beers, and it's only rain. I'll be all right. You go on, have fun. I was just filling in, anyway, right? When Barbara wasn't coming? You shouldn't have to split your attention."

Relief floods through Van. She's solving his problem for him! Such a good friend; she always knows exactly what he needs. No one else understands him better.

He leans in and kisses her cheek, catching her scent: something crisp and bright. He would bet anything she got it at some shop that sells crystals and incense. She smiles under his kiss, then turns to look him in the eye.

He notices her eyes are an intriguing shade of brown: light, caramel-colored. Almost gold, really, like those of a cat. He's never seen them before like this.

"G'night, Van," she says, giving him a light shove on his shoulder. "Go on."

He floats out of the bar, ready to go enjoy his beautiful date properly, thanking his lucky stars the whole way, for such an understanding friend.

CHAPTER 35
IRINA

For the first time in her life, Irina finds herself in envy of her older brother.

The band plays "Smoke Gets In Your Eyes," and at the center of the floor, he sways along with Barbara. She is a looker. Wavy auburn hair, creamy skin, and a slender body with enough boobs to fill out her dress but not so much that she's falling out all over the place. She envies Van not for his girlfriend — after all, Darius is smoking hot himself, and gets stares from women everywhere he goes — but because Barbara is only a girlfriend. At any time, he can walk away.

Oh sure, she can get divorced, and she most assuredly will. And she can even hand over the baby to Darius and wish him well. But, young though she is, Irina realizes she will be changed by this. In an elemental sense.

She's already felt some primal urge to

protect the baby, this baby she didn't plan and does not want. Which means, no matter how much she wants to carry on with her single, freewheeling life, some part of her will resist. Some part of her will cling to that bundle and not want it taken away. That thought fills her stomach with a heavy dread.

And Darius will never forgive her. She will inevitably feel guilt over that. Unlike what Katya seems to think, she doesn't just screw everything with a dick within a twenty-five-mile radius, to hell with consequences.

Just that the consequences have never been steep before since she always made the guy wear a condom.

Stupid old condoms aren't supposed to break. She should sue Trojan. At the time, they made a joke of it. "No condom in the world can contain me," Darius joked, standing over her on the bed, flexing his muscles and posing like a comic-book superhero. She laughed until she cried.

Two weeks later, she just cried.

Darius, sitting to her side, tries kneading her shoulder, but she gingerly shifts it out from under his hand. She begged off from dancing, pleading exhaustion, which was partly true. And the music was too loud for easy conversation, so they've been sitting in silence, watching the party.

Irina fingers an ivory cocktail napkin, with gold script reading, "Max and Mirabelle Zielinski, 35th anniversary, June 2, 2007."

Irina couldn't conceive of it. She'd known Darius barely thirty-five days before he knocked her up, and already she wanted out.

Maybe Kat was right about her after all.

"Hell of a storm," Darius shouts over the music.

She nods vaguely. She hasn't been paying attention, since they returned to the party. Inside the reception hall, everything is twinkle lights and candles refracted in crystal. Easy to forget the turmoil outside. She has to give Katya that much. It's pretty, and her big sister is really good at pretty.

"Reenie!" Irina turns to see cousin Angela with her daughter propped on her hip. The kid's name escapes her. Britney. Christina. Some pop-star name.

Angela plops down uninvited next to her. She's wearing a dress that couldn't be more unattractive if she'd gone out of her way. It's the color of shit and hangs like a sack straight down from her shoulders. Angie's hair is so flat to her head she might as well not have any. The kid has grabbed a fistful of it and is chewing on it. The sight makes Reenie's stomach turn, especially when the candlelight glints off some fresh snot on the kid's face.

"Congratulations!" chirps Angela. Reenie squints at her, and she says, "Oh, my mother told me after she heard from Grandpa about you fainting on the balcony. I take it you're OK now and anyway, congrats!"

"Thanks." An uncomfortable silence passes. "How's your little one?" Reenie asks, hoping she'll answer with the kid's name.

"Oh, she's great. Fifteen months now. She's up way past her bedtime, and she's so cranky because I won't nurse her right now. She's still loving the breast!" The band was just winding up a song, so Angie ends up shouting the word "breast!" across a nearly quiet hall. She doesn't seem to notice.

Reenie looks down to adjust her shoe, which doesn't need adjusting, because she's afraid that her disgust at imagining a toddler sucking on Angela's boob has registered on her face.

She steals a glance at Darius, who looks not one bit disgusted, and in fact, he's playing peekaboo. The nameless boob-loving toddler buries her face in her mother's hair, smiling shyly.

Irina finds she can't stand to sit there any longer. "Restroom," she says over the sound of the band, which has drifted into some other ballad she doesn't recognize.

She parks herself in a stall and just sits there, like she used to when she worked at that horrible accounting firm with the boss and his roving hands, and the women with frosted hair and dagger-length nails who gossiped about her in the coffee room. So sometimes she'd hide in a bathroom stall. If she balanced just right, she could almost nap that way. It was rejuvenating, anyway.

They probably all thought she had dysentery.

As she comes out of the bathroom, she nearly collides with Patty, her mother's neighbor. Patty has teased her yellowy white hair into cotton-candy froth. Patty takes Irina's arm and her grip feels wiry and claw-like. She wobbles in place, and though Irina knows some of that is age, it appears some of the wobble might have to do with the drink in her hand, which is almost empty but used to be pink and frozen. She licks some of the sugar off the rim and bites her lip as she looks into Irina's eyes.

"Oh, honey. You're going to have a baby." Christ, she thinks. Everyone must know by now. Did Katya take out an ad or something?

Irina is about to say "thank you" when

she realizes that Patty didn't say "Congratulations." She replies, "Yes, I am."

"Take special care of your mother." Patty squeezes Irina's arm as she says this. Her watery eyes remind Irina of old Katharine Hepburn movies.

"What did you say?" Irina asks, in case she misheard over the band. Mira hasn't needed anyone to take care of her in all the years Irina can remember.

"She'll tell you when she's ready, but just be kind to her. She needs your support."

Irina plunges into a lie, unsure why she's doing so. "No no, she did tell me. I just wasn't sure I heard you right. Yes, we'll have to take care of her."

Patty makes a great show of sighing, her shoulders drooping. "I'm so glad you know, it's awful hard to walk around with a secret like this. It must be terrible for Mira, after all these years of being the spitting image of health and vitality."

"I know just what you mean." Irina steps closer so she can hear better, and puts a commiserating arm around Patty's shoulder. Tell me more, she urges silently. What's going on?

"It just seems wrong." Patty gazes into Irina's face, now just inches away. A tear drips from one eye, tracing a particularly deep wrinkle down the side of her face. "It's never the rapist and warlords dying of cancer. It's always the good people, like your mother." At this, Patty wraps Irina in an awkward hug, one hand still clutching her drink. "Excuse me," she says through a choking sob, and shuffles into the bathroom.

Irina stands with her arms still slightly open for hugging Patty.

Cancer?

Without realizing she's doing so, Irina sweeps her eyes over the party, searching for Mira. She spots her mother talking to Paul, her old boss at the university, in front of the memory display Katya created, lined with photos of the family through the years. Paul bends over her like a tall, old tree. He has one hand on her shoulder, and Mira looks away, to one side, as if she can't bear to meet his gaze.

Chapter 36
Mira

I can't believe how young we look.

Katya put together a wall of memories for this shindig. It's been mostly ignored since dinner was served, and this is the first chance I've had to study it.

I've seen these photos before. Katya raided my own collection to put it together. But now I see them as part of a finite collection of memories that will come to an end. Maybe that picture, there, will be the last time I'm ever photographed wearing that dress.

Maybe I'm naïve. Maybe other sixtyish women have long been contemplating the downhill side of life. After all, cancer or not, I crested the mountain probably twenty years ago.

Maybe I've been fooling myself these many years by acting young. Refusing the old-lady conventions of sensible clothes and cropping my hair short. Having a late-life baby helped in that, I think, though for those middle-of-the-night feedings, I certainly felt older than the pyramids.

Maybe this same photo wall will appear at my funeral, with a few photos from tonight tacked on. Maybe a few from next Christmas, too, a few more holidays if I'm lucky.

I imagine other photos: cheerful me putting up a brave face while wearing some dopey headscarf, hollows under my eyes, a rubber boob. All skin and bones.

I hear Dr. Kevorkian just got out of prison, though he swears he's retired now from the "putting out of misery" business.

"Reminiscing?"

Paul has appeared at my side, offering me a glass of champagne. I'm feeling not the least bit bubbly, but I take it anyway. It gives me something to do with my hands.

"How can I do anything but at my own anniversary party?"

"Max is a lucky man."

"Of course he is," I say with a smile. Paul and I have had this exchange at least once a week. I like to pretend it's all in fun.

"You're going to tell me what's wrong yet? Or do I have to get you so drunk you spill the beans?"

"I'm sick."

I don't know why I just said that. It's an

immediate betrayal of Max, after swearing him to secrecy and using every emotional manipulation I could muster to get him to keep this from our children, his parents, everyone close to us. And then I go and blurt it to Paul.

"What do you mean?" Paul puts his hand on my shoulder, and I want to shrug it off, but I know that would hurt him. He's always hated to be pushed away.

"Don't tell anyone I told you. It's not common knowledge just yet."

"Mira, what is it? Exactly?"

So I stand closer, and he bends his head down so I don't have to shout. Thunderclaps drown out my words, and now and then I have to repeat the story. Of finding the lump, ignoring it until I found a second one. Of Dr. Graham talking of surgery, chemo, radiation. I don't mention the fight with Max the following morning though of course it leaps back to center stage in my mind.

How I manage this all with dry eyes is beyond me. Maybe I'm well schooled in managing my emotions around Paul.

"You can do it, Mira. I don't know many other people stronger than you. Remember when the faculty strike dragged into its thirtieth day? Remember the dissension in the ranks, the death threats?"

I wave my hand in the air, wrinkling my nose. That whole fracas was so melodramatic. "I never believed anyone would kill me over protesting a wage freeze."

"That's not the point. You're tough enough to beat this, and you'll have all the support in the world. Max, your family. And me."

Paul squeezes my shoulder gently, and a warm shiver runs down my spine. It's my own anniversary party, damn it, but I've never been able to control my physical reaction to his presence. You'd think that all those years of working side by side, of watching him get more gray and paunchy, of watching my own skin slide downward like a melting glacier, you'd think I would have gotten over it.

I bring my eyes to a picture of Max and me, clowning on the dock behind the house. He's hoisted me up in his arms like he's going to carry me over the threshold, only you can already see his knees buckling. Some of that was comic exaggeration, but only some. He's no athlete, my Max. I wonder if Max appreciates how hard it has been to keep to my vows all these years. He can't appreciate it because he doesn't really know. What am I supposed to say? Max, you should be glad

I've never screwed around, because I'm really horny for my colleague. That would go over well.

"Mira?" Paul prompts, and now I do shrug gently out from under his hand, unable to stand the distraction any longer.

"I don't want to be tough. I don't want to be one of those posterchild cancer patients with the yellow bracelet and the bald head with the funny hats, trying to make light of dying." My voice is getting louder, even though Paul is close by and the band isn't all that noisy in this part of the hall. "I'm getting old, too old to put on a brave face and go through all that shit."

"Stop talking like an eighty-year-old dowager. You're as young as you've ever been. I've seen you wheeling around campus on your bicycle while the rest of us slobs drive an eighth of a mile to our next lecture. You have to fight this."

"Don't tell me what I have to do!" I push him at this. I actually put my hand on his arm and push him. Paul is much larger than me, but the surprise of it makes him stumble back.

"You're not making sense," he persists, stepping back to the space I just shoved him out of.

"It's my body, and if I choose not to have

parts of it chopped off, irradiated, that's my choice."

"Think of your children!"

"My children are adults and stopped caring about what I think round about the time they hit puberty."

"What about Max?"

"He doesn't own me!"

Paul gingerly sets his champagne flute down on the memory table, near an album of pictures from the university years. It's open to a newspaper clipping of the strike, where I'm leading the picket line, my mouth open in a most unflattering fashion, like I'm about to swallow a zeppelin. I drain my own glass quickly and put it down next to his.

"So that's it?" Paul crosses his arms and juts his chin forward. "You're going to stamp your foot and tell the whole world, 'You're not the boss of me.' "

"If you think belittling me will change my mind . . ."

"I don't care what it takes. I just want you here, on this planet, for as long as possible."

"No matter how sick I get or how miserable I am? Now you sound like the child. You want what you want, no matter what the cost."

"When it's this important, yes, I do." Paul steps in close, and this time puts both hands on my shoulders. "I love you, Mira."

I'd like to answer him, but my lungs have frozen, and I can't find my tongue.

He says quickly, "You're my oldest friend, and I love you dearly." This he says more quietly, and he lets go of my arms, casting a glance over my head. He must also be wondering if anyone else heard him, if Max has witnessed our exchange.

He would go on, I can tell, but Katya has borrowed the microphone from the singer. She's telling us that the storm has worsened, and now the weather service has declared a tornado watch. She calls off the party, recommending that everyone get to a hotel if they have a long drive.

This launches a flood of partygoers coming up to me to say good-bye, or say hello if they haven't done so earlier. An impromptu receiving line forms, during which Paul melts from my side before we can exchange another word. Max walks up to take his place, pecking my cheek between handshakes with guests.

I don't hear what any of them are saying. I can see their smiling, nodding faces, receive their enthusiastic hugs and kisses on my cheek. Several of them I might never see again, barring another family funeral or wedding in the coming months.

I practice my *uijayi* breathing like my yogi taught me, or else I might fly apart in all directions like an exploding star.

Chapter 37
Katya

The siblings may make fun of Katya's SUV, but she notices that none of them complain when it's time to go back to the house in a rainstorm, and she's the only one who drove to the party. Even so, there was not enough room for the whole family. Paul gave Max and Mira plus Darius and Irina a lift back to the house in his own SUV.

Charles taps his fingers on the steering wheel, staring fixedly out the window, though there's nothing to see but darkness and streaming rivulets of water. He worked the room, glad-handing and small-talking, after their spat, resuming his typical distance both physical and emotional. Katya curses herself for not taking advantage of this rare display of spousal availability, but then, why should she have to "snap to" just because he decides to be husbandly for once in a decade?

Maybe Tara is out of town this weekend.

"Oh Charles?" His head inclines slightly, silhouetted in the light of the parking lot. "I think I'll stay with the family tonight, instead of at the hotel." He doesn't reply.

Katya massages her temples. The sudden interruption in the flow of martinis has resulted in a sensation of billiard balls rolling around in her skull.

In the rush to escape the rain, Ivan ended up in the front passenger seat next to Charles. With the three kids in the back, that left Katya sitting next to Ivan's silly date, Barbie. To Katya, she looks like a Barbie with a drugstore dye job. Barbara smells aggressively like Calvin Klein's Obsession. Katya is baffled as to why this girl — who only yesterday had rebuffed Van completely — was riding back to the house with them like a proper sister-in-law. How had she gotten her hooks in so deep, so quickly? And what happened to the disappearing Jenny? Weird-looking girl, but nice enough. She'd ask Van later.

"Are we all loaded in?" Katya has to shout over the rain lashing the car.

Barbie's cell phone trills, and she jumps on it like a heart patient waiting for a transplant. Then her face lights up, but she keeps her voice even. None of them can help hearing her, trapped in her conversation by the storm.

"I didn't think you'd call me back after the last time we talked. . . . Yes, well, after you said you didn't want to see me . . . Oh, I see, you feel differently now . . ."

Katya can't hear the words on the other end, but the voice is distinctly male. Ivan is slumped against his armrest, his tall frame curved over like the letter C. And still she keeps talking.

Katya snatches the phone out of her hand and punches buttons until it stops. It feels good, and she decides to have martinis more often.

"Hey! That's my phone!" Barbie snatches it back, cradling it to her chest like an infant.

"And that" — Katya points to Ivan — "is my brother, and I'm not going to sit by while you humiliate him." Katya stretches across Barbara, nearly prone in her lap, to reach the door lock on her side. She flips it open and sits back up with some effort. "Maybe you'd better get your car. Just across the street is a motel. Once you get past the shag carpet and fake wood paneling, it's quite a cozy place." Katya smiles into Barbie's searing glare. "I'm sure there's a vacancy."

Barbara cries out to Van. "You can't just send me out in this rain! Are you going to let her talk to me like that?"

Van rouses himself from his slump long enough to say, "It should be perfectly clear by now that no one has control over what Kat does and does not do." Katya leans again to slide the Escalade door open. The furious rain sends a damp mist into the car. Barbara looks around, as if searching for an ally, and is greeted only by silence and muted giggles from the children. So she releases a disgusted snort and jumps out into the downpour. Katya slams the door.

Katya catches Van's eye just long enough to see a faint, sad smile before he turns back to face forward.

No one pushes around Kat Peterson, nor her family, thank you very much.

"Mom?" Kit says, her voice sounding smaller and more girlish than usual. Katya prepares for her to ask for something outrageous.

"What, honey?"

"Can we come to Grandma's, too?" Too? For a moment Katya forgot that she decided to stay at the house instead of the hotel.

Katya turns to face her daughter. In the darkness of the car, she can only see her in silhouette. But Kit's shoulders are hunched around, and she's sitting close to her big brothers.

"We? All of you?"

"Yeah," says Chip, without elaborating.

"Well, of course, if you want to." Kat can't keep the skeptical note out of her voice. Since when do they want to spend time at Grandma's?

Kit might be afraid of the storm, but she doesn't know why her boys want to hang around.

"Charles? You going to stay at the hotel, or are you coming to the house with the rest of us?"

A silence falls. The noise of the rain has almost disappeared in the way that constant noise does. Now, the *whap-whap* of the wipers is discernible. In the rearview mirror, Katya catches a reflection of Charles rolling his head around, stretching his neck. Considering his answer. What is he weighing? In one hand, family togetherness, in the other hand . . . what? Solitude. Work. Maybe a porno flick on the pay-per-view. He'd pay the bill, and she'd never know.

Katya shakes her head. Her mind does wander after a bit of liquor.

"I'll just drop by the hotel to pick up my stuff. Meet you back there."

Katya rests back in the seat. Tonight seems to be the night for family surprises.

Chapter 38
Ivan

Ivan rests spread-eagled on his childhood bed, in his childhood room, doing the math on his weekend. Friday equaled "no date." Saturday dinner equaled "two dates." Saturday night was back to "one date" but here, in the real nighttime hours, he's alone.

Again. Stop the presses.

His eyes trace a crack in the plaster ceiling from the corner of his room, wandering across the middle like a river on a map. The river seems to be longer and wider than he remembered from his childhood habit of gazing at the ceiling. The house is getting older, along with everyone and everything else. Little Reenie getting married, soon to be a mom. Mira is a little slower in her step these days, his dad even more distracted.

Katya was seemingly born old, though. Always so organized with everything color-coded and filed and lined up. Even had her colored pencils arrayed in the color spectrum. What kind of artist is so anal retentive?

And yet, here's Van. Still operating on a school-year calendar, still single, still plucking away at his guitar. Still getting upstaged by his domineering older sister with the fabulous home and beautiful family and successful business of her own.

Bartleby saunters in through the door he left cracked open and meows beseechingly. Van pats the quilt, and the old cat backs up on her hindquarters, wriggling her little cat butt, taking all the time in the world to gather up her strength, then pow! She unfurls and lands lightly next to him. Then she turns her butt to him and plops down, as if she couldn't care less he was there. Her and every other woman he knows.

In the SUV on the way back to the house, Van slumped into the seat, wanting to throttle Katya for butting into his life, yet collapsing with gratitude that she'd solved his problem for him. The call Barbara took in the SUV from some other guy was just the topper. Any illusion that Barbara genuinely liked him had already flaked away by the third time she tried to drag him across the dance floor to accost his father.

Barbara must have had other plans with some other guy, and they fell through, and still Van was not appealing enough until she decided he could help her get her stories published. He was just a pawn. Not even a pawn. The chessboard? Lower yet. The little felt feet that keep the chessboard from sliding across the counter.

Only, marginally less useful.

A soft tapping at his door. Must be his mother or Irina. Katya would pound. Even when she tries to knock softly, Katya pounds.

"Come in."

"Hi." Reenie slips into the room. She's changed from the yellow dress into a tank top and pajama pants with pink stripes. It's like she's leapt backward in time to her preteen years, and Van half expects a gaggle of girls to follow her in, slumber-party style. Then Van is surprised to see Katya slip in behind her, carrying a plastic cup, still wearing her party clothes. "Got a minute?" Reenie asks, closing the door.

Ivan snorts. "Gee, lemme see if I can fit you in between, hmmm . . . No One and No Body."

"Isn't that a poem?" Katya mumbles, squinting as if the light is glaring from the small forty-watt bedside lamp, which it's not.

Van looks back at the crack on his ceiling.

" 'I'm Nobody, who are you? Are you nobody, too?' Emily Dickinson."

The rain has eased up outside, but lightning flashes come so close together, the effect is strobelike. Once everyone made it back to the house, Mira had sent Max and Charles off to search for flashlights and candles. The Big Tree's branches has taken out power lines more than a few times in its long life.

Irina perches on the edge of Van's bed, almost teetering off. She strokes Bartleby absently. Katya leans against the door and folds her arms. "Reenie said she wanted to talk to us."

"Reenie, what? What's on your mind?"

"I think Mom has cancer."

Van props himself on an elbow. "What? That's crazy."

Katya nods. "Yeah, nuts."

Reenie tells them about Patty and the conversation, including her tipsiness. Kat just rolls her eyes and sips from her cup.

Next to her, Van sits all the way up. "She must have gotten her wires crossed. She always was a little daffy."

"Wires crossed how? How do you imagine that your friend told you she has cancer? That doesn't make sense."

"It doesn't make sense that Mom has

cancer," jumps in Katya, her voice dripping with irritation, as if no one could be so stupid. Van thinks she's probably right, but he could do without her nasty tone. "Has she seemed sick to you at all? Has she even seemed worried? If anything, she was in a better mood than usual."

"Except when I brought Darius home." Irina juts her chin at Katya.

Van says, "Well, even Mom has her limits. That was a bit of a shock."

Irina rubs her bare arms and hugs herself tight. Van slides over and wraps his own bony arms around her. "Hey, look, she's fine. If anything I bet it's a skin cancer or something. A spot on her nose. They never used sunblock back then, you know."

"She sounded pretty sure. I think we should ask her."

Van stands up and crosses the room to the window. "No, definitely not. If she has something to say and hasn't told us, there's a reason. We need to respect that."

"Yeah, don't hassle her, Reenie. Not tonight," Katya says, already edging toward the door.

"Even if she's dying?"

Van catches his breath. In the yellow lights along the harbor's edge, he can see boats and yachts pull away and slam back into the docks. Thunder growls, the next crash beginning before the first one dies off.

"She's not."

"We don't know that."

"I do."

"You can't be sure . . ."

"Look, Reenie. Don't ask her. This is her anniversary. She's trying to have a good time. It must be minor, whatever it is, or she would have told us. Don't bug her with it."

"Van . . ."

"Promise."

"OK, Jesus. I guess you're right. Patty was probably being a bit dramatic, being drunk and all. God, I could do with a drink right now. Or six."

"There's wine downstairs."

"Speaking of," Katya says, looking into her cup and slipping out of the room.

"Hello? Pregnant? Bun in the oven and all that? My fun is over."

Van returns to the bed and nudges her with his shoulder. "Ah, come on. It's not over. You'll have fun again. And anyway, the baby will be fun."

"Oh yeah, I'm sure she and I will be doing Jell-O shots in no time."

Van lets himself fall backward across the bed. "Jell-O shots. Grow up, Reenie."

"Easy for you to say. You've had your fun."

Van props up on his elbows and squints at her. "Oh yeah, that's me, living the high life. Eating pizza straight from the box alone, six out of seven nights."

"Don't dump your hang-ups on me because you wasted your twenties."

"Shut up."

"Where did Jenny go, anyway?"

"Home."

"All the way home? That's like a three-hour drive!"

"She left a while ago." Van looks at his watch. "She's probably halfway home by now."

"In this?" Irina gestures to the window. "You let her leave in this? Your head is so far up your ass."

Ivan puts his indignation on pause to think about Jenny struggling down the road in her fifteen-year-old Cavalier.

"Well, she said she wanted to go, I didn't think she needed my permission."

Irina stands up and rakes her fingers through her hair. "You are one piece of work, you know? This Barbara chick so much as hints that she likes you and you've got stars in your eyes and you're drooling down your chin. Jenny, who you say is your best friend, goes out into a monsoon to drive three hours home, and you're like, 'Bye, have fun!' " Irina goes to the door and pauses with her hand on the doorknob. "You better call and check on her at least. Dumb-ass."

Irina leaves him alone, and a guilty flush creeps over Van's ears at the ring of truth in her words. No one can spell out his screwups so vividly as his angry sisters. He looks for his phone and speed dials Jenny.

Ringing. Still ringing. Ringing some more.

Jenny's voice mail. Van hangs up because he can't think of anything to say. He pulls on his earlobe and tries to remember other times he might have shoved Jenny aside for the interests of a fickle girl. Might have? Must have.

Now there's pounding on his door.

"Come in, Kat."

She stands in the doorway again. Her hair has gone all askew, and her makeup is smeared or faded off. She's still in her linen party dress, but barefoot. "There's a tornado watch, still. 'Conditions are ripe' they're saying on the radio, and advising everyone not to drive. Just thought you should know. We're all going to have some more cake downstairs. You coming? Might as well, no sense in hiding up here all alone."

She leaves without an answer, with full

confidence that he'll do her bidding. And of course he will because otherwise he'll lie in the dark thinking about Jenny white-knuckling her way home.

Chapter 39
Irina

Irina curls up in an overstuffed living-room chair, a piece of cake balanced on her folded-up knees, trying to replace an alcohol buzz with a sugar high by eating a piece with frosting flowers the size of brussels sprouts.

Darius laughs at a story Max is telling, one of the favorites in the Zielinski repertoire, about the time his Uncle Lukasz convinced Van at a family picnic to try the hot and spicy salsa. Van, about eight years old then, scooped up a huge chunk of it and chomped it right down. This resulted in Van streaking toward the lake, mouth wide open, as if he was going to dive in and drink the whole thing. Max's impression of Van never fails to get a laugh, though they've all heard it six thousand times. Having a new face in the crowd makes the story seem new again.

Irina licks her plastic fork and watches her husband laugh. It's a warm, smooth sound.

Bass guitar in a jazz band, syncopated rhythm.

She steals a glance at her mother, who has changed into a purply pink tie-dyed dress, and braided her hair into pigtails, which might look ridiculous on any other sixty-five-year-old woman, but Irina can't imagine her looking any other way. She's reassured that Van and Kat are right. She seems just fine. Perfectly normal. She must not have remembered properly what Patty said.

Charles is laughing, too. His presence here is the biggest surprise of the night. Instead of his usual business suit, or Dockers-and-golf-shirt combo, he's wearing flannel pants and a T-shirt from some road race. His feet are bare, propped on an ottoman. Irina doesn't believe she's ever seen the soles of his feet before. Nor his teeth, for that matter, for how little the man smiles.

Not that Katya is enjoying herself. It's like she's trying to hide behind her wineglass. She's not even sitting next to her husband.

Irina squeezes Darius's hand and tries to catch Katya's eye. See? She wants to say. Look what I've got. A handsome husband who truly loves me.

Irina puts her empty cake plate down on the floor. So it's hypocritical to gloat about a husband she intends to divorce. She doesn't get many things over on Katya, with her big fancy house and successful business and rich man.

As she glances around again at her family, Irina thinks that everyone looks happy. Together, contented, relaxed, all that sappy stuff. It won't last, she knows. They all know that.

"At least they're not dull," she murmured to Darius on the plane on the way back to Michigan, after she'd complained through a whole time zone about their various offenses. And he replied with the gravity of a guru, "All happy families are alike; every unhappy family is unhappy in its own way."

"My, aren't you profound," she said, staring out the window at the flat glaze of white cloud.

"It's Tolstoy," he said, opening one of his textbooks. "From *Anna Karenina.*"

Irina catches Van staring at their mother. For all his confidence in his room about how nothing was wrong, he seems worried now. But then, when isn't he worried? He'd worry if there was nothing to worry about, just to fill the time. Irina was just a kid, but she could remember him pacing the house, tugging on his earlobe, and holding his notes or a textbook. He liked to walk and study at the same time. How he didn't crash into walls was a mystery for sure.

Van's cell phone bleeps, and they all pause in their conversation. He flushes pink and looks at the screen, then the color drains from his face. He scurries from the room.

In the silence that settles after him, the storm takes up residence, crashing and roaring like a fairy-tale giant.

Katya sighs. "I wonder where the kids have got to."

She weaves a little getting up from her chair. For someone who normally polishes every aspect of her appearance, she looks like someone mopped the floor with her at the moment. Still wearing that dress, no shoes, runs in her nylons, makeup smeared all over. Hair coming loose from its updo.

All of a sudden, Irina can't look. Katya looks old and more than a little wrecked. Her step is heavy as she passes into the kitchen.

Bartleby the cat dozes on Max's lap. Her father's gaze is a million miles away, like always, but there's something different about his face. It's not slack, as it usually is when he's thinking over one of his books. It's got a tightness to it that Irina is not used to seeing.

Van appears back in the living room. His cell phone is so loose in his hand he could drop it any moment. The shock in his face exaggerates the long, gangly look of his body, and he seems almost spidery.

"There's been an accident."

Mira bolts straight up in her chair. "Who? What happened?"

"Jenny." Van tugs his ear with his free hand. "I have to go get her. She slid off the side of the road on 66. She's not even to East Jordan yet."

"Will you need any help?" Darius stands up, seeming very strong and tall to Irina just then.

Van stuffs his phone into his pocket and stands up straighter. "I can handle it."

"I didn't say you couldn't. I was just offering to keep you company. Maybe you'll need help pushing the car completely out of the lane." Darius stands with his weight on one leg, arms folded loosely. The picture of coolness, the flip side of Van.

Van cringes, still yanking the earlobe like he's going to pull it right off. "Sorry. No, it's fine. From what I gather, it's completely out of the lane and halfway in some guy's yard. She was calling me from some gas-station convenience store. She'd walked up the side of the road."

Irina chews on her tongue, wanting to say, "Told you so, moron," but she'd sound like her big sister, and, anyway, Van has figured out his mistake all by himself by this point.

"Take it easy," she says instead. "We don't want to have to come rescue you, too."

Their father shakes himself out of his reverie. "Is she okay?"

Van pulls on his ear again, and Irina feels like yanking his hand away from it. "She says she's fine, but she sounded . . . I don't know. I think she's okay."

Mira stands up to give Van a hug. "Let me get you Max's old raincoat. I wonder why she went out in this storm, anyway? She would have been welcome here."

Van slides his eyes over to Irina. She gives him a pitying smile and looks away. She can't be too hard on him. Considering.

Max jumps to his feet, and Mira drops something in the hallway when Katya screeches from upstairs, "Mother! Come see what you've done to my kids!"

Chapter 40
Mira

Oh, bollocks.

In my office, I see exactly what has got Katya screeching and grabbing fistfuls of her own hair.

Chip is cross-legged on the floor, head lowered like a kindergartener sitting in the corner. His eyes are bloodshot, and despite his mother's raving frothing anger, a dreamy smile keeps floating to his lips. Taylor is next to him, similarly bloodshot, but looking distinctively gloomy.

And the place reeks of pot.

"I'm raising to try . . . trying to raise . . . two, er, three young people in this crazy stupid world, and giving them all the 'just say no' speeches and making them sign their little DARE pledges and where do I catch them getting high? In my own mother's house. With her very own weed."

Kat's disgust radiates like heat from a sidewalk in August. She thinks she's standing up straight, in her usual position of indignation, but she's drifting in place and has to keep moving her feet to stay upright.

"You're so drunk you can barely stand, and you are going to lecture me about substance abuse?"

Taylor gasps, and Chip stifles giggles with his hand.

Kat wipes at her face, smearing more makeup. "Fine. Keep getting high like it's 1968, keep wearing the same old ratty clothes like you're still twenty-two years old even though you look insane. I couldn't care less. But when you leave it lying around so my kids can get to it, in fact so they'll not only get to it but think it's cool because Grandma does it . . ."

"It wasn't lying around." Chip lifts his head to his mother. The vapid smile has gone for now, but his voice has a lazy, syrupy quality.

"Yeah," chimes in Tay. "We had to really work to find it." He points over his shoulder at a stack of books they piled on a chair to reach the top shelf of my closet. The little jade box where I keep my pot — the box was a gift from Paul after one of his overseas trips — is open on my desk.

"Ask them why they were snooping in my study."

"My kids are in here getting high, and you're concerned about your drugs?"

"I'm not concerned about the drugs. I'm wondering why they thought it was okay to rummage in the farthest reaches of my closet."

I haven't had to put on a stern look for a small child in many years, and I'm not sure I can remember how to do it. My own high has long faded, but even so, the most I can manage is to look sad. And I am.

Chip is staring at the floor again, fascinated by a pattern in the carpet. Taylor is the one who gazes up at me with a quivering chin. "Don't be mad, Gramma."

"I'm the one who's mad, Taylor Richard. I'm the one you should be worried about." Katya starts to tap her foot, then leans on my desk for support instead.

Taylor darts a quick glance at his mother and turns back to me. Tears tremble at his eyelids, threatening to fall. "We went into your purse. You left it on the table, and Chip wanted to see what was in it."

Chip giggles some more. "We found a *joint.* I mean, wow. A joint."

My emergency escape hatch, I'd thought that morning as I slid it into a lipstick case and dropped it in my purse. It was still there last I looked.

Now it's Katya's eyes that are shiny with tears. "Go downstairs." She enunciates each syllable, whether out of anger or because she's trying not to slur, I don't know. "Talk to your father. This is going to be one long summer for you two. And where is your sister?"

"Taking a bath," Chip answers, pulling himself off the floor like he's climbing out of a tar pit. "Don't worry, Mom. We wouldn't have let her do it. She's too young."

"I'm so glad you have standards," Katya chokes out, as they pass. Chip is nearly as tall as she is, and Taylor not far behind. Katya closes the door behind them and turns back to me.

The smell in the room and the expression on her face make me want a joint in the worst way.

"I can't believe you."

"What I do on my own time is my own business. I didn't ask them to go through my purse and my closet."

"I should not have to worry about their finding illegal drugs in their grandmother's house."

I grab my jade box and put the lid back on. I swipe the books they used to reach the closet onto the floor. "It's not like they've never seen pot before."

"I'll have you know we live in one of the best school districts in Michigan. Their friends come from some of the best families in the city, thank you very much."

I put the box back where it goes, and I know I shouldn't do this, I shouldn't throw this in her face, but Katya can't keep living like she's in the pages of *Better Homes & Gardens.* I step down from the chair carefully.

"Did you notice they were smoking joints? Already rolled? I didn't leave any joints in here already rolled. Just the papers and the weed, loose."

Katya just stares. She's so drunk she can't follow what I'm saying.

"They, or at least Chip, already knew what to do. He expertly rolled that joint." I picked up the roach from my ashtray. "Yep. He's done this before, you can bet your big fancy house on it."

"He does not know how to do drugs. You left a joint in there, and you just don't remember."

"Run down there and ask him, quick before he comes down and realizes how much trouble he's in. Did you see how high he was? He didn't have that much time in here after he found the weed. He got right down to business. At the bare minimum, he's seen it done. Seen it enough times to do it himself."

Katya's face has gone pearly white under the remnants of her makeup. She can only shake her head. "That still doesn't resolve the question of why you think it's okay to have illegal drugs in the house?"

"You don't know anything about it."

Katya's face is pulled into a sneer. "I know marijuana is illegal. I suppose next you'll tell me it's medicinal. What, are you dying of cancer?"

The noises of the house ring loudly in my ears. Bartleby's paws click across the kitchen floor. The spirea bush outside scrapes the window in the gale-force winds of the storm. The grandfather clock, an heirloom and the only thing of my parents I kept in the house, ticks sedately in the hall. Katya thinks she's scored quite a rhetorical coup. Her eyes gleam with malice and victory, having momentarily forgotten her shattered illusions of her perfect sons.

"It just so happens that yes, I am."

Katya laughs, a harsh barking sound. "Oh, very funny. You're such a card. That's what everyone loves about you. Isn't Mira charming? Isn't she funny? Isn't she so wacky?"

"I'm not kidding."

Her laughter spirals down. "This isn't funny."

"It damn well isn't funny, no."

"You're not serious."

"Very."

I should have eased into this announcement, but then, I didn't expect to be spilling it this way, in my office, which reeks of hash smoked by my grandchildren.

"What kind?" Katya sinks against the edge of my desk and grips with both hands. "What can they do?"

"Breast cancer. And they can do things, but I don't want them to."

"Don't want them to what? What things won't you do?"

Katya shakes her head. She always used to do that when she was a girl, struggling over a vexing math problem. She'd sit there over her homework, squinting at the paper and shaking her head as if she could shake out the correct answer.

"I'll talk to the family. You'd better get everybody together."

"They don't know?"

"Your father knows. Go get them all together. Well, except Van. He's driving to get his friend off the side of the road."

"I can't believe this," she says, drifting out of the room, one hand on her head like she's checking for a fever.

I can't believe this, either. Any of this.

The girls look like members of a jury. Their bodies are crossed and locked in positions of judgment and anger. Only Max is in motion. He paces the perimeter of the screened-in porch, stopping now and then to peer outside at the storm, which has let up a bit, the thunder more like a low hum than destructive crashes. Kat has finally changed out of her fancy dress and is wearing a huge nightshirt, which reaches to her knees, and flip-flops. She's also finally washed off that makeup, but I see she hasn't laid off the wine, yet.

Can't say as I blame her.

The grandchildren lounge on pillows in the center of the room, seemingly unaware of the reason for the meeting. Chip keeps chuckling about God only knows what, Tay is eating a bag of Cheetos that must have come from Katya's stash of snacks, and Kit strokes Bartleby, who lies splayed out on her back.

I raise an eyebrow at Katya, gesturing with my head at the kids. Does she really want them here? She merely glares back at me.

With the wind dying down, we've opened the windows and the night breeze slips in.

Still muggy, but at least it's moving.

The still inside air was choking in its closeness.

Katya and Irina are sitting side by side on a wicker love seat. Katya pats Irina's hand, and Irina lets her. That's surprising, but then, crisis is supposed to bring solidarity, so I'm told. Darius leans against the door to the outside, as much on the fringe as he can be. He inspects his cuticles, his face passive.

Charles is out of his laconic pose in the recliner and sitting up straight now, ankle crossed over his knee, hands gripping the sides of the chair.

"So. Tell them, Mom," Katya says, her voice hard like the crack of a whip. "Tell them how you're dying."

Irina jabs a finger at her sister. "You make it sound like a personal attack. Like she arranged to be dying just to mess up your life. God, you're self-centered."

"I suppose you're glad she hid this from us? Maybe that suits you just fine. Ignorance is bliss, right, Reenie?"

So much for solidarity.

From his post at the window, Max turns to face the room. "Girls. Stop."

He didn't raise his voice, but his speaking up at all in such a way is enough of a surprise. The girls fall silent, glowering at each other. Irina leans on the arm of the love seat, aiming her body away from her sister.

"I found a lump, then I found another. Dr. Graham says I have breast cancer. She says I need surgery. Probably chemo and radiation, too, depending how much it's spread."

"So when is the surgery?" Reenie bites her lip, tucks her feet underneath her on the love seat. "You've scheduled it, right? Mom?"

Katya slurps her wine audibly.

"Reenie, listen . . ."

"You're not going to do it?" Irina nearly shrieks this, mouth open and her eyes glassy with shock.

"When did you learn about this?" Katya interjects, not willing to let me off the hook for keeping the secret.

"Ten days ago."

Max says, "Your mother says she's given this a lot of thought."

His voice comes out strangled and forced, the use of "your mother says" signaling that he doesn't believe this himself.

"I'll bet," Katya spits out. "When has she ever given anything a lot of thought?"

"Mom," Reenie persists. "Are you really

going to let yourself . . . die?"

"Honey, I know it's hard to explain . . ." In my effort to be gentle about something that hurts, I flash back to removing a sliver from a tiny finger, using a needle to probe the top layers of skin, all the while cooing, *Almost there, it will be all right, almost got it . . .* "But it's not like this surgery and all that is a walk in the park. And it might not even work."

"You look fine." Irina now slumps back, drumming her fingers on the love seat armrest, taking in her air in quick gasps.

"So far, yes."

"It can't be that bad, then."

"It is, sweetie."

"How could you do this to me?" Reenie curls up even farther, and starts chewing on a thumbnail, an old habit I haven't seen in years.

"Now who's self-centered," Katya says.

"I have a baby coming," Reenie shoots back. "I need your support, Mom."

Katya, predictably, takes offense. "Oh, and I'm a potted plant? I've been around that block three times."

Reenie acts as if she hasn't even heard. "You have to fight this, Mom."

A crushing weight is settling on my chest again, pressing me down in my chair.

"Don't tell me what I have to do," I say, before I realize the words are out of my mouth. "When your doctor looks at you and tells you to get parts of yourself lopped off and you just say 'Roger that, Doc, whatever you say' then you can get on your high horse about what I should or should not do. As it is, none of you know a damn thing about this. If I'm going to shuffle off this mortal coil, it's my own damn business."

Katya tries to smack her wineglass down on the end table but misses, spilling it on her nightshirt. Since it's Shiraz, she looks like a stabbing victim. "We almost made it through the whole weekend before quoting Shakespeare. And *Hamlet,* of course. Why don't you arrange for some sort of duel so you can go out like a true tragic hero?"

"I didn't expect any of you to understand. Why do you think I didn't want to say anything?"

"Mira . . ."

"Leave me be, Max."

"Gramma?"

I'd almost forgotten about the kids, sprawled on the floor, below my line of sight.

"Yes, Kitten?"

"Are you really going to die?"

I crouch down, though my knees give me

a punishing jab of pain. "Not right away or anything. But it looks like, well . . . Not years and years, either."

"Aren't you scared?"

Her big brown eyes search my face in awe. I don't see fear, or grief even. As precocious as she is, it probably hasn't dawned on her what I'm really saying. The only death in her tiny world has been a goldfish.

"You know, I'm not. I've had a good time, and it doesn't last forever for any of us." This makes her flinch, so quickly it's like a firefly flash. "But honey, you've got decades and decades. Ages. So have your mom and dad."

The boys haven't moved from their sprawl. Tay seems to be asleep, with his hand in the Cheetos.

"Is there anything we can do?" This is from Charles, who fiddles with his watch-band. Fastening, unfastening. Action-oriented, my son-in-law.

"Thanks for offering, but I don't really think there is."

Standing seems like too much effort, so instead I sit back, cross-legged, rooting my tailbone to the earth like my yogi taught me. I join Kit in stroking Bartleby.

Darius crosses the room and takes Irina's hand. He pulls her up to stand, wraps his arm around her, and leads her from the room without a word.

Katya watches them go and shoots a glance at Charles, who now stares out at the storm, gathering strength again outside.

"Ivan should have taken the Escalade," he says.

CHAPTER 41
KATYA

Of course Reenie would fall apart. She's such a child. Katya remembers that by her age, she herself was a college senior, engaged, and already ramping up her design business on the side.

And of course Mother would choose this moment to go all "Circle of Life." Katya could see the wisdom in eschewing caffeine and pesticides, and carrying groceries in her own canvas bags has a certain kind of economic sense.

But cancer? A growth eating her alive from the inside out?

If that were me, thinks Katya, *I'd be first in line for the scalpel.*

And now her mother has scared Kit by all this death talk. *The boys will probably have to hear all this again tomorrow, when they're no longer high, thanks again, Mom.*

Katya tries to picture what exactly Chip was doing when she walked into the study.

Whether or not he looked like an old pro at using drugs.

The wind grows shrieky and in a blink, everything goes black.

Katya wonders who leaned on the light switch, until Max says, "Nobody move, nobody panic. I've got a flashlight on one of these tables . . ."

"Oh, terrific," she hears Charles mutter from across the room. He probably wanted to get on the computer again tonight.

"It's OK, kids, nothing to worry about," Katya says.

"Duh, Mom." So much for Kit being vulnerable.

At her house, a blackout would be instant cataclysm, at least if the kids hadn't been charging their phones and laptops. Their house sucks down so much power, she's surprised the power grid doesn't spit them out from pure disgust at their gluttony. Between Charles's work computer, Katya's work computer, the desktop in the office, the kids' computers for homework, the televisions, DVD players, chargers for all their iPods and more . . .

At Mira's the only thing missing is a few lamps, shortly to be replaced by candles. Probably organic beeswax candles manufactured by Rwandan villagers or some shit.

Katya stretches out in the space vacated by Irina, led away by her doting husband. Her wine is gone, most of it spilled on her shirt.

Max's flashlight beam slices the dark, making the surrounding blackness even more startling.

"I'll get some more flashlights. Other than Irina and her husband, we're all in here, right?"

No one answers.

"Hello? Am I alone?"

"We're all here, Dad," Katya says with a sigh.

She could just find her way to her room, though. As well as she knows the old house. She should probably lay off the wine anyway, as Charles is always saying. Katya wonders how late it is, whether Tom would be awake.

Kat is possessed by two powerful urges. More wine, to keep her headache at bay, and to talk to Tom. Because Tom knew her before she was old.

The flashlight beam stops in front of her, and her father's hand holds out a candle and a book of matches from Nanny's, the restaurant on Ferry Avenue Beach that used to be the scene for all the Zielinski birthday dinners and other celebrations.

Katya takes them wordlessly and shuffles into the darkened house.

"Wait for me," Charles says from behind her, and she stops for him to catch up. "Are you going to light that?"

She wasn't going to because she can find her way around by memory. But Katya hands him the candle and the match flares up, bringing his face into view like something out of a Vincent Price film. With his stubble and the lines around his mouth, he looks a decade older than her mental picture of him.

The candle reeks of that hippie incense stuff her mother is fond of. The Yankee Candle scents Katya has given her over the years are probably in the closet next to the pot. Or maybe Mira gave them away to a thrift store.

Katya moves into the kitchen, which lights up in the stuttering flashes from the storm lightning. Between those bursts, and outside the soft orb created by the candle, there are only shapes of black. She tries to peer out the window, but all she can see is wetness on the pane. There's not even a moon, and with no streetlights, or neighbors' lights, the night looks primeval. She feels her way along the counter until she encounters the wine bottle. Since she left her glass in the living room, she takes a swig right from the bottle.

"Charming," says Charles. "I thought you were going to bed."

Katya casts a glance behind him. The kids are talking to Max on the porch. He's probably telling them one of his fanciful stories, like he used to when she was a girl, when he wasn't away on a tour, or holed up in his study with a manuscript. She doesn't see Mira.

"We have to talk about the kids. I caught them getting high. The boys, anyway."

"Oh."

"Oh? That's all you have to say is 'Oh?' We've got two druggies on our hands . . ."

"Get over yourself. Everybody experiments. Even you, Mrs. Peterson."

"Trying a joint at a frat party does not count, and I was in college. For God's sake, Taylor is not even in high school!"

"Where did they get pot?"

Kat snorts and swigs from the bottle again, unable to believe what she has to say. "My own mother."

"She gave them weed?"

"She didn't give it to them. They were snooping and found it."

"I'll have a talk with them when we get home."

"What's wrong with now?"

"Besides the fact that it's late, we're in the middle of a storm and blackout, and they just found out their grandmother is dying? A lecture can wait."

"You just don't feel like dealing with it."

Charles sighs roughly. He's moved the candle away from his face so it illuminates his T-shirt from the 5k instead. Katya was supposed to run that race with him, but she got busy with some last-minute client projects. "No, I don't feel like dealing with it. I've got a lot on my mind. Can't we just go to bed?"

"Do what you want. I don't feel like it. I'm upset."

Charles steps forward with his arms out to embrace her, but Katya steps back, fearing the candle will set her hair on fire.

Charles stops, arms frozen outward. "Fine. I'll be upstairs. If the power comes back on, wake me, because I should log into the office computer if I can. Some stuff was going on that I should take a look at."

"Oh, great." Katya knows just what "stuff" he means, and she nearly spits out what she knows about Tara, but stops. There will be a more advantageous time.

"Hey, I held up my end of the deal. I didn't check e-mail or take one phone call through the whole party. Party's over."

Is it ever, thinks Katya. *Is it ever.*

"Just take the candle," she says. "I can feel my way around."

He steps away into the enfolding darkness, and Katya sighs, relieved at being left alone. After two tries, she succeeds in hoisting herself onto the kitchen counter, and plunks the wine bottle next to her. In doing so, she bumps against her phone, which she left on the counter after the party. She flips it open and dials a number, the phone providing its own little glow in the blackness of the kitchen.

"H'lo," mumbles a voice.

"I'm sorry, is it too late? It's Kat."

"I had a long day so I turned in early," Tom says, clearing his throat gently. "How are you?"

"Fine, I guess. Sort of. Actually, I'm having a rough day."

"Oh?"

"I just found out my mom is dying, and she wasn't telling any of us. And she can probably save herself, but she won't have the surgery, and my kids are smoking pot and my husband doesn't care about me at all, he's forever walking away from me. I didn't know it would be this way, being married, I thought we'd always talk, but lately we're more like co-managers than lovers, but maybe you know just what I'm talking about? And I really miss being young, that feeling in your stomach like Jell-O when your phone rings, and it's a boy you like? I always felt that way talking to you."

"Wow, um. Are you OK?"

"I've had too much wine."

"Maybe you should call me back when you're sobered up a bit."

"Well of course I will, but did you hear me? I said I feel like Jell-O talking to you."

Katya grips the phone with both hands and holds her breath. She closes her eyes and imagines Tom's youthful face before hers, his soft lips tweaked in a playful grin, and her stomach is indeed quivering, just like it did when he asked her out, then on their prom night. Graduation night, when they sneaked away from the party . . .

A third voice interrupts them. A feminine voice. "Tom? Who is that?"

Tom's answer is muffled, as if he's covering the phone with his hand.

"Look, Kat, it's been nice to talk to you, but maybe we've done enough catching up for now. I wish you all the best. I've gotta go."

"Tom, I'm sorry, that was really inappropriate . . ." Kat draws herself up straighter on the counter, grasping the air with one hand as if trying to find her dignity.

"G'night."

And he's gone.

Katya closes her phone and sets it down on the counter with utmost care.

She picks up the bottle for one more drink, then tips it way, way back. She feels her way along the counter and drops the empty bottle in the sink, where it lands with a clunk on the enamel.

Her tongue tastes like a strip of duct tape, and she puts one hand over her eyes. Then she laughs.

Laughs because she just drunk-dialed a high-school love with a woman already in his bed. Because her kids are using a gateway drug, and Charles is bonking his assistant, who isn't even particularly pretty.

Because Mira gets to escape it all and leave the mess for everyone else to clean up.

She sniffs and wipes her damp face with her hands. Just as well she'd polished off the booze. If she drank any more, she might end up dancing naked in the rain, and she'd be hauled off to a loony bin.

This is why she's not a carefree, impulsive person, she reflects. She places one impulsive call and spits out her feelings and ends up sitting alone on the kitchen counter with tears drying on her face and an empty bottle of wine the only thing to show for her effort.

Max comes into the kitchen, the flashlight beam bobbing ahead of him, the kids following behind. Katya hears a protesting mewl from Bartleby, in the clutches of one of the kids, apparently. Katya wipes her face again and hops down from the counter, landing unsteadily but without actually collapsing.

"Katya, we should get to the basement."

"Why? What's in the basement?"

"There's a tornado coming."

Chapter 42
Ivan

The sheets of rain drape over the car, and Van navigates by following a set of taillights ahead of him. M–66 is a twisty two-laner along Lake Charlevoix, threading the woodsy countryside between Charlevoix and the main highway south. With every slip of his tires as they surf through the storm water, Van curses himself for sending Jenny out in this.

"Stupid insensitive jackass," he mutters. He distracts himself from the real possibility of crashing his own car by coming up with more insults. "Nutter. Imbecile."

Jenny didn't sound hurt on the phone, but it could happen yet. She's stranded on the highway and could get run over if a truck plows off the road.

Van swears as the car fishtails again. He'd been pressing down harder on the accelerator without realizing it.

If he lost Jenny, she'd leave a huge tattered hole in the fabric of his life. Even without working side by side anymore, they saw each other weekly, called or e-mailed every single day. Only Jenny knew how inadequate he felt in comparison to his father, his older sister. Only Jenny knew about that night and Irina, about which he'd never told another soul.

He casts his mind back to the first day they had met, before he had grown so cynical at Death March High. He was wearing a blazer over a Rolling Stones T-shirt, khaki cargo pants, and Converse Chuck Taylor sneakers. It was all at once an attempt to look self-consciously cool to his students, clutch desperately to the filaments of his own youth, and walk the line of the dress code.

The music room was just down the hall from the languages corridor. He'd gotten lost and turned into Jenny's room by mistake. Her hair was black, then, so black it shone blue under the classroom lights. She had a nose ring. In a teacher! It was tiny, barely to be seen. But still. Van was intrigued. She started to give him directions, then slipped into French, and kept talking to him as if he could understand. Van was confused, then panicked. Had he gone insane and was hearing in other languages?

Did he indicate he could speak French? Had this girl chosen this precise moment to go completely barking mad? He stammered and perhaps turned pink, and she tossed her head back and roared.

"You should have seen your face! I knew I was speaking French to you. It was my own little private joke. *Pardonez moi.*" Then she took his elbow and steered him toward his room, depositing him there with a wink tossed back over her shoulder.

Van slows the car, peering through the sheets of rain, looking for Jenny's hazard lights. That's when he notices it's even darker than before. The car ahead of him — whose taillights he'd been following like bread crumbs in the forest — has turned off, or sped up and away. Based on her description, she should be . . .

He sees it. Her Cavalier, with the dome light on. She'd skidded off the road, and her car is parked on the lawn of some cottage, her front bumper aimed right at the front door. In Van's headlights he can see the deep, muddy ruts made by her tires. He pulls into the driveway of the cottage and is nearly alongside her car when he hops out into the rain. The storm slaps him in the face, which Van decides he richly deserves.

She opens the door before he gets there.

Her wet dress sticks to her, and her hair is matted to her head.

"I've been trying to get it off the yard, but I can't, driving or pushing, either one," she says without prelude, not meeting his eyes.

"I'm sorry, Jenny . . ."

"Let's just move the car!" she shouts over the sound of rain hammering metal.

Van nods and gestures for her to get back behind the wheel. He stands between the car and the house, bracing himself to push it away from the house and back toward the road. The lightning is coming more frequently, and Van questions the wisdom of putting his hands on a metal car in an electrical storm. Jenny looks down, then gives him a thumbs-up in the dome light to indicate she's put the car in neutral.

Van's shoes — still his good shoes from the party — slip pathetically on the slick grass. He can't even see where he's pushing the car. The interior of Jenny's car is the only thing visible. All he can see is her face, frowning, her hands tense on the wheel.

Then it starts to roll. Toward him.

Van backpedals but the slick grass offers no escape traction, either, and the car under his hands is tilting forward, giving Van the sense that it's about to gather speed and run him down, even with no motor.

So Van hops on the hood, causing Jenny to yelp and cover her mouth with her hands.

The car rolls forward about six feet, Van grasping the windshield wipers to keep from falling off, Jenny starting to laugh, then it bumps to a stop against what looks to be a heavy concrete planter filled with geraniums.

Jenny continues to laugh, and Van laughs, too, nearly drowning at the same time, as rainwater pours down his face and into his open mouth.

He gestures for Jenny to get out, and together they dash into his car.

For whole minutes they can't do anything but start partial sentences and guffaw.

"You jumped on the . . ."

"I thought the car . . ."

"Looked like a maniac . . ."

"Car was trying to kill me!"

Jenny finally wipes the rain off her face and picks up her cell phone. "I guess I better call a tow truck. I should have earlier, but I thought you could push it out of the way." She smirks at him. "Guess I should have remembered I was calling Ivan Zielinski, not Mr. Universe."

"I should have brought my soccer cleats instead of my dancing shoes."

Jenny tosses her phone back into her bag.

"No signal."

Van tries his, with similar luck. "Not here, either. I guess we'll have to leave it for now."

Jenny nods. "It doesn't look like anyone's home at the cottage, anyway. Will you drive me back here tomorrow? Then I'll get the car and leave the owner a note. Does insurance cover lawn damage?"

"Ah, who cares. Some rich prat with a summer home can spare some money for grass seed."

Van cranks the VW's engine and puts his arm on the back of Jenny's seat to brace himself as he peers into the dark, backing out onto the road. "I'm sorry, Jenny. I don't know what I was thinking to let you go home in this."

"You should be sorry."

Both of them jerk back slightly in their seats as he punches the brake. In the years he'd known Jenny, much as he occasionally deserved it, she'd never been angry at him. Not for one minute.

"Well, I am." That familiar regret settles in his stomach. A combination of nausea and that dizzying feeling of an elevator dropping too quickly. If only he could go back, before he behaved badly enough to lose his best and only friend.

"You should have just told me you invited

Barbara. I wouldn't have come out here and spent the gas money and made it so awkward for all of us that I risked the monsoon rather than stay there anymore."

"I didn't invite her. I mean, I didn't think she'd come."

"You thought wrong."

Van resumes driving, gingerly taking to M–66 again, keeping more or less to the middle of the road, straddling both lanes, as no one else is stupid enough to be out in the weather.

"Are you cold?" Before Jenny can answer, Van pulls to the side and shrugs out of the raincoat Max loaned him. "It's wet, but not as wet as you are. The inside is dry."

Jenny regards it for a moment, then wraps it around herself, shawl style. She nearly disappears in it.

"Maybe we should wait out the rain," he says, before pulling back to the road.

"We could wait all night, in that case."

"Never mind."

They drive for a few more minutes, Van longing to look at Jenny, to see her eyes and determine if their friendship is over or only damaged. Maybe he could patch it up, yet, make this the first relationship in his life he saved instead of destroyed.

"Jenny? Are you OK?"

"Fine. I bumped my knee on the steering column, that's all."

"I meant besides that."

Van exhales as the strip malls on the outskirts of Charlevoix appear in his headlights. It didn't seem like such a long drive this time.

The streetlights aren't working. A blackout. No wonder it was so pitch-dark on the road, no streetlights, no lights from the surrounding homes.

"I guess I'm OK, except that I love you."

Van jerks forward against his seat belt. He's hit the brake too hard at the intersection. "What?"

"You haven't gone deaf, have you?"

Van shakes his head. No, he hasn't. But he may have had a coronary.

Van thinks of writing a song called "Coronary."

Chapter 43
Irina

Irina bounces on her tiptoes, paces the room, stops to bounce again, hugging herself. Her shadow slices back and forth along the wood floor in the light of a single candle on a bookcase, the flame bouncing around in a draft.

Darius sits on the bed, leaning back against the headboard, long legs stretched out in front of him. He'd given up trying to hold her.

"I want a drink so bad."

"You can't have one."

She shoots him a glare from behind her hair, which has gone all askew from raking her fingers through it. "One can't hurt."

"We're not taking any chances with my baby."

"It's not just your baby."

"You're just upset. It will pass."

Irina stamps her foot. "It will not pass. My mother will not suddenly get cured. I can't believe she didn't tell us. If I'd only known . . ."

"If you'd only known . . . then what? What, Irina?"

"I can't do this alone."

"Who said you're alone?" Darius stands up next to the bed. "Why are you acting like this is only on you?"

"Because it's only *in* me. It's my problem."

He steps forward with his arms out. "It's not a problem, it's a baby. Our baby. Son or daughter."

"Don't touch me."

He stops short. "What did I do? I'm just trying to help you."

"You shouldn't be here, I shouldn't be pregnant, none of this is right."

Darius's voice grows tight and strained. "But I am here, you are pregnant, and you married me."

"That can change."

"No, you're not doing this. You're not doing what I think you're thinking about doing."

Irina turns her back to him, facing the weather outside. "I made a mistake. Mistakes can be fixed."

The hairs on Irina's neck stand up when she hears Darius's footfalls on the wooden floor. His voice comes from high above her, right behind her. “You will not abort my baby.”

Irina flinches and closes her eyes. How can he think her capable of that? Of doing that to him?

“No. But I don’t want it. You can have it. I’ll file for divorce on Monday, and you can have the baby as soon as I push it out.”

“You silly little bitch.”

Irina sneers into the glass, her reflection flickering with the candlelight. “Yes, go ahead, Darius. Let it out.”

“I should have known you were too much of a child for this.”

Irina doesn’t turn around, but she hears his feet stomp toward the bedroom door. “Why did you even marry me?” he shouts from the doorway.

“Why did you ask?”

She closes her eyes against her reflection, and listens to his steps, now less sure in the darkness of an unfamiliar house. His hands smack against the hallway as he feels his way along.

Van was right. She should have listened to him after that night and stopped dating for a while, even as long as a year. Clean herself out, he said. Give her heart a rest. And her vagina, she added, laughing, though there was nothing at all funny going on.

It was easy for Van to say, though. He's probably never had a real connection in his life. So how could he know what it feels like to connect to man after man, then try to live without one?

Irina drags herself over to the bed and crawls in, wincing because the sheets still smell like sex. Was it just a few hours ago that she and Darius made love before returning to the party?

Irina fingers her wedding ring. Darius is probably right; she is a silly bitch. And he reached that amazing conclusion without even knowing about Alex.

She was living at her parents' house, between jobs and apartments. Also between men. She was getting bored with the same few Charlevoix bars, so when she drove by a wedding party arriving in three limousines at Castle Farms, she decided to crash. She ran home to change into a silky sundress and spiky heels, and turned up prepared to pass herself off as a cousin, if anyone asked.

No one did.

A few sauced groomsmen chatted her up, but none of them lit her pilot light. They all seemed to be mere varietals of the same species of pub rat that she'd been dallying with since she'd been living back at home.

So when Alex sidled up to her in the

courtyard, she was ready for a change.

"You're far too beautiful a woman to be alone," he said, lighting a cigarette.

"You're far too smart to be using a tired old line like that," she replied, grateful for the cloudy night hiding her smile. She got a charge out of that in spite of herself, probably because he'd said it with such cool reserve, like he was simply reading off the bus schedule.

"Oh, I'm not that smart at all," he said. "Or I wouldn't be smoking these things."

He was not handsome exactly, but he was interesting to look at. His face was craggy and lined, his hair graying but still mostly there. Not the first older man to proposition her, not the first one to attract her attention, but the first one who was so arresting. She tried to convince herself to go back inside and find someone her own age, but he'd quirk an eyebrow at her, and she'd stay a little longer.

He had a condo on the lake, and they screwed all night long.

Alex was a Chicago businessman, but he came up to Charlevoix every weekend he could, and every time he did, he'd call Irina. She never said much about him. Though it wasn't her parents' business whom she slept with, and Mira was open-minded enough to accept almost any pairing, something about this relationship felt naughty and illicit, and Irina liked it that way.

She even liked it the first time he started talking nasty to her. Not dirty, she was used to dirty and could dredge up a phone-sex dialogue at a moment's notice. Nasty. Mean. He called her horrible names, and once he grabbed her hair in his fist and yanked her face to his lips. Then yanked her face somewhere else.

It scared her. It also thrilled her. She didn't tell him to stop.

Afterward, he would be his usual laconic, cool self. No hint of genuine meanness. It was all play, Irina decided. She could play with the best of them.

Irina scrunches herself farther down in the sheets as she remembers that one night. *Was it almost a year ago, now? A little more than that.* Van was home visiting on his school's spring break. Fortunately, as it turned out.

She couldn't pinpoint a single thing that had started to make her uneasy with Alex. The last few times they'd met, she would vow to herself never to see him again, but then he'd call, and she didn't know what to tell him. "I can't see you because you slap me and call me a whore" didn't make sense, because he'd been doing that for weeks, and in fact, she'd been enthusiastic in her response to him.

That night was much the same. They had a candlelight dinner on his balcony, then retreated inside. He grabbed her dress and yanked the shoulder strap apart. He would always send her two more dresses for each one he ruined, always with a thin strap at the shoulder. He started to toss her around, kissing her hard, pushing her up against walls. He grabbed her chin and pushed her head back against the headboard of his bed and kissed her so hard she thought she'd suffocate.

"Let's cool it a little, hey?" she finally said, the first time she'd ever asked him anything.

That time, his slap left her with a bloody nose.

"Bitch," he said, throwing her off the bed and onto the floor. He pinned her down, and bit her shoulder. She cried out again, and he hit her again.

"Stop!" she cried, but whether he thought she was playing, or just didn't care, Irina would never be sure. But he stopped nothing.

He stood up and growled, "Wait here," and stormed out of the room, slamming the door behind him. Irina was trying to piece together her clothing when she heard a funny rattling outside the door. She ran up to yank the handle, and it stuck. He'd locked her in.

She searched his room for a phone but couldn't find one. She was contemplating how to get through the window — and then, how to survive a drop from three stories up — when she remembered she'd had her bag still in her hand when he dragged her through the door. She scrabbled on the floor until she found it under his bed.

She didn't dial 911. She sent Van a text message that read: "HELP. COME GET ME" followed by the address of Alex's condo, praying Ivan would understand, wouldn't question, wouldn't call back, he would just come right away.

Irina was starting to panic about what would happen if Alex came back in the room before Van got the message — wait for what exactly, she wondered — when she heard a pounding on the outside door. Then muffled voices growing louder, and then a thwack sound, like a fiercely served tennis ball.

She was cowering in the corner when the door to the room burst open and Van stood there, sweaty and red.

"Come on, Reenie."

Alex was in his kitchenette, a hand over his eye, which was turning several unhealthy shades of yellow and purple already. Irina stumbled out clutching Van's arm.

She refused to let him take her to the police. Refused to let him tell their parents what had happened. Refused, also, to explain how complicit she was in Alex's behavior, at least at first. She only said that it was a game, and he had taken the game too far.

She told her parents a story about falling down the stairs, and they wouldn't have believed her except Van backed her up.

After Alex, she'd reverted to her usual quarry of men her own age who only wanted a simple screw and a "call you sometime," which meant never. Until Darius came along, who wanted more than the simple screw but never raised a hand to her in play or any other way.

Maybe she'd been so thirsty for kindness after Alex and all the empty fucks after him that it was all too easy for her to marry Darius.

So Darius is right about her. Van was right.

Irina turns her head to find a spot on the pillow that's not wet.

Even Alex was right.

CHAPTER 44
MIRA

I hate our basement. Houses like mine don't have basements so much as they do cellars. Dark, windowless, and thick with spiders and dust. At least we put in a cement floor, so we wouldn't all be perched on dirt and potentially sharing our storm shelter with a groundhog.

So I volunteered to go hunt for Reenie and Darius, to keep myself out as long as possible.

Max and Katya are in a frenzy of worry and hand-wringing, made worse because Kat can't get a cell signal to check her weather reports. It's nonsense. We've lived through countless tornado warnings and never had more than a few tree limbs down. It would probably dissipate before it reached civilization. Or veer out over the lake. Or maybe it wasn't even there, and some hysterical weather spotter was just trying to get on TV.

I hear pounding feet on the steps in front of me so I call out, "Darius?" mainly to alert him to my presence so he doesn't run me down.

"Excuse me, Mrs. Z," he says as he pushes past me.

"There's a tornado warning, we need to . . ." But he's off somewhere in the house. He doesn't know where the cellar is, and he doesn't have a candle or light. He's stumbling like a drunken man.

First, I have to check on Reenie.

I knock with one knuckle, tapping out "Shave and a haircut . . ." It was cute when she was little, and she'd call out, "Two bits!" or rap the side of her dresser twice.

As a teenager she would say "Go away!" and once chanted a two-syllable obscenity in response. I gave up that charming little tradition.

At no response, I push the door open slowly. The candle is jittery on the dresser across the room. All I can see of Reenie is a rounded shape under the covers.

"Reenie, sweetheart. There's a tornado warning. We should all get downstairs."

The lump under the covers is impossibly small for an adult woman. She's curled herself so tight.

"I don't care," she finally murmurs. "It

won't hit us anyway, they never do."

"C'mon, it's not safe to be in this room with all these windows."

"What do you care? You're killing yourself anyway."

Some days, on the receiving end of my children's ire, I can shrug it off. Realize it's their issue, not mine, just like when they were toddlers having breathless screaming tantrums on the floor, and I'd know it had nothing to do with me, or whether they wanted jelly on their bread, and was just a kid thing. I'd count to ten and carry on with my day.

Then there are times, like now, when it's like an ice pick right in the heart.

"Haven't you ever felt something that didn't make logical sense?"

Irina sits upright in bed. Her hair is all over her head, and the candlelight glints on a face wet with tears.

"Don't you feel obligated? I mean, you have kids."

"Look, it's not like I have total control over this, like I flip a switch between life or death. None of us can control our fates."

"You didn't answer my question. Don't you care about your new grandchild? Or is it, 'been there, done that' because you've already got three. Just like when I came along and you were barely ever there because whoops! Didn't plan on Irina."

"No one ever said that; it's not true."

"Right. Fine. Anyway, we have to go downstairs, do we? If I can find my husband, I'll bring him down and we can all sing 'Kum Ba Ya' and hold hands."

Reenie yanks a sheet off the bed and wraps it around herself like a shawl.

The insults that sting the most are the ones with a ring of truth. We weren't prepared for Reenie.

I was forty-four years old. Kat was sixteen and well into those fraught teen years. Ivan was eleven and doing well in school, even though he didn't make friends easily. I was reveling in full nights of sleep and no training pants or pacifiers.

Irregular periods weren't so strange for me, so it was a while before I thought to question why I was so tired all the time, and why my normally favorite foods made my stomach turn.

I remind myself that it's impossible for Irina to know that I cried all day after the doctor told me I was pregnant. That I briefly considered terminating the pregnancy. That Max was so alarmed by my state, he actually considered letting me do it.

But maybe somehow in the womb she felt

it. Maybe my uterus bathed her in ambivalence. A polluted atmosphere.

She came out over a week late, feet first. As if unwilling, as if she knew.

I loved her, though. After my initial panic, I settled into acceptance, and when she actually was born, after that grueling, horrid labor, I looked into her tiny dark eyes under that swirl of black hair, and thought, *Well! How did I ever think I could live without you?*

It's true she spent more time in her baby swing than the other kids, and Katya was pressed into service as a babysitter more than was healthy for either of them, I'm sure. But I had just been elected president of the faculty union, had taken on a big load of classes, and Max's career was taking off, and his editors were always leaning on him to hurry up and finish the next book.

When I did get time with her, I tried to love her extra hard. Did she notice? Did it matter?

Did anything I ever did for the kids make a slightest difference in how they turned out?

If I go ahead and put myself under the knife and pump myself full of chemicals in an effort to extend my life, will it matter? The kids think they will feel better, but will they? Watching me get sick in order to get well, if I even do? What if my last years are marked by side effects and medical treatments, the good times left long behind?

I should have told them right before they left to go home, when they could have digested the news in their own environments. Now we're all shut up here together like inmates.

The screen door clatters downstairs, and a voice calls, "Mom? Hello? Where is everyone?"

I grab the candle and get downstairs as fast as my knees will let me, shielding the flame from this drafty house.

"I'm here, Van!"

I approach them with the candle and the circle of flame expands on them to reveal a couple of soaking-wet kids. Jenny in particular looks like a shipwreck survivor.

"Oh goodness, let me get you some dry clothes. My stuff will be too big, but maybe you can borrow some from Irina . . ."

"Oh, I'm sure you've got something that will do. I'm sure she only brought a couple things for the weekend."

"As long as you don't mind old flower-child clothes."

Jenny looks down at herself and grins, then I chuckle, because of course she doesn't mind.

"I take it you're OK?"

Van answers, "Yes, we're fine. She's fine. Everyone's fine." He looks like his father suddenly, his eyes unfocused ahead of him, his mind gone traveling somewhere.

"We have to get downstairs, there's a tornado warning, and your father and sister are in a tizzy."

As if on command, Katya comes storming up the stairs. The running is uneven and frantic.

"Funnel cloud!" She's breathless at the top of the stairs, and her flashlight beam bounces all over the place. "The radio! They think they spotted a funnel cloud outside Charlevoix!" Funnel cloud. If it touches down, it's a tornado.

Reenie comes out of the downstairs hall. "Where's Darius? I can't find him!"

"Get downstairs, now!" Katya yells in her demanding-mother voice.

"Darius!" Irina flies past us, still dragging that sheet behind her like a cape, and she runs toward the back door, clattering against a chair and cursing on the way. She peers through the dark. "He's out in the car!" She sheds her bedsheet then and darts out into the maelstrom. Van shoots out behind her, and we all follow to the doorway. Darius is slumped in the seat, illuminated by the dome light. In a moment, he sits up, and the trio runs back to the house.

The screaming gale chases them into the house, and Max slams the door on it.

"Mira, grab some clothes for the girls, and I'll get everyone downstairs."

The wind picks up faster, and, finally, their urgency affects me. Maybe it really is happening this time. "But my mother's clock, we should get it downstairs."

"There's no time!"

Max tosses me an extra flashlight from a drawer, and he and Katya lead the troops to the cellar. I dash up the stairs as best I can, going by memory as well as by the meager yellow light. I have a mental image of this lovely old house ripped from the ground, with me still clinging to the stair railing, and it's a picture both frightening and oddly exhilarating.

In my room, I yank open my wardrobe doors and grab a couple of big old dresses and sweaters, then stop by the bathroom long enough to seize a couple of towels. I wonder if Katya's children are terrified, and if the boys have come down from their high enough to know what's going on. Kit probably has Bartleby by now. She wouldn't stand for leaving her upstairs in a tornado, though Bartleby is probably yowling in protest at being held there.

Now I come to the cellar door, and I hold my breath before descending.

It's cold down there, despite the heat that has wrapped itself around the house all day, even in the night with the windows all shut against the storm. I don't want to go, but I have to.

"Mom! Hurry!" I'm not sure which girl said that, Katya or Irina. Doesn't matter.

I pick my way down the old wooden stairs, closing the door to the kitchen behind me. I duck under the low ceiling, though I'm short enough it doesn't really matter. I shine my beam around, and there's my family, sitting on an old red-plaid blanket we always used for picnics at the beach, at the far corner of the cellar, well away from the tool bench with the screwdrivers and saws. An old mattress is propped up behind them. In the center glows a Coleman lantern that I can't believe still works, from the days when I used to drag Max out camping, after he'd made a deadline and could finally be pried out of his office. The result is a greenish glow resembling the moon on a spooky autumn evening.

"We can put this over us if a tornado hits the house, so we're not injured by debris,"

Katya explains as she sees my gaze light on the mattress. I nod, unable to shake this wistful desire I have to go back upstairs, like a captain going down with the ship. Would it be so bad, to just fly up into the air?

I hand the clothes down to Irina and Jenny, who are huddled on either side of Van. I give him a towel, and he towels off his hair. The radio crackles in the center of the blanket, repeating its entreaties to get to an interior room, into a cellar, or a bathroom, clutching the bathroom pipes.

The grandchildren cluster around their parents. Kit curls up in her mother's lap, twirling a piece of hair. Tay has his head on her shoulder, and even Chip is sitting as close as he can without actually being in her lap. Charles sits cross-legged behind the three of them, talking in a low voice to Chip.

"Where's Bartleby?" I ask, trying to ignore the keening wind outside, the trees raking the wood exterior, as if it's even too much for them, and they're begging to be let inside.

"Stalking spiders," answers Katya, nodding to indicate she's behind me, in the dark outside the circle of lanternlight.

Katya looks older than I've ever seen her, and she keeps wincing. No wonder, with all the booze she's had tonight. Looks like she'll be having her hangover without the benefit of sleep.

We should have grabbed pillows and blankets, or at least a measly deck of cards. We could be up all night long, waiting for the tornado that might never come, Max's anxiety slowly dissipating like air out of a leaky tire.

"Mom, sit down."

Max and Darius are holding the mattress up as a privacy screen, and Jenny and Irina are taking turns changing. Irina comes out first in one of my old dresses, the sweater wrapped around her shoulders.

I fold myself to the floor, and Jenny emerges wearing a tie-dyed number I chose for her. I'll let her take it home; it suits her. She curls on the floor next to Van, but they don't touch. They don't look at each other. I wonder what happened on that drive back from her car? What was said?

Because the studious way they avoid each other's eyes reminds me of how Paul and I have maintained for years a steadfast professionalism. At such great effort.

But what a wasted effort for Van and this nice girl, who have no other attachments or obligations so far as I know.

"It's so quiet," Kit says. "Wish I had my

iPod. Oh, Mom, what if it all blows away?"

"It won't. And even if it does, we'll replace it."

"But all my music!"

"Dipwad," jumps in Chip, "it's all saved on your hard drive. You can just download it again."

"Shut up, pothead."

All faces jerk toward Kit. She answers our unspoken question. "You reek like pot. Duh."

"Be quiet, Kit."

"But Mom, he . . ."

"Katherine! You will shut up, for once in your life, shut up."

The radio static surges and swamps the voices, and Max shuts it off. The wind outside sounds preternatural. Lightning goes off around us, flashing through the high, dusty basement windows.

Kit whimpers. Darius murmurs to Irina. Max scuttles to my side and wraps his arms tightly around me. I look around at my family, take them in. Van and Jenny are holding hands. Charles has his arms around Chip and Katya, Katya holds Tay and Kit. Reenie clutches Darius, who looks expectantly at the ceiling. One large brown hand covers her belly.

Even Bartleby has joined our circle, mewling lightly, circling on the blanket.

Then there's a fearsome crack, a creaking, and a thunderous vibration runs through all of us, from the floor to our skulls.

My house, my house.

My family.

My life.

I can't tell if the scream is from a person, or crashing metal, or just inside my head.

CHAPTER 45
KATYA

Katya thinks, *don't hurt the children,* and she's not sure if that's a plea to God or a reminder to herself not to crush or smother them in her clutches. She's grateful for Charles's strong arm around her, though she knows how useless that would be if a twister ripped the house apart and exposed them to the ruthless sky.

What about that mattress that Dad dragged down here?

Too late. A crash echoes through the earth surrounding their cellar hiding place. Someone screams, and she can't tell, maybe she did it herself, even. She squinches her eyes shut and grips her family, maybe if she holds tight enough they can all blow away together . . .

Then it's not so loud. The wind is still present, but only blowing instead of roaring. The lightning has stopped its mad flickering.

For a moment Katya thinks she's still drunk, and only dreamed it all. But she looks up and sees the ashen faces of her family in the light from the lantern, all doing the same thing, cautiously uncurling from their instinctive fetal positions, still gripping their loved ones, unwilling to relax yet.

"I think it's OK," says Darius, his warm, firm voice a balm to Katya's shaky fear. "I don't think it hit us."

"Is it really?" Reenie's voice sounds so small.

"I'll go look."

"I don't know if that's wise." This from her father, who has released Mira long enough to fiddle with the radio. Still just static.

Sirens in the distance. They all look to Darius, and, wordlessly, he steps past them and walks up the steps.

Irina looks bereft without him, and she scoots toward Van, who offers his hand.

Other than the sirens, the quiet is scarier than the noise. It might be still raining, the cellar is too far removed to really tell, but it's definitely not the driven, pounding, drowning rain that it's been all evening.

Darius's footfalls move through the whole house, and he comes down the stairs without anyone else saying a word.

"Hard to tell because the power's still out," he says, "and it's still too cloudy to get much moon. But the house seems intact. No broken windows. Couldn't see outside too well, so I don't know how your neighbors did."

"Oh. Patty . . ." Mira peels herself off the floor and makes an unsteady path for the stairs. Max rises to follow. "Don't go outside, honey, just look through the window."

He turns back to the rest of the family. "I'll grab pillows and things. I'd like us to stay down here. We don't know for sure that it's over."

No one argues. For once.

Katya and the rest start looking over the cellar, picking out places to sleep. She suggests that Irina and Darius be given the mattress, given her condition. Kat expects a nasty look from Irina over the term "condition," but Reenie only stares at her belly, her hand touching it all around, as if feeling for damage.

Katya knows that feeling so well. She remembers falling on the ice when she was pregnant with Tay. Chip had darted out ahead of her into some store's parking lot, and she shouted after him to stop while trying to rush as much as her girth would allow. She never saw the ice or even felt the falling, she was just instantly on her back. She remembered the gasp from the surrounding shoppers, though only one person stepped forward to help her up while the rest simply gawked. Chip was too little to understand why Katya was crying when she yelled at him for running ahead.

A store security guard helped her to the car, and she squeezed Chip's hand so hard he whined about it. Once he was in his car seat, Katya settled behind the wheel, she picked up her bulky car phone, and dialed the doctor's office.

She cried the whole way there, cried in the exam room, and continued crying even after the ultrasound showed Taylor bobbing and weaving in the amniotic fluid, oblivious to all the drama.

So, although Irina's stomach didn't suffer one iota of trauma, she understands down to her marrow.

Mira comes back down the stairs, loaded with blankets. Max follows behind with stacks of blankets and some old musty sleeping bags, and a few flashlights balanced on top of the pile.

He hands out flashlights to all of them, saying he doesn't think lighting the candles and going to sleep would be safe, so they prop up the flashlights as best they can to get situated, and ignore the spidery dust of the basement. Bartleby keeps mewling at the door until someone brings down her food bowl and litter box. She won't have it, and finally Mira reluctantly puts them back where they belong upstairs, leaving the kitchen door slightly ajar. Trusting kitty instinct that she'll come back down if the storm returns.

Katya makes a nest for her family along one wall. Chip insists on his own island of blankets, but otherwise, they all pile in together. She notes with some surprise that Irina and Darius have not zipped their sleeping bags together — as her parents always did on camping trips — but have lain side by side, a pall over both of them.

Of course there should be a pall, thinks Katya as she snuggles into Charles's side to make more room for Taylor. Mira is dying and letting herself go.

Why should someone with such self-conscious verve and spirit want to die? She should be wearing irreverent T-shirts that say SCREW CANCER or something, and replacing her luminous silver hair with funky hats and bandanas until it grows back. She could crack jokes about prosthetic boobs, flirt with the doctors.

And of course she doesn't want her mother to die. Especially if her marriage goes under, and she loses herself. Especially if her kids turn to drugs and lose every opportunity she worked so hard to give them.

She still needs her mother. What is so wrong with that?

Katya feels herself drifting off, relieved she doesn't yet have to go upstairs to face whatever devastation awaits them.

Part 3
Departure

Chapter 46
Ivan

Ivan is startled to see Jenny's sleeping face just inches from his. For a moment he thinks they're in his apartment, and they've made love.

Then his eyes focus, and he remembers the cellar, the storm, rescuing Jenny from the side of the road.

She said she loved him.

Ivan sits up, and his joints screech and grind at having slept on three centimeters of sleeping bag over hard cement floor. Flashlight beams still glow through the basement, but the lantern has burned out. Or someone put it out. He glances around and seems to be the only one awake. He turns away from Darius's long arm draped over Irina's waist.

Van takes the stairs a few at a time, lightly as he can, stepping around the squeaky spots. He nudges open the kitchen door to find Bartleby mewing accusingly.

He blinks against the sunlight. It rushes in, so bright it feels tangible, like he's swimming in it.

Van thinks of writing a song called "Swimming in Light."

The windows are dappled with raindrops, which look like jewels in the dawn. But there are leaves too close to the house. The view outside is not what it should be.

Van steps through the screened-in porch and opens the back door.

"Oh, God."

The first thing he sees is Katya's Escalade, smashed by the southern neighbor's tree. It's gone U-shaped, as if it were a toy, and a spiteful boy has taken a bat to it. The leaves and branches of the felled tree rise two stories into the air. Even on its side, the tree is magnificent.

He trots down the driveway, though he's barefoot, and the drive is soaking wet. His bare feet splash in little puddles here and there.

He glances south down the street and sags with relief. The houses are still intact. Porches are smashed, shutters ripped off and dangling, lawn furniture all over the street and scattered in random yards. Some windows are broken by limbs jutting into upstairs bedrooms, but no one's house did a Wizard of Oz.

Van can see other people doing the same. Stumbling out into the daylight, surveying the damage.

He turns to face the north, to check out Patty's house and the exterior of his parents' home, and what he sees makes him sit right down in the driveway, right into a puddle.

The Big Tree. The maple, taller than the house, a century old, is felled. Van feels a stitch in his chest and holds his breath to keep from breaking down. It's only a stupid tree, anyway. They're all safe . . .

But seeing that giant splayed out like that . . . It stretches all the way across Dixon Avenue, its leaves brushing the porch of the house across the street.

The roots have ripped up nearly the whole front lawn. They make up a massive labyrinth taller than two men, clumped with mud. The mass of tangled wood dangles in the air, useless. Dying already. The crater they've left is vast. Van knows that the morning light will crash into the house unfiltered by fluttering green.

"Oh, wow."

Van turns to see Jenny on the porch. She's wearing his mother's old purple tie-dye dress, is wrapped in a sweater, and she has stepped into his own shoes. She looks like a girl playing dress-up.

She was talking about Katya's truck, but then she follows Van's gaze to the Big Tree.

"Oh, no. That was such a beautiful tree." As she approaches, Van stands up and wipes the grit off his pants.

"Thank God it fell across the street, though. Can you imagine if it had fallen the other way?" Van shivers, imagining that massive trunk slicing through the kitchen, the upper boughs tearing into his old bedroom.

"Maybe we can blame my car in the yard on wind. The tornado blew it there."

"Except tornadoes don't leave tire marks in the turf."

Jenny pulls the sweater more tightly around her. That's when Van notices the cool breeze raising goose bumps on his arms. He's still wearing his undershirt and suit pants, having never gotten around to changing clothes.

The silence grows bigger than casual, and Van tugs on his earlobe.

Jenny squints up at him in the morning light. He can see her freckles. "Look, I'm sorry about what I said last night."

"You didn't mean it?"

She looks down briefly at her tiny feet in his shoes. "I meant it. But it didn't need to be said."

Van notices that she looks so small, all shrunken down and hunched over. Virtually unrecognizable compared to the firecracker of a girl that he's known for years.

She says, "But I don't expect you to do anything about it. I don't even know why I said it, except that . . . Well, it's been getting harder not to say it."

Van steps closer, looking down at her quizzically.

"Promise me something," she says, brushing her hair out of her eyes. "It's OK if we're never more than friends, or even if it's too weird to be friends now, I'll get over it. I won't die. But you have to date better girls."

"Better?" He thinks back to stunning Barbara.

"Yes, better. I'm not talking about selfish cover models like whatsherface. Not girls who treat you like shit or girls who don't take the time to get to know you before writing you off as a weirdo. Date nice girls. Even if they're quiet, even if they're a little weird themselves."

"I do the best I can, Jenny." Van folds his arms, uncomprehending how bad treatment at the hands of other people is his own fault.

She laughs. "That's just the point! You don't do the best you can. You very deliberately, for as long as I've known you, do everything *but* the best you can."

"That's uncalled for."

"It's true. Your songwriting for example."

"What does that have to do with anything?"

"You're not really trying to be successful. You're not doing what you know you have to do."

Van steps back from her, warily, as if from a friendly dog that has suddenly begun to growl. "I liked it better when you didn't love me if this is how you show it."

Their attention is drawn away by shouting from the house. They look back, and it's Katya standing on the porch, her hands on her head, shouting, "No! Oh, no . . ."

But she's not looking at her smashed car. She's looking at the front of the house and the ruined Big Tree.

She starts to jog down the driveway, then winces and stops, walking hurriedly instead.

"Oh," she says again as she reaches Jenny and Van. Jenny steps to the side, turning her eyes away. Van reaches around his sister's shoulders and looks in her eyes. Katya's eyes shine with tears. "It's stupid to be upset with everything going on, but . . . I loved that damn tree."

"I know. What a weekend. Irina brings

home a new husband, then this huge storm." Van decides not to bring it up, but there was also that remark last night from his niece about Chip reeking like pot. As soon as she said it, Van realized, oh yeah, I thought I smelled something . . . He catches a whiff of it on his students now and then. Katya's son was doing drugs? Here?

Katya gasps, putting a hand to her mouth. "You don't know, do you?"

"Know what?" Van asks. "What else is there to know?"

At the sound of the screen door to the porch slamming, Van and the girls look up to see Mira on the porch, clutching her purple bathrobe up around her neck.

Chapter 47
Irina

Irina rubs her eyes and turns to look for Darius. Gone, and she sighs with relief. The sound of running feet filters into the cellar, which is now lit by a slice of light coming in from the kitchen.

She follows the noise, nearly tripping over the hem of her mother's old dress.

Katya comes flying back into the house, her eyes red. "Where's my sketchbook?"

"Your what? What's wrong?"

"Go look outside."

She steps to the back porch and breathes in fresh morning, astounded at how good the air feels reaching into the deepest pockets of her lungs, but shocked at the sight of Katya's SUV smashed by the neighbor's tree.

Just like Katya to be freaking out over a stupid car, when their mother is dying and her kids are smoking pot and they could all have been sucked into the sky by a twister.

She turns the other way and grasps the doorframe for support: The big maple in the front is down, having ripped a chasm in the yard. Some official-looking men in hard hats with lights on them are circling the tree, which is straight across the road.

Why did Katya want her old sketchbook anyway?

Irina sees Van, Jenny, and her mother deep in conversation and hangs back from walking out into the driveway. It hits her that no one told Van about the cancer, since he wasn't home for the big revelation. She wonders how he'll react, gloomy as he always is even on the best of days. He won't take it well.

Who can be expected to take it well?

She glances around, listening to the silence in the house. Must be no power, yet, or someone would have the TV on, listening for news reports.

Katya trots past her again, still in her pajamas but now wearing her sneakers, too, carrying her old sketchbook and a pencil. She parks herself on the wet grass right in front of the old tree, puts the pad on her lap, and starts going at it with the pencil. Her hands skate over the page nimbly, her left hand pushing locks of hair behind her head as she keeps checking the tree and going back to the page. After a few moments she turns the spiral bound pages and starts anew.

She looks like a crazy person.

Irina sees Van hugging their mother. Jenny stands to the side, both hands over her mouth in the manner of shocked bystanders. So, now they know.

Irina wanders back into the house, suddenly famished. She sticks her head into the refrigerator, but it's mostly bare, and anyway, she's letting the cold air out in a power outage. Instead, she hops up on the counter and helps herself to an orange from the fruit bowl.

She gets orange rind under her nails as she shreds the peel. It's strangely satisfactory, and even after she gets the peel off, dropping it in the sink next to her, she goes to work on the tiny stringy bits.

It's like their mother has clocked out of being a mother. Distracted and unavailable as Mira was during Irina's own childhood, she really can't imagine her mother would just let herself die if she still had a child living at home.

Irina peels the orange in half, then sections it out, lining up the other sections on the counter.

Maybe Mira has been counting the days

until retirement as a mom, that when Irina turned nineteen and moved out, Mira threw herself a party and thought, I'm free!

Irina does mental math, and calculates she'll be forty when the baby is nineteen. That's not so old, really. Some women are just having babies then. She could start over, recapture her youthful life.

The orange is biting and refreshing, like a cold dip in the water.

Then again . . . nineteen years. In her head, she hears a fearsome judge with an echoing voice pronounce her sentence, and she feels like weeping. Nineteen years, for one broken condom? Unfair! Call the ACLU!

Irina stuffs another orange slice into her mouth and wonders if she's gone completely loopy.

The last person she wants to see comes in the back door.

"Hey."

"Hi."

"How are you feeling?" Darius remains distant. He's asking in the same detached voice he used when he talked about the storm last night. His eyes are shuttered against her; she can't see what he's thinking.

"I'm hungry, but I'm eating, so I'm fine."

Silly bitch. Irina would have preferred more heat and anger. His coolness is frustrating and more than a little spooky.

He takes a few steps closer, but remains more than an arm's length away. "I just went for a walk. Power's still out, and downtown's a mess. Boats are tipped all over the place out there, smashed up pretty good, too. There'll be some pretty pissed off rich folk today."

Irina snorts. "They're insured. They'll buy newer boats."

"How are you doing about, well, your mother?"

Irina can't finish the orange. Her stomach roils suddenly, and the pleasant tang turns to acid in her throat. She gulps. "About like you'd think. Um, excuse me . . ."

She dashes past him and up the stairs. The bathroom is still dim. The only light is the soft morning creeping in around the window shade.

She lifts the toilet seat and the medicinal, sterile water sets her off.

She hears no footsteps behind her. Darius has not pursued her. Katya is still freaking out over the tree.

Her mother has not come to help her.

Chapter 48
Mira

I already miss the light.

The special morning light, as it would weave in around the leaves of our own Big Tree, felt like magic. It would carry in golden bits of dust and you'd think they were spirits of your ancestors come to wish you good morning. It was a dappled, playful light that would dance around the room as the breeze stirred the old maple's branches.

Out my office window now, all I can see is mud and broken roots. Her leaves rest on the porch of the house across the street. These are the last lush, green leaves she will ever wear, in fact. She can't be put back together, after the wind ripped her from the earth.

I twist the ends of the joint I just rolled. I'm not quite the expert at this as Chip. My fingers aren't as nimble as they used to be.

What a lousy grandmother I am. My most

significant contribution to his life in recent memory is to provide him with drugs. Of course Katya should be furious. She has every right.

Not that fury needs permission. Fury comes when it chooses, and it can stay long past its welcome. My own anger simmers. I can almost feel my lid rattling with the pent-up force of it.

I tuck my joint and a book of matches into my bra — next to the renegade left breast — underneath my favorite blouse, silky and in the colors of peacock tails.

It takes a few good yanks for me to open the stubborn old window, but the screen pops out easily. I swing my legs over the sill with some difficulty, but my yogi says I have supple hamstrings for a woman my age.

I'm on the first floor so it's a short drop into the muddy garden. I land smack on some yellowed tulips flattened to the earth by the rain. I'm on the other side of the tree from the main exit of the house. It's a simple matter to walk where I choose without anyone needling me: Where are you going? What are you doing? When will you back?

None of your business, nothing, and when I damn well feel like it.

This is why I've never gotten a cell phone.

It would be like wearing your family around your neck. I'm glad I raised my children in a time when you could leave the house and really, truly leave.

I set off toward town, walking, in no particular rush, my Birkenstocks sloshing through puddles, cold rainwater splashing over my toes. My neighbors pay me no mind as they inspect their own damage. They're righting patio furniture, picking shingles out of the yard, inspecting tree limbs. I note some smashed porches and tree limbs poking into windows. I hope no one was hurt. The unfortunate neighbors across the street had the wind blowing the large old maples toward their homes, instead of away.

Our tree must have been more rotten and aged than she appeared from the outside.

Couldn't have been a real tornado. The damage would have been worse. Much worse. I suppose if people make it to church this morning, they will be praising God for sparing them.

What if a tornado had hit? Would they be praising God for that? Maybe for their own survival, but what if it killed others? Is that worthy of praise?

I wonder if people will try to drag me to church, now that I've got cancer. I turn onto Michigan Avenue. Hardly anyone's up yet. I cross in the middle of the street to the west side. I drop my head so my hair will fall a little, shielding the side of my face from the early-morning rays.

I grimace to myself. I can't imagine being one of those deathbed Christians who find themselves terrified into believing. Patty always asks me, but what *do* you believe? I don't have a good answer for her. I can't say "nothing" because the world is too powerful to be an accident of rocks in space banging around.

Maybe I should figure that out, then. Before I kick off.

Should. I've never been good with "should." I should have been more cunning and political in my dealings with university administration, but that's precisely why I was anything but, why I threw their hypocrisy right in their faces when they tenure-tracked men at twice the rate of women. I should have dropped my old flaming-liberal, feminist leanings in the eighties, some told me, because the battle was over. The women won. Time to cut your hair short and dress like a man and fight it out on their turf.

If not for Paul, soaring past me on the career ladder, then protecting me from his position on high, I would have been teaching freshman comp forever if I even managed to keep my job.

And maybe if I weren't so belligerent, Roxanne wouldn't be threatening me with freshman comp to drive me out of work.

I cross the bridge, which during the day bounces with the weight of cars that stream across. It's only just morning, though, and the bridge is still. I walk down the concrete steps to the walkway beside the channel and turn toward the big lake.

I did toe the line with some of the "shoulds." I stayed with my husband even after he cheated on me. Katya would be shocked. She'd say, *Mira, the original feminist, stood by her man after he had an affair?*

What can I say? I loved him. The kids loved him. He was sorry. He'd been lonely and drunk on a book tour, heady with recent success. He confessed and tortured himself with his mistake for far longer than seemed reasonable.

It hurt anyway, oh, did it ever. I'd been in meetings all day, then went out after work for a drink with the faculty, and the crowd dwindled down to me and Paul, and we flirted and smiled and toyed with the electric current that ran between us, letting it zap us, then retreating. It took everything to pull myself away and go home, chaste, and later I discovered Max was, perhaps at that very moment, screwing some bookstore clerk who wore cat's-eye glasses.

I kept the family together. I gave up working on my poetry, which I'd abandoned decades ago in the crush between children and paying work. I gave up spontaneity and stayed home from more than one protest march or petition-gathering session because I had babies to raise.

I've outgrown shoulds. It's my time, now.

I kick off my Birkenstocks and pick them up loosely in my fingers.

The sand of the beach is pockmarked by the hard rain, and it resists my step the same as hard-packed snow. I pause by the swing set and look out over the lake, which rests languid against the beach, looking exhausted after last night's excitement. The brilliant sun warms my back, but my face is brushed by a cool breeze.

I pull my feet through the sand and settle down against the stone wall that separates the beach from parking. I grind my toes into the sand. A couple of inches down, my toes find the smooth grains untouched by the storm.

It's not Irina's place to tell me what to do, nor is it anyone else's.

Even poor Van will have to learn to grow up. I wish I hadn't had to tell him separately from the others, watching his face crumple inward like it always did when he was a boy. In some ways he's the youngest of the three, with none of Irina's fierceness or Katya's resolve.

I've given them the best start I can, and they have to go on without me. I will not cut myself apart for them.

I fish the joint out of my brassiere and light it up, breathing in the smoke and holding my breath against what everyone else expects of me.

Chapter 49
Katya

Katya's pencil skims the page, and the tree appears before her. It's beautiful in a terrible way, on its side like that.

She breathes fast as she sketches, having forgotten what it was like to pour out everything through the tip of her pencil. She has shifted her position from the porch steps, where she mainly saw roots, and gone around to the far side. She's sitting on an old bath towel in the yard, recording the side view: now she is working on the knots in the bark, the splits where the tree grew wider than its old skin, then grew more to replace it.

If only her mother could just grow a new breast after surgery, maybe she'd go ahead and let them operate.

Katya feels a cramp of regret in her stomach for all the time she's fought with her mother this weekend, this year, this life. Was it really worth it? It always seemed so at the time, so critically important.

"It's just a dress!" her mother had yelled, in that week before the prom, when Katya was a sophomore in high school and had been invited by a handsome senior named Danny Morrow.

But it wasn't just a dress, as any normal high-school girl would tell you. It was never just the dress.

Kat was shopping in Traverse City with the popular girls, friends of Danny's, who'd invited her along after they'd heard she was going to prom with him. She'd been plotting how to cobble together a reasonable dress given Mira's hippie sensibilities. She could use something handmade by Patty, but time was running short, and she had other sewing projects. Kat had yet to find a pattern she liked at the Ben Franklin Five and Dime, anyway. She could troll second-hand stores or garage sales in fancy parts of town, where the styles might not be so out-of-date yet. But she hadn't had the time between her schoolwork and the National Honor Society volunteering, and her after-school job at the corner grocery.

Bottom line: Mira didn't believe in shopping as recreation and thought buying old clothes was a good way to recycle.

Also, a good way to commit social hara-kiri.

One of the girls that day in Traverse City had complimented Katya's denim skirt and asked where she got it. Katya paused for half a beat before making up the name of a store. They looked at her quizzically, and she said, "It's a boutique in Chicago." Patty had made the skirt.

They started trying on prom dresses as a lark at first, claiming they were not seriously shopping. They'd do that later, with their mothers.

But then Katya had tried on a royal blue dress, with a short flouncy skirt, an acre of sequins, and a ruffled, one-shoulder neckline. All the girls had exclaimed over the way it showed off her legs and made her eyes sparkle.

Nowadays it would be ugly and kitschy, but in the eighties it was the height of fashion.

They started urging her to buy it, as she stood in the fitting room, wearing the dress and thick cotton socks. Katya shrugged. She didn't have enough money on her, and hadn't expected to buy anything, she told them. That was true, but she was skating over the real heart of the matter. Mira had other plans for Katya's dress, involving consignment shops or a sewing machine. She would never permit Katya to buy the polyester faux-satin ruffly dress.

That's when Tiffany stuck out her hand with her mother's credit card. "I'll buy it," she said. "And you can pay me back whenever. You have to have that dress. You are gorgeous in that dress."

Katya couldn't miss the significance of her phrasing. "Gorgeous in that dress" meant "Not gorgeous without the dress."

Katya's palms were filmed over with dampness when she got home, the dress wadded into a ball in her oversize purse. She took the stairs two at a time to make it to her room before Mira came out of her office to say hello. She shook the dress out, smoothing the wrinkles as much as she could, and hung it in the far-distant reaches of her closet, where old, ill-fitting clothes silently yellowed away.

She wiped her hands on her denim skirt and stashed the plastic bag from the store in her underwear drawer, also shoved toward the back.

Katya knew she couldn't very well hide the dress from her mother if she intended to wear it. She just didn't want to fight that battle just yet.

Days went by, and Katya held hands with

Danny in the hall and sat on his lap at lunchtime, and laughed with the popular girls at the poor idiots like Peggy Mae, who could politely be called "heavyset" and looked like she wore her mother's clothes from the seventies.

Katya rehearsed her speech to her mother when she was supposed to be paying attention in algebra, and as a result, got only a C on the exam that covered the quadratic equation.

She walked in the house after getting off the bus and surprised her mother in the kitchen. She'd come home early from university that day. It was exam week, and her hours were all jumbled up. They never knew if she'd be there or not.

"Katya! You'll never guess what Imelda just gave me. You're going to love this."

And Katya knew already what it would be, and knew with a desperate, cold certainty that she would hate it.

Mira flourished a satin-and-tulle cream-colored dress, with orange satin trim on the bustline, wide shoulder straps, and a cascading lace appliqué in matching orange, a floral pattern. Mira turned it over, and the appliqué reached around the back of the dress and trailed off.

"Isn't it stunning?" Mira hadn't yet looked

at Katya. She carried on, "It's a 1950s dress, just gorgeous, like a glamorous film star would wear. Ava Gardner, maybe. You're going to really stand out in this."

Kat threw her backpack on the floor. "Of course I will, because everyone will be laughing at me!"

"Don't be silly. It's a beautiful dress, and it's a good thing that it isn't what everyone else is wearing. Trust me on that."

"My God, do you live under a rock? Don't you know what it's like for me in school, always wearing these hand-me-down clothes and trying to pass them off as new? I'm barely hanging on to a social life now, and if I show up in that, they're going to laugh me out of the dance, and I might as well drop out."

Mira placed the dress over the back of the couch. "Now you're just being melodramatic. I suppose you want to spend $200 on some designer piece of trash you'll wear once and never want to see again? So you can be like everyone else?"

Katya stormed up to her room and grabbed her blue dress out of her closet. She yanked off her school clothes and stepped into the dress, stealing a glance at herself in the mirror. She looked like something from MTV, and the dress really did do wonders for her eyes, not to mention her legs, which were not swathed in tulle and could actually be seen.

She flew down the stairs and stood behind her mother, who had gone back to preparing dinner. "There. This is what I am going to wear."

Mira turned slowly, distracted. She froze, and her mouth set in a hard line when she saw Katya. "And when did you get that?"

"When I went to Traverse City."

"And with what money?"

"I'm going to pay for it."

"With what money, Katya?"

"Tiffany paid for it. I said I'd pay her back."

Mira smacked the knife flat side down on the cutting board. "So one of the rich girls tells you to buy a dress, and you just say 'Sure, whatever you say!' You are not wearing that. Leave the tags on, you're taking it back."

"What?" Katya hugged herself as if Mira were about to rip it off right then. "You wouldn't!" She knew her mother wouldn't like it, she knew she'd get a lecture and probably have to pay for the dress herself over several weeks of reimbursing her mother. She never expected this.

"You lied to me and sneaked around to

buy this dress behind my back. You will not wear it."

"I will not wear that thing!" Kat jabbed a finger at the fifties dress, in a heap on the couch. She imagined looking like Sandra Dee at the prom, and she started to cry.

"So Patty will sew you something, but you're not wearing that one."

"You're being so unfair! You're going to ruin my life!"

She turned back to her vegetables. "You'll survive."

"I'm not going then. I will not go to the prom if I can't wear this dress."

Katya crossed her arms, tapping her foot and staring at her mother. Mira's black hair was escaping from the loose braid she wore over a tunic and long floral-print skirt. She was barefoot, as usual. She turned slowly to face Kat and leaned back on the counter, her face still, except for one fine line across her forehead.

"I guess you'll have to call Danny and tell him to find another date."

In the end, Katya feigned a stomach flu at the last moment, when she couldn't bear the sight of herself in the fifties dress, and Mira did not relent about the blue dress. Mira returned the blue one and gave her the money to give to Tiffany, who never knew about the fight.

"I'm so sorry you missed it!" she'd told Katya at school the following Monday. "But I'm sure you can wear the dress next Homecoming."

Next Homecoming, Danny took Tiffany to the dance. Katya sold concessions at the football game and watched a video Saturday night.

Katya shivers in the cool breeze off the lake as she smudges parts of her sketch where the line is too heavy and dark.

She wonders if teenage Katya would have done anything differently if she'd known that in just over twenty years, her mother would have cancer. Maybe she would have smiled indulgently and worn the stupid dress.

"Kat, when are we getting out of here?"

Charles stands above her, wearing some jeans and a polo shirt, his hair combed, face clean-shaven.

"What's the rush?"

"There's no power. I have to get to the office, or at least to an Internet connection. I can't get through to the insurance company about the truck, and we'll have to rent a car, which will take time. There's . . . I just need to."

Katya slaps her sketchbook shut and

shoves the pencil into the spiral binding. She struggles to a standing position without Charles offering her a hand.

"You need to tell me what's going on," she says, brushing a piece of hair out of her face. "Are you having an affair?"

"What? Jesus," he looks around, but no one seems to have heard. She sees his jaw clench and wonders if she's gotten it right. He really is screwing somebody. "I told you, it's just business. A work crisis."

"What's the problem?"

"It's complicated."

"I'm not a drooling moron. Try me."

"You wouldn't be interested." Charles shifts his weight from foot to foot, looks over her head, and chews on his lower lip. Anything but looking her in the eye.

"I have never been more interested in your business. I demand to know what's happening that is of such critical importance that we have to leave my mother's house the morning after we find out she's got cancer."

"It's just . . . We're having . . ."

"Out with it." Katya throws her sketchbook at the ground. "Out with it, damn you!"

"Stop shouting and be reasonable."

"I'm fucking sick of reasonable!" Her shriek startles a man who had been sawing off a tree limb across the street. He stops in midstroke and openly gapes.

CHAPTER 50
IVAN

Van savors the trippy echo in the boathouse as he strums a chord. A tune has burrowed its way into his brain, but he doesn't yet know what it's trying to tell him. He picks out a few notes of something that might be a melody. Typically, he hammers out some lyrics, then whaps together a melody that seems to fit.

This one's different.

Everything's different, now. His mother is dying. His best friend loves him. He tries to imagine loving Jenny. It's easy enough to imagine sex with Jenny, because he's already considered it, in his most lonely of nights. He's even pondered asking her about it, but somehow asking his best friend for a pity fuck was too pathetic, even for him.

The boathouse is empty, not rented at the moment, it seems, as there aren't even any signs of recent use other than a few liquor bottles from kids sneaking in. One open end frames the harbor, with boats tipped on their sides, some turned completely over; still others in the public marina across the way are smashed and scraped. And all around them a sky so blue it pierces the eye.

He feels terrible having snuck out on Jenny while she was showering. But since her profession of love and needling him about his pathetic career, he couldn't bear to look in her direction.

The sound of heavy steps on the old boards makes Van nearly topple off the barrel he was using as an ersatz stool.

"Oh, I'm sorry. I didn't know anyone was in here."

Van appraises Darius, who looks imposing, poised in the open end of the boathouse closest to the house. His long arms hang loosely at his sides, but there's a taut expectancy in him, as if he's ready to draw his six-shooter at high noon.

"Trying to escape?" Van adjusts his seat on the old barrel, intently studying his fingering, to avoid having to look at his brother-in-law.

"Just walking around. Irina is getting dressed, and the house is a bit crazy right now." He leans his long frame against the doorway. "And what did you mean exactly by 'escape'?"

"Nothing."

"Hmm. Like it meant nothing yesterday when you said 'if you stick around long enough.' There some reason you assume I'm going to run out on your sister?"

"It's not because you're black." Van wishes he could grab those words and stuff them back down his throat.

"Damn, what is it with you? I never said you thought that. We're talking man to man, here. Black's got nothing to do with it. Right?"

Van forces his eyes up from his guitar. "Of course not. Look, you don't know this about me yet, but I'm like an idiot savant, except I've just got the idiot part. I'm excellent at saying the wrong thing at the worst possible time."

"So why have you been looking at me sideways the whole time I've been here? That is when you're not stammering and trying not to sound racist."

Van takes his time resting his guitar carefully against a pile of canvas next to his barrel.

"Why do you act like you own my sister?"

"Excuse me?"

"I heard you bossing her around about the coffee. Yes, OK, she's pregnant, and caffeine isn't the best. But you're not her boss, you don't own her."

"I do look out for her because someone's got to."

"She's got a family for that, not to mention she's not helpless herself."

"She's just a . . ."

"Kid? Then why did you marry her? Why did you knock her up?"

Darius cracks his knuckles. "I didn't knock anything. It's a two-party system. She seduced me, if you have to know."

"I didn't have to know, but I'm not surprised. Reenie can't be alone, for whatever reason. She's gotta always have a guy, and sometimes she's not choosy."

"You think I'm that low-down to leave her while she was pregnant? Like you said in the hallway, 'if you stick around long enough' I believe was your phrasing."

"I don't think it's going to be you that leaves."

Darius folds his arms tight and looks down at the knotted and gnarled boards in the floor of the boathouse.

"I don't know you at all. I just know my sister's track record. For all I know, you're just like . . ." Van stops himself. ". . . Just like the others."

"She married me."

"Well, that is different all right. You got siblings?"

Darius drops his arms to his sides. "None living. I had an older sister who died in childhood. I don't remember her."

"I'm sorry to hear that. If you did, you might understand the protectiveness. Especially for Reenie."

"Who says I don't understand?"

"Because you married her. I'm sorry to say it, I love her more than life, but since you married her, it shows a fundamental misunderstanding of my sister's temperament and attention span."

"You don't give her enough credit."

"And you don't hardly know her." Van pulls on his ear, his stomach churning with a sudden desperate desire to change the subject. "Look, forget it. You seem like a good guy." Van smirks at him. "You know, for being black and all."

Darius laughs, his warm voice bouncing around in the boathouse, the water giving the sound a ringing quality, like church bells.

"You're all right, you know that?"

"You only say that because you don't hardly know me, either. Give it time."

"I will. Because I don't quit. If your sister quits on me, that's her business, but that baby is my baby and my blood no matter what she decides, and it's your blood, too. So. Looks like we're connected. For a long, long time."

Van considers this, studying Darius again. He tries to imagine their gene pools mixing.

Darius sighs, takes one more look out at the water, then turns back toward the house, striding up the grassy slope with long, purposeful steps.

Van strums another chord, feeling a growing admiration for that composed, mature gentleman who inexplicably married his ditzy sister in what will surely end up as another sordid page in Irina's colorful romantic history. It's as if Katya got all the good karma, meeting her dashing and successful husband in college, having three beautiful healthy children and raising them in a showplace home. Running her own successful business. She used it all up, like she used to use all the hot water on school days, when they were trying to catch the bus.

Of course that's silly. Good fortune is not a finite, concrete substance that gets passed around like a potluck dish. She wanted her life to be perfect, and she went out and made it that way.

"What's her secret?" Van whispers. And he decides to go find out.

He slings his guitar over his back and steps out of the boathouse, blinking in the morning sun. That's when he spots his dad coming down the hill, hand over his eyes, and calling out, "Ivan! Have you seen your mother? I can't find her anywhere!"

CHAPTER 51
IRINA

Irina slaps her yellow dress into their suitcase, along with her still-damp pajamas from chasing after Darius out into the rain.

Her shorts that morning wouldn't snap, so she left them undone, hoping the fly wouldn't unzip at an inconvenient time.

The door creaks, and Irina whirls around. Darius slides into the room, his eyes on the floor. He studies the floor for a time, then gazes out the window. The silence swells in the room until Irina feels it pushing her away like an expanding balloon.

He looks just past her shoulder when he finally speaks. "Will you need help finding a new place? Or maybe you will stay here because of the baby."

His voice is hard and brittle as fresh ice.

"I haven't thought about it." She takes his dress shirt and shakes it out with a snap of her wrist, before folding it in the suitcase. "I'll pack my things first, then decide."

"I'd like you to be staying with someone, anyway. Someone to keep an eye on you. Might not be a bad idea to stay here, during the pregnancy. Your mom could . . ."

"You don't get to say where I go. Ex-husbands usually don't."

If Darius was hurt by that, he didn't show it. "I'm looking out for the baby. If you should pass out like you did at the party, but alone . . . You could hit your head, lie on the floor unconscious. It's not good for the baby. Or for you."

Irina couldn't help but notice the phrasing, how the baby came first. Well, what did she expect? She was divorcing him. She's become simply a brief affair turned quickie marriage. In fact, she's become a baby-mama, something Darius probably never wanted to have. He doesn't like clichés.

"I like living alone," Irina says, needling him, knowing it's childish and not caring. Realistically, she wouldn't be able to afford a decent place of her own, and in all likelihood would end up in her childhood room, with a few boxes of possessions, just like she did last year during the affair with Alex. She always seemed to zoom back toward home base after every relationship went up in flames, brushing ashes out of her hair.

"Just think about it," Darius says. "I'm

not asking for my sake, because I know that doesn't matter. But the baby needs to be safe."

"I know." She speaks so quietly he likely doesn't hear. He doesn't acknowledge her, and instead reaches around her to put his shaving kit in the suitcase. She leans her head against his muscular arm, and takes that arm in her hand, caressing it.

Darius jerks his arm away. "Do you think the roads are passable? The traffic lights are out, but that just means all the intersections are four-way stops, I think . . ."

"How are you so calm?" Irina swallows back a rising sob.

"I don't know why you're upset. You want to split up, in fact, you say you didn't even want to get married."

Irina turns away from the suitcase to face him. The bright morning light cuts a shaft across his body, and she wants to throw herself into him. "I'm all at loose ends, with my mom's news, and the storm tearing up the tree . . . Oh, that doesn't make sense, but, I don't know. I'm confused."

"You're young, is what you are. I don't mean that to be insulting, so don't go getting all indignant. It's true. I was wrong to convince you to marry me, I should have seen this coming. This is all my fault. But I did let myself believe we'd be a family, for a while. Now I believe we will not be, and I'm getting used to that. Don't confuse the issue."

"What are you talking about?" Irina steps toward him, and he visibly stiffens.

"I mean, you didn't want to marry me, you don't want to raise our child together. So don't think you can still use me to get laid or get a hug or whatever."

"I wasn't trying to use you!"

"At least this time I'm only losing the wife, and not the baby, too." Darius steps toward the door, then turns back. "Assuming you take good care of yourself. You really need to take good care of yourself, Irina."

He steps out through the door as quietly as he came in, shutting it so gently it doesn't latch, and swings back open with a creak.

Chapter 52
Mira

I stub out the joint and bury it as deep in the sand as I can. The sand feels beautiful in my fingers, silky and also soft like the hand of a lover. It's cool in the lower layers underneath the hard, rain-speckled surface.

I'm so grateful for that sand, and the lake, and the breeze, and yet soon it could all be gone for me.

Then I'd better enjoy it while it's here.

I'm halfway to the pier before I realize I've left my sandals by the wall, but I don't care. My toes love the sand, too.

I'm surprised the pier is deserted on this incredible morning, this morning so fresh it feels newborn and unscarred. But then, most everyone else is picking shingles out of their landscaping.

Katya will have to get that tree off her truck somehow. She's probably so angry, her head is spinning like Linda Blair's. The images make me giggle, and I immediately feel rueful. It's not what I wanted for my daughter. I had such great plans for her.

She'd be a free spirit, independent, brave, and strong. Yet from the beginning she was determined to follow. And follow what? A cause? A religion? An ideal?

A glimmer in the distance, that's what she's been running toward. She probably doesn't even know what exactly, but it's always on the horizon, and she will never, ever catch it.

All kids want to fit in, I guess, but Katya was relentless in her demands for the newest and latest and most popular. Even though I took the family to a soup kitchen on Thanksgiving to serve the homeless, still Katya wanted to spend more on designer jeans than the cost of an entire week's grocery budget for a poor family.

Katya would have gladly traded mothers if given half the chance. She probably still would.

Van loves us, but he's grown distant in recent years, refusing to talk about his music or his songs, when he once had such hope.

And Irina . . . Always so quick to take offense and assume the worst, treating herself so carelessly. She thinks I don't know that a man beat her up last year. Falling down the stairs indeed. I may be a wilted flower child, but I'm no idiot. I didn't press her, though. Van was there to help her, and he didn't want to tell me, either, so I understood that I was not relevant and left it alone.

Even the university doesn't want me anymore. Roxanne pulled out all the stops to get me to take the buyout and retire. Budget cuts, she said. The state is cutting the school's financing. Think of the young professors, she implored.

"People with families, Mira," Roxanne said, leaning on the edge of my desk. I was sitting in my chair, grading papers, and, when I got tired of that, making notes on the next week's lecture on *The Tempest*. My reading glasses were on my nose, soft music was playing on my radio, and a fragrant spring breeze was rustling the leaves of the plant on my desk.

"I have a family," I told her.

"You know what I mean."

I do know exactly what she means.

I'm irrelevant. But my family won't let me go, like a child who clings to an outdated toy meant for someone much younger.

They're going to drag me under the knife, aren't they? They're going to drag me along and cut off my breast, then what? Go back to ignoring me while I'm left with scars and pain and big hunks of flesh simply gone?

The breast gone that nurtured my children and made me a woman? And then they will be gone, too, wrapped up in their lives again, and where will I be? Irradiated and pumped with chemicals to chase away any fugitive cancer cells. Hairless and sick.

An image of Max's face rises up in my mind's eye. His normal pleasant countenance screwed up with rage . . . His hands on my arms.

I'm at the foot of the lighthouse now. It rises ahead of me like a cyclops with its huge triangle eye. I shiver in its shadow and move around it, back into the light. I lean out over the blue-metal railing around the edge of the pier. The lake is gossamer-clear over the rocks, only detectable by its light movement. It looks refreshing, and my feet have started to ache from walking on the concrete pier with no shoes.

The lake beckons with her waves, reaching out for me, then pulling back toward the horizon.

I put one foot up on the blue railing but the pot has made me dizzy and I can't get my bearing once I leave the concrete surface. So I fold over and slip through the horizontal rails.

I feel like the prow of a ship out here. The breeze pushes my hair away, I allow my body to lean out over the water, my feet still on the pier, for now, my hands holding the railing behind me. The stretch feels good in my shoulders.

The lake's deep green recesses beyond the rocks look soft, like moss on a forest floor. Like a pleasant place to hide.

Chapter 53
Katya

Katya slams through the cupboards in the kitchen, finding only herbal tea. The slamming hurts her head, but she revels in it anyway, in the spectacle she's creating, though no one is there to witness it but Charles, who has put on the "patient endurance" face he uses when the children are acting up.

"If you're looking for the wine, I think you drank it all last night."

"Shut up." The thought had occurred to her, though it was only midmorning on a Sunday. But people have mimosas with brunch. Bloody Marys, too. Mira might even have tomato juice, though the vodka isn't likely. Katya abandoned her search and wheeled on Charles. "Now you need to tell me what the hell is going on. I've seen the e-mails. Are you having an affair?"

Charles whips his head around. "Jesus, what if the children were in here?"

"The boys are picking up branches in the yard, thinking that will get them out of being grounded for getting high. Kit is in her room, listening to her iPod until the batteries die. I notice you didn't answer the question."

"I can honestly tell you, no, there is no affair."

Charles rakes his hand through his hair and frowns into his instant Folger's, which he made with lukewarm tap water.

"You're not exactly filling me with confidence. If it's not an affair, then it's something."

"You don't want to know."

Katya's heart goes twitchy in her chest, and she wipes her clammy hands on her flannel pants. "No, I don't. But now you have to tell me, or I'll lose my mind."

"Those e-mails are from Tara, but it's not an affair. It's blackmail."

Katya's world shrinks to the size of a pinprick, and when she shakes her head to clear it, she's holding the side of the kitchen counter. "What did you do?" Her voice comes out as a whisper.

"Times have been tough." Charles stares intently at his coffee, and Katya sees a glimpse of his father in the new furrows across his forehead, fresh lines around his eyes. She hadn't noticed them before. He continues, "We made some bad investments, in some technologies that seemed promising at the time but turned out to be a bust." His speech had a studied, rehearsed quality. Katya realizes he's been planning this for some time, this confession. Charles shifts in his chair. "Normally, we can handle a few bad investments, that's the whole point of our business, but we never really recovered from 9/11."

"Hard times aren't cause for blackmail, Charles."

"You know how I'm on the Literacy for Kids board with Tara?"

Katya frowns and searches her memory. She recalls a charity function where he had cajoled his assistant into joining the board with him. Tara had joked that he only wanted to run her life after hours, too, but there had been a hard edge to her voice, the way people have when they are not truly joking. In the end, she had joined the board after all.

Charles could be going over the same memory, because he's stopped speaking and has begun turning his coffee mug in a circle on the kitchen table.

"Charles, please."

"I started borrowing a little money from

Literacy for Kids."

Borrowing. Otherwise known as embezzling. From a charity. A headline flashed into Katya's mind: "Businessman indicted for stealing from illiterate inner-city kids."

"I always intended to put it back. I figured it was a stopgap measure, and no one would ever notice."

Kat forces her vocal cords to work. "I take it that Tara noticed."

"I never realized she was paying such close attention."

The hair on Katya's neck stands up. "Are you going to the authorities?"

He narrows his eyes at her. "You want to see me in prison?"

"This can't go on forever."

"Maybe it can. Tara won't want to mess it up, she's got a pretty sweet deal."

"How are you paying her if you can't afford to keep the business afloat?"

Charles doesn't answer but Katya makes the assumption. More embezzling. He'll never be able to stop.

Katya sinks to the floor, next to the counter, and puts her head in her hands.

"This is no picnic for me either," Charles says. "I'm the one she's got by the short hairs."

"Which she couldn't have done if you

hadn't stolen money in the first place."

"As if I had a choice."

Katya drops her hands from her eyes. "You had no choice but to steal? Oh that'll go over well with the judge."

Charles flinches. "There will be no judge unless you decide to rat me out. You're not going to do that to the children, are you? The media attention, sending me to prison. Losing the house because who's going to pay for it otherwise? Assuming we didn't lose it to restitution or a civil suit."

Katya feels like a hand is closing on her throat. "I fail to grasp how you had no choice. We could have done something, gotten a second mortgage . . ."

"We already have a second mortgage."

"We could have made it work!"

Charles smacks his hand on the table. "Don't you think I tried! But I had to do something to keep our life going because you wouldn't have settled for anything less than what we have."

Katya feels her blood drain out of her face. "Are you putting this on my doorstep?"

"Would you have stayed with me if I came to you, and said 'Honey, we're broke, I invested in junk, and now we've got nothing? Let's declare bankruptcy and sell the house.' You think we would have stayed together through that?"

"And you expect me to stay now?"

"You're going to leave me in this position? Break up the family? And what will you tell the kids?"

Katya feels the anger drain out of her limbs and lets herself go limp on the floor like a corpse. Any action she takes will result in the explosion of everything she's ever worked for.

Her eyes meet Charles's from across the room. His eyes look damp, and a sheen of sweat films his forehead. He looks hunched and defeated, and never more vulnerable since the night he proposed to her, with a ring at the time that seemed so extravagant, but at their fifteenth anniversary he replaced it with a new setting, befitting her status as Mrs. Peterson of Peterson Enterprises.

Kat looks down at the ring as it catches the light and bounces it across the room. So that's her life — nothing more than pretty-colored light reflecting off a cold stone.

CHAPTER 54
IVAN

In his search through the house for Katya — and now his mother, too, since Max can't find her — Ivan is distracted by the unmistakable sound of sobs. Something he heard often growing up in a home with two sisters.

He knocks and opens the door at once, not giving her a chance to order him out of the room. Darius is nowhere in sight. The room is empty of their personal effects, and the result is a curious absence of pulse. Like the room prepped for an estate sale: bloodless, a commodity.

Van's never thought of his childhood home as just a house before. But his mother and father will be gone someday, his mother, perhaps quite soon.

Irina wipes hard at her face, leaving pink marks on her skin from the pressure.

"Hey, hey . . ." he says, coming around to the side of the bed, where she sits hunched like an elderly woman. She shakes him off, and he leaves his hands in his lap, not knowing what else to do. He thinks back to his chat with Darius, getting the impression that it was Irina who wanted to leave him. So why did she look so devastated?

"What do you want?" she croaks out, sounding eerily like herself ten years ago, in her preteen years.

"Is it Darius?"

Irina looks up at the ceiling as if searching for her answer in the air above her head. A breeze from an open window stirs the loose hairs around her face, and for a moment his sister's beauty hurts him, because he knows the price she has paid for that beauty and how the men in her life have used it.

"Yes," she says, letting out a shuddery breath.

Van stands up from the bed. "Bastard." He was lying all that time, he really was going to ditch her, leave her with his baby after . . .

"Bad choice of words."

"Oh, Reenie, I wasn't talking about . . ."

"I know. And anyway, it's not him that's the jerk. It's me."

"What do you mean?"

She draws herself up straight on the bed, which is high enough that her feet barely touch the floor. As she talks, one hand drifts to her abdomen. Van doubts that she has noticed the gesture.

"I told him I don't want the baby, and I don't want him. We're splitting up, and I'm going to let him raise the baby without me. And it upset him, I mean I think I really hurt him."

"So why are you the one crying?"

She chuckles and wipes her face again. "Men. They just don't get it." She points at her face. "This . . . this is regret. This is thinking that maybe if I cry hard enough and feel bad enough, God will spin the world backward and I can not sleep with him, or not even meet him, or I can get the morning-after pill or whatever. Or not that far, maybe just far enough for me not to marry him and lead him on into thinking he'd get that family he really wanted. I'm a terrible person, Van. Really terrible."

Van kneels down so he can peer up into her face and take her hands. "You haven't done anything yet, just take it back. Change your mind. Women do that all the time. Believe me, I know." He tries a rueful smile, but she doesn't react. "You can keep the baby, tell Darius you want to stay with him. I mean, if you want to. Do you love him, Reenie?"

There's a long pause while Reenie gazes

out at the harbor. "I might. I don't know. I'd really like to, because that would solve a lot." She chuckles and rolls her eyes, wiping off her face again. "It doesn't matter though. He'll never take me now. Not after I've jerked him around like this."

"Then live here . . ."

"Mom has cancer, remember? She'll be getting sick, I can't expect her to take care of me."

"Then live with me."

"What?"

"I'm serious. I'll ask my apartment complex about finding a two-bedroom apartment. I've got the summer off, I'll be around for a while anyway, and I'll take a leave of absence. I like being an uncle, and Katya's kids think I'm an idiot." Van smiles at Irina's midsection. "I've got a fighting chance with this one yet."

"It's not that simple."

"Why can't it be? I'm tired of everything being so damn hard all the time. Keep the baby, Reenie. We'll help you."

"Won't it crimp your style?"

Van laughs. "Right. My style. I've got girls banging down my door. Hell, a cute niece or nephew might be just the ticket for changing my romantic fortune."

Reenie's expression softens a little, a smile

playing around the edges of her lips. Then she closes her eyes and shakes her head.

"No. It won't work and, anyway, I don't want to be a mother. It's not a matter of where I sleep or who will take the baby for walks. I fundamentally don't want to be a mother, and this baby is better off without someone who feels that way." She turns a hard glare on Ivan. "This baby deserves to be wanted."

Ivan hears her loud and clear. "You were wanted, Reenie. Unplanned isn't the same as unwanted. Mom loved you, loves you still."

She shakes her head. "No, I'll give Darius the baby as soon as it pops out, then make my own way, like I always have. I have some old friends I can stay with. Alex's number is still in my cell phone."

Van feels both hot and cold, and leaps to his feet. "You will not go back to that sadistic asshole. Anytime you have to be rescued from a man is a pretty good indication he's bad news."

"He was nice to me lots of times."

Van jabs a finger at Irina. "Why do you treat yourself like you're disposable? You go back to him, you can forget I exist. I'm serious. I'm not going to stand by and watch you go through that again."

"So you'll throw me away, too?"

Van closes his eyes, and the memory of Irina cowering in that man's room, blood trailing from her mouth, looms large. "I won't watch you destroy yourself."

He crosses to the door, and, before he goes out, he tries once more to get through to his baby sister, the one who once grabbed his hair in tufts, while riding his shoulders as he galloped through the house. She screamed with glee and terror, and he made horsey noises, even. And she thinks she wasn't loved? What twelve-year-old boy makes horsey noises out of anything but love?

"You think you're not important? You're important to that baby. If you feel so terribly unwanted, how is your child going to feel growing up, knowing his mother gave him away?"

He doesn't stay around for her reaction, continuing his search for Katya, to unravel the secret of her life, and their mother, who still seems to be missing.

Chapter 55
Irina

Irina slams the door after Van, not caring if he's right because he sounds like a freakin' Dr. Phil. And he's a fine one to talk. Mr. Go-Nowhere with big-shot dreams to be a songwriter and nothing to show for it but a crappy job at a crummy high school.

As if.

She could call Alex right now, even. See him on her way out of town. He'd probably get an extra kick out of it, smacking around a pregnant woman. That'll show that stupid Ivan, thinking he can tell her what to do.

And then a coldness runs down her neck and over her shoulders. Did she really just consider putting herself in physical harm's way? While carrying a child?

She checks the mirror on the back of the door. She smooths her loose shirt tight over her abdomen, and there's an unmistakable arch that wasn't there before. It's real. The baby is real and could be hurt.

She feared for it during the storm, realizing that if a tornado sucked them out of the house, what chance did a tiny fetus stand? Darius must have felt it, too, holding his hand over her stomach as if he could magically keep it safe.

Maybe it wouldn't be so bad, being a mom. Irina ponders her examples: Katya, whose children use her like a combination ATM machine and whipping post, and Mira, who was barely available for Irina's own childhood . . .

And now will be unavailable for her adulthood as well. And irrational anger bubbles up in Irina because her mother didn't choose to get sick. Yet, when was the last time she had a mammogram? And she is choosing not even to let the doctors try and help her. Choosing her own priorities over whatever her children might want. Or need.

Irina slams the door open and stomps down the stairs. At the bottom of the steps she finds Katya and Van in the kitchen, and at the same time, her father comes in from the back porch, with Patty shuffling along behind.

"You kids won't believe what Patty just told me."

Katya pushes her hair out of her face — unlike her to appear willingly so disheveled

— and asks, "Is your house okay?"

"Lost some shingles, but I don't care about that. Look, I saw your mother climb out of her window."

"What?" Van says, gaping at Patty.

"She climbed out her window. I was brushing branches off my porch and plain as day I saw her slip out of her study like a cat burglar in reverse, and she marched off toward the lake. I thought maybe you all had a stuck door or something, but then your father here said he couldn't find her . . ."

Max was pulling on a ratty old university sweatshirt, already wearing a moldering pair of swimming trunks and sneakers made green by a thousand lawn mowings. "We have to go find her. Something's wrong. Something's really wrong."

Van says, "My shoes are on the porch."

Katya goes sprinting for the stairs. "I'll get my sneakers, I'll catch up to you."

Irina looks down at her sandals and follows Van to the porch.

He turns to her briefly, in his crouched position, lacing his shoes. "You should stay here. You need to take it easy."

"I feel like a walk. I need the air."

He seems to swallow back some words. "Okay. If you get tired, just sit down on a bench, and we'll swing by on the way back."

He stands up to his full height, and with that determination written on his face, Irina gets a glimpse of him as he looked when he burst through the door in Alex's condo.

"Do you think she's okay?" Irina asks.

"I don't presume to know anything anymore," he answers, already stepping out onto the porch.

Chapter 56
Mira

Are the rocks talking to me? It seems like they are . . . I hear voices, but they're far away. Maybe underwater? I release one bar of the pier, and for a moment the swinging motion alarms me, then it's thrilling. A heart-stopping swoop toward the lake. My fingers are much too far above the water, but I want to touch the rocks, the pretty mottled things that must be ancient, so sturdy . . .

"Mother!"

I can't kid myself. That was meant for me. Seeing as there's no other mother here on the pier.

I can't seem to pull myself back, though, and the metal of the railing seems more cold and slippery than I remember, but a hand slaps over mine, and more hands pull at my blouse. This fresh tethering allows me to turn my feet back again, to face the shore. It is with more than a little regret that I leave behind the unending vista of the lake stretching ahead to kiss the sky.

Kiss the sky, Jimi wailed, back in the day when my life was endless.

Now I see Ivan's face, and he's red and wild, and for a crazy moment he looks like the day he was born, when he came out screaming like a little angry tomato with all that black hair.

So I laugh, because how could I not?

Now all their voices bubble together like a stew, and I don't hear anything, but I can see Irina holding herself a few yards back and Max seizing my other arm — ouch, he'll leave a mark — and Katya is bellowing something, and she's drawing out her cell phone.

That I definitely don't want.

"Stop!"

That must have been loud because some gulls explode away from the pier in a puff of white wing. Kat freezes, with her phone not quite to her head.

"You better not be calling 911. I'm not a cat in a tree for God's sake."

Katya closes the phone and shoves it back in her pocket. The eyes of my eldest daughter betray confusion, anger, and impatience. Probably the way I looked to her many times in our growing-up years when she behaved in a baffling teenage way.

Ivan and Max have my arms so tight, and my son is reaching past the pier to my waist, and I realize he's fixing to haul me in like a sack of flour.

I brace my knees tight, much as I can anyway, and lock my elbows. "No."

"Mom," Ivan pleads, quietly. "Come back over here. It's dangerous out there."

Max's voice quavers. "Mirabelle, don't do this."

"Do what?" I laugh again, this time I'll admit a little harshly. "Oh, you think I'm trying to drown myself. Ophelia, I'm not."

Katya's voice is cold, like cracking ice. "So what are you doing out there?"

"Enjoying the view."

"And you're high, too, I suppose?"

"I just want to be left alone!" I try to yank my arms free of my husband and son because they feel like jailers; they feel like chains around my limbs, and I won't yield. I jerk momentarily backward, and a screech comes from Irina. I didn't mean to scare her.

Katya steps closer to me, while Ivan and Max continue to hold me, Van trying to nudge me closer to the pier, but I'm bracing myself away from them.

"I don't know what you're trying to do,"

Katya says, her skin so pale I can trace a blue vein through her temples. "But in case you haven't noticed, your actions do have something of an impact on other people, and we'd rather not have to fish your dead body out of Lake Michigan."

Van barks at her. "Katya!"

Irina lets go of herself to step closer to Kat. "No, she's right. Because that's the whole point of all this, isn't it?" She turns her small frame square to me, glaring and shuddering. "Mom thinks her life is hers to throw away to hell with anyone else, and I don't know why I should be surprised."

Katya joins in gamely. "Well, exactly. So what if I'd like her to be there to watch my children graduate from high school? If I need her in my life. She'd rather lie there and die rather than even remotely consider doing what the doctor says."

I wonder if Van and Max can feel my limbs tremble. The sun has climbed higher in the sky, and it's behind the lighthouse, casting us all in shadow, but a corona of sun beams out around it, it hurts my eyes like an eclipse, and I wish they'd shut up and let me be, for once . . . Even Van whispers to me, "C'mon, Mom, we just want what's best for you . . ."

"How do any of you know what's best for me!"

All three of the children start to answer at once when another voice joins the fray, to my left.

"Shut up, all of you!" Max loosens his grip on my arm, moves his hand down to my hand on the railing. He turns to me. "Mira, I don't want you to fall," he says with perfect calm, his eyes the color of amber couched by wrinkles and bags, those eyes that have been smiling at me for four decades, much longer than I've deserved.

Van releases my hand, and I reach for Max, who helps me under the railing, the same way I got out there. Past his shoulder I see a spectator, some jogger who paused to gawk. I flip him the bird, and he gasps and turns away.

I pat Van's arm because he's the closest, and I fold into Max, letting him hold me, feeling where he's heavier and thicker than he used to be and not minding at all.

I don't look up as he addresses the children.

"In all your dither about yourselves and how this affects you, have any of you have given your mother a hug, and said 'Gosh Mom, I'm sorry.' Or, 'Is there anything I can do?' "

He starts to walk away from them, and I close my eyes and let him lead me, following with no hesitation because he won't let me fall.

CHAPTER 57
KATYA

Charles refuses to meet her eye when she and the children gather in the living room. Katya doesn't think she can bear the knowledge of his crime. Besides the logistics of it — is she an accomplice now, after the fact? — is the knowledge that her all-powerful husband who could do anything, of whom she was so proud, was reduced to thievery to install a SubZero refrigerator in the kitchen and Jacuzzi in the backyard.

Well, no one ever said it was easy being a wife and mother, and Kat Peterson is nothing if not stoic, thank you very much.

In their mother's living room, the children sit on the chocolate brown velveteen couch in ascending order of height. Kit steals glances at her brothers in a mixture of awe and glee. She could barely hide her delight at being included on the lecture and punishment.

Punishment will indeed come. But first,

Katya wants some answers, before she can figure out how to deal with her mother, who is probably programming Dr. Kevorkian into speed dial at this very moment.

Charles is on the overstuffed chair at the corner of the couch, looking for all the world like one of the children, awaiting his punishment.

"So, Chip." She paces in front of him like a TV lawyer. She's put on her slacks and high heels from Friday, and this has not only made her feel taller, but more secure in her own world, the world where she is in control, not sketching trees and pulling her crazy mother off the pier. "You seem to think it's a lark to use an illegal drug. Not only a lark, but apparently you're quite practiced at it. Did none of those DARE meetings do a thing for you?"

He laughs. He actually laughs, right there in her face. Katya could rip off his eyebrows. "DARE. Right. Ask how many kids in my school graduated from DARE and get high every weekend. And what about Taylor?"

"I'm getting to him, but I'm starting with you."

"It's no big. It's like sneaking a drink now and then, so what? You like your wine enough, and you're not an alkie."

Kat lets the wine remark pass, but she

could almost hear Charles's silent agreement, always needling her about "hitting" the bottle. A more pressing matter is Chip's casual dismissal of the dangers of drug use. She hadn't planned to use their neighbor's dirty laundry like this, but . . . "I suppose you think Mr. Johnson down the road started out using meth every weekend when his kids were at Little League? He started somewhere before that."

"I'll tell you how it started, it started with Mrs. Johnson moving to Ann Arbor with the little Johnsons. I'm telling you it's nothing. Everybody does it, and everybody knows that everybody does it."

"How did you get so . . . entitled? No, I mean it, answer me this, all of you. Why do you think it's okay to laugh in my face? And treat all your expensive things like they're disposable? Why do you act like I'm not even there when I ask you to do a simple thing like, heaven forbid pick your clothes up off the floor and get them in the laundry hamper. I'd fall over and die of a coronary if any of you actually used the washing machine."

"I don't know how." This from Taylor, who is plenty old enough, and Katya balls up her fists to keep from slapping him across the face, but in a moment she realizes he's in earnest. His face is blank and slightly puzzled, there's a hint of a crease between his eyes, an echo of the one Charles has permanently imprinted on his face in the exact same spot.

She's never taught him to use the washing machine.

"Well you'll know how soon enough, but why do you tune me out when I ask you to pick up your clothes?"

Taylor seems to be struggling with the question. He stares at his sneakers, scuffed and muddy, and shifts in place. He looks over at Kit, who has turned her attention to the farthest corner of the room, suspecting — rightly so — this conversation isn't just about her brothers.

Chip finally answers, not a whit of shame or embarrassment in his voice. In fact, his voice takes on a commanding resonance, much like his father's.

"I guess we always figured if it really meant anything to you, you would have made us do it. Because you never have. You might yell at us, but you always do it yourself in the end. So we figure it doesn't matter that much."

Kit pipes up. "I'm just busy. I have homework and dance class."

Taylor jumps on that train of thought. "Oh

sure, and band practice."

Band practice. Dance class. All these stupid classes that she spends half her life driving them to, so they will stay out of her hair and learn something and be well-rounded, or at least as well-rounded as the neighbors' kids. So when the McCartys ask, "What are the kids into these days?" she has something to say besides, "Guitar Hero and Dance Dance Revolution."

She points a finger at Chip, then Taylor. "You are both grounded the entire summer."

Taylor launches into a whine that surely must have dogs cowering for blocks.

Chip just rolls his eyes and elbows his brother. Katya reads their silent communication. Chip doesn't think she'll stick with it.

Kit believes it, though. She's covering her mouth in shock and glee.

Finally, Katya turns to Charles, who has been clearing his throat like a thirty-year smoker. "We should talk about this," he says, and Kat knows he doesn't want to stick with it either because it means both boys underfoot and sullen, and making sure they don't sneak out, and it's a hell of a punishment for them, too.

"We just did talk about it." She turns back

to the kids. "Get out of my face."

Kit scampers down the hall, Taylor snivels along behind her, and Katya could swear she hears Chip mutter an obscenity as he passes by.

And Katya thinks, I pick adolescence years to start disciplining my kids? Must remember to buy more wine. Her mother was probably onto something when she suggested Katya be more strict all those years ago, though at the time Katya had blown her off. Right, the flower child telling me to be tougher on the kids? Though, she had to admit that she herself and her siblings were — mostly, anyway — well behaved.

"Wow, it sounds like you really meant it."

Katya whirls around to see Van standing in the doorway from the kitchen.

"How long have you been there?"

"Not long. I just came to tell you Mom's lying down in her room, and later on we'll have some brunch. She has the stuff already, assuming the fridge stayed cold, it should be OK . . ."

Katya waits for Ivan to finish up and leave, but he starts tugging on his ear. She can feel Charles simmering behind her.

"Van, what?"

"I just wanted to talk to you."

She points a finger toward the kitchen.

"Look, just wait a minute. Whatever it is can wait."

Katya glances at her watch and starts counting the minutes until her own personal happy hour at 5 P.M.

Charles stands up and moves close to her. She inhales his musky aftershave and looks up at him. He's so close she has nearly an Adam's-apple view.

"Kat, what are we going to do?"

"If you don't want to deal with the kids, fine, I'll handle the grounding and stay home all summer long —"

"Jesus, not that. Though I do think that's crazy. I'm talking about our other trouble. You know, with Tara."

"That's for you to figure out."

"What do you mean, exactly?" Katya sees his jaw clench, lines around his mouth growing more severe.

"Solve the problem. I don't care how, and I don't want to know another thing about it. Just make it stop."

"You're not leaving me then?"

"No." Katya grinds her teeth, hating the sound of that word because it sound like capitulation. It's not though, it's the braver choice. For the children. "But this can't go on. It just can't."

He slumps a little, and Katya can see that

he was holding his breath. He really did care about losing her.

He moves past her without another word, brushing his fingers through hers quickly as he passes.

She sinks into the chair Charles had occupied and puts her head in her hands, elbows on her knees. She pushes the heels of her hand into her closed eyes until she sees stars. She just wants normal back. She wants to know that their paychecks can cover the mortgage and the credit-card bills and they're still saving for retirement and college . . . Katya bolts up in the chair. The retirement accounts. She hasn't looked at the balances in months. Years, maybe. Did Charles clear them out before raiding the charity? He must have. Why else would he have been so desperate?

Which means even if they manage to keep Charles out of jail and out of the headlines, they have nothing to live on in their dotage. Unless they start selling all their expensive toys and saving again, as if from scratch. Katya gazes down at her ring, which disgusts her suddenly. For baubles like this, Charles felt driven to embezzle. She yanks it off her hand and crunches it into her palm, squeezing until the diamonds' sharpness burns into her hand. She would like to crush it down to the tiny thing Charles bought her when they first got engaged. Katya cringes now to recall her disappointment back then. And he must have registered that disappointment, because he patiently explained that they had to save for a long, long future together. "I'll take care of you, Kat," he said then, tipping her chin up, looking into her eyes. "You can trust me to take care of you."

Katya blinks several times and rubs her eyes with her free hand. She will sell the ring. Sell it, and build their retirement back up. Maybe in her own account at first, just her name. Because Charles's crime could still blow up in their faces, and she might need it to feed and house the children.

"Hey, you OK?"

Ivan's back.

Katya slumps back in the chair and kicks off her heels, which feel superfluous in Mira's house, decorated with beads and silk wall hangings and framed prints of unrecognizable things. She slips her ring into her pocket, unwilling to look at it again.

"Nothing. It's fine. What did you want to ask me?"

Van sits on the couch closest to the chair, scratches his nose, and takes a couple of tries before he speaks, as if he's working up to something. "How did you do it?"

"What?"

"Get such a perfect life?"

Katya glares at him. "I don't need sarcasm. Anyway, that's Irina's gig."

"I'm serious."

Katya laughs bitterly. "Did you not just witness me ground my children for an entire summer because they're doing drugs? And you noticed how seriously they took that? Chip is probably texting his friends right now about what a joke I am. And you ask me about perfect?"

"Every kid gets in trouble. But you seemed to get everything you wanted. Successful husband, beautiful house, healthy kids. Your own business. What did you do? More to the point, what am I not doing?" Van smirks. "I wouldn't mind a little bit of perfect."

"There is no perfect. Only real life and liars."

"Oh, come on."

"Van, if you only knew." Katya narrows her eyes and tries to clue him in without actually having to tell him what a joke her life is with a criminal husband and how her "healthy" kids are going to hell in a handbasket, as Charles's parents would say, not because of one time smoking pot. But because they respect nothing and no one. He stares back at her, blank, just like Tay did when she asked why he didn't do laundry.

She tries again. "Don't aspire for someone else's life because you won't want it if you get it. Then you'll just get restless and start grasping for something else."

"To thine own self be true."

"Yeah, yeah, *Hamlet.*"

"Mom said that to us all the time."

Katya's hand rests on her wedding ring, still tucked in her pocket. It makes a frightfully big lump, gaudy thing that it is. She wonders what happened to the original one. Maybe they let the jeweler keep it. Maybe Kit used it as a Barbie doll crown.

Ivan says, "That's what Mom is doing, you know. True to herself and all that."

Katya looks up. "Oh, you mean the whole dying thing? She'd like us to think that, I'm sure."

"Why are you so nasty about her?"

"I'm not nasty, I'm just . . . tired. I'm tired, Van. I think I've been tired since I was born."

Van stands up and stretches out. "Point taken." He ambles to the stairs in an unfocused way, as if he's trying to take the long way around. He pauses at the bottom of the stairs. "Real life and liars, huh?"

He goes upstairs without waiting for a reply.

Katya strokes her temples, willing herself not to think of Charles and what he'll do to get himself — correction, both of them — out of his mess.

Not her concern. She told him to solve it, and he will, like he's always solved everything, and they can all get back to normal, or something like it.

But does she want that, considering what their normal has been?

Katya stands up and brushes off her slacks, though there doesn't seem to be anything on them. She steps back into her high heels and clicks off to check her phone upstairs, to see if the insurance agent has called back yet about the Escalade. Also, maybe the radio has a weather update. The air feels muggy.

Chapter 58
Ivan

The closest paper he could find was a take-out menu from Wing On Lau.

He's cross-legged on the sleeping porch upstairs in the house, the cool breeze ruffling his hair and scooting the paper around the scuffed wooden floor when he doesn't have his pen to it, scribbling.

His guitar in his lap still trembles from the most recent chord when a creak in the boards causes him to jerk his head up.

Jenny. She's wearing a new dress, this one rather simple compared to her usual wild patterns. It's loose and pale gold, embroidered with something in the same color thread. From his vantage point, he can see the tattoo on her ankle, a swirly pattern of black shapes weaving around in a circle. He likes the way the breeze swirls the hem of her dress around.

"You look nice," he tells her.

"That's supposed to make up for you

disappearing on me all morning?"

He would tug his ear, but he has a pen in one hand and the guitar neck in his other. He bites his lip instead, unable to think of a suitable excuse.

Jenny folds herself to the floor in front of him. She leans forward, balancing her elbows on her knees, and at this he gets a glimpse of the freckles on her chest and a shadow between her breasts.

He glances away.

"I have never regretted anything more in my life than what I told you last night."

He stares at his guitar, and from his peripheral vision, he can see Jenny lean closer.

"OK, then, you don't have anything to say. Fine, I don't blame you. I'd undo it if I could, now that I see the feelings aren't mutual. Because you've been a terrific friend to me. I've never met anyone so loyal and sincere, who can also quote the whole Monty Python dead parrot sketch. And now I'm afraid that's gone since you won't even look at me." She stands up and looks out over the backyard and the harbor. "Then, to compound my whopper of a misjudgment, I get on your case about songwriting at the same time. So. I guess this is a rambling apology and a desperate wish I could unsay what I said. If I could have one superpower right now, I'd choose the ability to give someone selective amnesia."

"You'd have people lining up around the block. You'd make a fortune." Van was smiling before he realized she was being serious. He couldn't help himself.

"I hadn't even thought about charging. I'd just do it pro bono." She smiled back, though her eyes were still sad. "Hey, what was that tune, just now? It was pretty."

"I don't know. Something I'm fiddling with. Something my sister said got me thinking."

"Irina?"

"No, Kat."

"About your mom?"

Mom. Van feels a thud in his chest as it hits him again. Cancer. Pulling her off the pier had felt like a hallucination, same as when he'd clocked Irina's deviant boyfriend in the face a year ago. Not only is Mom sick, she is apparently in denial, or otherwise just reflexively stubborn about doing what other people want.

"Did you hear what happened on the pier?"

"Irina told me. She looks awful, by the way. I think she's been throwing up."

Van set the guitar down next to him and

stretched his legs out along the wood floor. "My mother has always been the most vivid person I know. That's the word, vivid. Doesn't that come from the word for life?"

"*La vie.* Yes, you're right."

"So why she won't fight for it now is completely beyond me."

"Maybe she hasn't had time to let it sink in. Maybe she'll change her mind."

"My mother doesn't ever change her mind. About anything."

"That kind of certainty must be comforting."

Comfort? He'd never thought of certainty as comfortable. After all, he was certain his days would remain much the same the entire school year and all the foreseeable years after that, and he found only life-crushing drudgery in that fact. Or did he? Maybe he'd grown comfortable himself.

Did his mother find death more comfortable than an uncertain prognosis?

"So what was it then?" Jenny asks, her gaze still out on the water.

"What was what?"

"The song. That melody, you said it didn't have anything to do with your mother. Can I hear it?"

Van shrugs, picks up his guitar, and starts picking out the chords, humming the melody, lilting along, knocking the body of his guitar now and then where he imagines a drum.

When he finishes and looks up to Jenny, her eyebrows are up, and she's smiling, with her whole face this time. "Van, that's lovely. Why didn't you sing the words?"

"Still working on them."

"You should sing it for your family."

"They wouldn't be interested."

"They might enjoy it. Give them something to think about besides your mom."

"Nah. I'm sure it sucks as much as every other song I've written."

"Your songs are good, Van, and that one's really good. You're just . . ."

Jenny stops, biting her lip.

Van finishes for her. "Not trying hard enough."

"That's not what I meant, not really. But you've told me before all the songwriters are in New York or Nashville, and that to break in from way over here in Michigan is next to impossible. So why not go? Give it your best shot? Wait tables and ply your art in the great American cliché?"

"I've got a job, an apartment . . ."

"You hate that apartment, and the job isn't much better."

"Are you trying to get rid of me? Won't

you miss me?" Van tosses off the remark casually, like he's joking, but he's not, in fact. The thought of being thousands of miles from Jenny has caused his chest to ache.

Jenny looks him in the eye, softly smiling, her stripey orange hair standing out like feathers, dancing in the wind. "I'd rather miss you than have you miss out."

Then he feels something, like something rising in his chest, something that might burst free and fly off, only it can't, so he stands up himself and crosses the room to Jenny, pushing his guitar behind his back as he does it, leaving his hands free.

Jenny doesn't return the kiss for a moment, freezing in place, then she grabs his face with her hands and rises on tiptoe. Van wraps his arms around her, lifting her off the floor.

CHAPTER 59
IRINA

Irina's knees tremble so hard she can hardly balance, awkward as her position is, poised over the toilet. She grasps the countertop for support, and the side of the tub.

It's blood.

Just a drop or two, but definitely there, scarlet beads in the water.

"Darius," she murmurs, wanting him but knowing he's out with Max buying ice at the corner store.

"Mom?" she calls. Her bedroom is close, and she knows Mira is lying down, but it's her mother she wants now. "Mom!"

Irina nearly reels with a sense of déjà vu, when she saw blood in the toilet all those years ago, more than a decade now. She'd been terrified, thought for sure she was bleeding to death, and she'd had to call out four times before her father shouted through the door. Her mother was not home from her night class, yet.

So it was Max who dug around under the sink until he came up with a maxi pad, her father who assured her it was perfectly normal and that her mother would explain when she got home.

After the fear and embarrassment ebbed away, Irina was enraged that her mother hadn't told her. Mira apologized, consoled, made her tea, and let her stay up late, cuddled under a quilt, eating cookies.

She said, I didn't know you would start this young, you're barely ten years old. She said, I'm surprised your school hasn't had "the talk" yet, I guess I'm out of practice, all those years since Katya . . .

And Irina shrank smaller into the quilt, reminded again that she was an afterthought, an unwelcome echo of her accomplished older sister.

"Mom!" tries Irina again, her voice breaking.

She hears light, quick steps before Mira bursts into the bathroom without knocking. Her hair is wild and ratty, her eyes shiny and face marred with red splotches. "What's wrong?" she says, shutting the door hard behind her.

"I'm bleeding . . ." Irina chokes out, standing up with considerable effort, checking her panties. There are small dots there, too.

Mira moves over to inspect the toilet. "It isn't much. A little bleeding is normal early on, it's probably fine."

Irina pulls up her panties and shorts, finding herself pinned to the corner of the bathroom by her mother's position, damn these tiny bathrooms and old houses.

Mira says, "Did your doctor say bleeding was normal at your appointment?"

"I haven't been yet." Irina gulps at saying this aloud, realizing she'd failed her child at least once already.

Mira gulps hard. "I could drive you to emergency. If you want."

Irina shudders. That long wait, a strange doctor poking around. "There's nothing they can do, is there?"

"I don't think so, baby. If there's anything wrong, which there probably isn't."

"But you don't know that for sure. I could be . . . it could be . . ."

"No, I don't know for sure."

Something breaks inside Irina's chest, she feels it giving way. "Mom," she says, falling into her mother's arms. "Mom, I wasn't sure I wanted to do this, but I don't want to lose it, I don't want the baby to die . . ."

Irina feels her mother sway in place, the

breath of "shhh" blowing past her ear.

"I don't know if I can do this," she says again. "I'm going to screw it all up, I know it."

Her mother whispers, "Sweetheart, we all screw up our kids. You just try to keep the screwups small and love them like anything."

Irina pushes back from her mom, and finds herself eye to eye with her chest. "Mom, I'm sorry I've been so hard on you this weekend."

"It's okay, sweetie." Mira brushes a lock of hair behind Irina's ear. "It's a lot to process, and I haven't handled it well myself."

"I just . . . the thought of raising a child without you around to help me . . . But maybe now there won't be one."

"Think positive, sweetheart. I'll brew some raspberry-leaf tea. That's supposed to help at times like this."

Irina gulps air, now feeling winded and claustrophobic in the airless bathroom. "Darius would be crushed. He lost a baby before this. I can't bear to tell him because he's already upset that I'm leaving him."

"Are you?"

Irina looks away from her mother, not sure what she'll think. "I thought I didn't want the baby, so I told him he could divorce me and keep the child. He got very upset; now if he thinks the baby isn't coming, either . . ."

Mira searches out Irina's gaze until she has no choice but to look at her mother, right into her reddened eyes. "Tell him how you're feeling, Reenie. Tell him you are scared for the baby and you are not sure about anything yet. Tell him you spoke rashly because you're not sure, are you? You don't want to give away your baby so much as you want to hit the panic button and reset everything back to normal."

Irina nods. How easily her mother can read her.

"There's no panic button. But there can be a new normal, and you might love that new normal."

Irina wonders if her mother speaks from experience, if she was reaching for the panic button twenty-two years ago when Irina was conceived. She decides not to ask. Not today.

Mira pulls her into an embrace again. "Call the doctor on Monday, see if they'll see you, see if they'll reassure you the baby bean is just fine."

Irina nods into her mother's shoulder,

clutching her hard, and finds herself praying that her mother is right.

Chapter 60
Mira

A chain saw whines outside, and it makes the hairs on my neck stand up.

I've retreated back to the bedroom, to our double bed with the snail's trail quilt handed down by Max's mother. I'm feeling loopy and wrung out from being yanked out of my nap by Irina's desperate cry for me. How that brought back memories, hearing that plaintive call of "Mom" that sets you running. Because it's a different tone, the "Mom" called out from genuine need as opposed to the persistent whiny demand.

The chain saw makes me wonder if they're going to work on our big tree or the one that crushed Katya's car, but the noise is too distant for that. Some other neighbor cutting away the debris.

Trying to shake off the high, and it's proving more difficult than usual. My eyes don't like to stay focused. But I should go downstairs for brunch with a semblance of dignity after my display on the pier this morning.

Must remember to flush any remaining pot in the house.

At the time it felt wonderful, to flee my family and this house and go commune with the lake, it felt freeing to be hanging over the water, eyes on the horizon. To think I almost jerked myself right off the edge when Max and Ivan tried to pull me in.

It was their hands on my arms that did it, made me want to pull away from them because it made me think of that day, after we talked to Dr. Graham.

As soon as we stepped into the kitchen after the long drive home, Max tried to fold me in his arms, and I shook him off like a sodden raincoat.

"Mira, I know you're afraid . . ."

"You don't know anything about it."

I'd forbidden him from talking to me in the car, and he obeyed, probably because he could barely concentrate on the road. I could tell that by the way he clutched the steering wheel. His hand shook when he flicked on the turn signal.

All the way home from Traverse City, I'd watched the highway reflectors along the side and in rhythm with their passing thought "no, no, no."

So the minute we got in the house, he tried to hold me, but to me it felt grasping and aggressive.

"Why did you leave? Why won't you listen to the doctor?"

"She says I have to let them mutilate me, and I won't do it."

"Mutilate?" Max repeated the word, his jaw hanging open and his voice strained by an effort not to shout. It was an effort that would soon fail. "And what do you think the cancer would do? Anyway, did you hear her say you could get reconstruction? They can build you a new breast, you'd look perfectly normal."

"How happy would you be if they said, 'Mr. Zielinski, we have to cut off your penis, but don't worry, we'll bring around a flap of your ass and you'll be good as new.' " And yes, I laughed. "Flap of ass" struck me funny somehow, and I was feeling a little crazy. It was all wrong, me in a doctor's office, being told I was sick when I felt just fine, and Max ordering me around like a child, like his little obedient wife.

"This isn't fucking funny!" he screamed, and it felt like a punch. My insides crumpled up, and tears sprang to my eyes. He ripped off his glasses and threw them to the floor at my feet. "Will you take your life seriously for once!"

"What do you mean, for once?"

"You've gone your whole life with your hands off the wheel, trusting someone would always steer you back to center, like your precious Paul protecting your job even when you pissed off the wrong people, me picking up your slack at home while you were at meetings half the night . . ."

"You're a fine one to talk about picking up slack! When you're writing, you're barely alive to the rest of us, and that doesn't count the occasional book tour. And don't you dare mention Paul to me in that tone. You have nowhere to go with that argument."

"I have never been flippant about our family." Max pushed his hands into his eyes and looked at me again, his mouth hard. "You know what that mistake cost me. Costs me, still."

"So you think I'm flippant, then? Careless?"

"Show me how you're not when the doctor says you have cancer, and in the middle of telling you how you can fight it, how you can win, you throw your hands up and walk out, and now you're telling me you won't do it. Boom, just like that, with practically no information at all. All the while those tumors are growing . . . Mira, you have to do this. For the children. For me."

"For you!"

He stepped toward me and I thought he was going to pick up his glasses but he grabbed my shoulders and put his face in front of mine, such that I couldn't look away, and there he held me.

"You have to do this. I won't let you die!"

"That hurts!" His fingertips bit into my arms and I tried to squirm away but he wouldn't let go. I scrunched up my face and turned it away.

In my ear, he yelled, "Mira, are you listening to me?"

My mother used to say that, as she stood above me, looking down her long nose, ticking off my failures as a daughter and a human being.

And then something inside me shut off, and I felt Max's heat dissipated by a coolness sprung from within me, and his voice seemed to echo and grow distant. It was from this place of coolness that I felt him let go of my arms and retreat.

I went to my studio to meditate, watching the gulls tease the harbor as I did so. It might have been minutes or hours later I don't know, but Max came back, positively soaking with apologetic tears. I accepted his apology but told him I considered the issue closed.

He shrank away, assumed his deferential, attentive pose, and that's the way it's been for the past nine days.

Until this morning on the pier.

My door creaks open. I lift my head off the pillow, and it's Max, his face crinkled up like it always does when he's worried.

"How are you feeling?" he asks.

"You won't have to lock me in to keep me from throwing myself off the pier." I push down the urge to giggle because none of this is actually funny. That's clear enough by the look on his face. He's aged a year since this morning. Ten years since ten days ago.

This has hurt him, too. I've failed to see just how much until just now. I've failed to realize how the fear of loss can turn outward, so panic looks like rage, love turns to screaming and demands.

I prop myself up and hold out my arms. "I could really use a hug about now."

He comes to the bed with surprising alacrity for a sixtysomething man who spent all night on a half-deflated camping mattress. He folds his arms around me and nuzzles the top of my head with his chin.

"You know," my voice comes out in a

whisper, though I didn't mean it to. "I'm scared shitless. Absolutely out-of-my-mind terrified."

"Oh, Mira. Who wouldn't be?"

"Katya, probably. She'd probably already be under the knife, telling the doctor to hurry up because she's got a meeting."

"She's as human as anyone, she just tries not to show it. Not unlike someone else I know."

"I don't know what I'd be like without both breasts." I didn't even know I was going to say that. It just popped out into the air. I can tell by a shift in Max's position that he's surprised, too.

"Why, Mira. What do your breasts have to do with how wonderful you are? Don't get me wrong, they're good breasts."

I laugh and wipe my eyes. "Good breasts? Is that all? And you call yourself a writer."

"Round orbs, glowing like the moon."

"Okay, go back to 'good' then."

Max scoots down on the bed until he's eye level with me. "I'd miss it." He strokes the wicked left one lightly, making my nipple perk up. "But not as much as I'd miss you."

My sweet, adoring Max. As I'm kissing him, his reading glasses fall from the top of his head and bop me in the nose. We giggle because it's not the first time that's happened, and he takes them off, tossing them carelessly so that they slide off the end table and clatter on the floor. That's happened before, too.

I need more moments like this, like hearing my husband's glasses hit the floor before we make love. I need many, many more moments like this.

He nudges my bathrobe off my shoulders.

Moments just like this.

I run a brush through my hair and wonder how I'd look without it. Maybe I have a weird-looking head. I try to remember baby pictures. Did I have a nice round one or a funky-looking potato shape?

Max has gotten dressed and gone off in search of brunch provisions in the pantry and to rally the troops.

Hair and breasts. Do I really need them? And anyway, the hair grows back, I think. Assuming I don't die.

A coldness snakes down my back because I can see the scalpel hovering over me, and I shake it off.

It's not that easy, like my family would have me believe. It's not that easy to let them cut you apart.

I smack the hairbrush down and go in

search of a dress to wear. Must get out of this room and this brooding. Time to be with my family before they all scatter again.

In the kitchen I find Katya, wearing the clothes she wore on Friday, business-meeting clothes, expensive and chic, if a bit wrinkled.

"Dad's got the camp stove out," she says, glancing at me before turning her eyes back to the contents of the counter. "So we should be able to manage a brunch, though we'll have to eat in shifts, with such small burners."

I'd anticipated my family's not-so-organic eating habits and purchased old-fashioned hearty breakfast food. Pancake mix from a box, fatty bacon. Syrup in a bottle shaped like an old woman. I'll have some muesli and juice, most likely. Also, I need to find that tea for Irina.

Katya rummages in the cupboard above her head. She's tied her hair back in a sloppy twist speared through with a pencil. Her face is drawn into a tight mask of anxiety.

I move to her side. "Are you feeling all right?"

"Fine."

"How are the boys?"

"Grounded all summer."

I toy with the ends of my hair, which I've woven into a braid and pulled over my shoulder. "You know how sorry I am. I've already flushed the pot that was left."

It's a through-the-looking-glass moment. The mother apologizing to the child for poor behavior. When did this happen to me?

The others start filing in, wearing their traveling clothes, casual stuff that will get wrinkled from hours in the car. Darius and Irina come down the steps, hand in hand. She looks pale and clutches her husband's hand. I notice he walks as close as he can to her without getting tangled in her feet, eyes on her, always.

"Hi, Mom," says Ivan, with a bashful smile, one arm slung over Jenny's shoulder. His T-shirt says, I MAKE STUFF UP. She has her arm wrapped around his waist, and she fits snugly next to his chest. They look like puzzle pieces. What was that Shel Silverstein book called? *The Missing Piece,* that was it. Ivan loved that story. But Jenny was never really missing. It was Ivan, missing the point, as usual.

"Hey, Van," says Katya, eyes on the mixing bowl. "Whatever happened to Barbie? Did she make it home in the monsoon?"

"She sent me a text this morning about what a bast—" Van stops, noting his nephews and niece. "What a jerk I am. So I'm assuming she survived the night. Oh, and Kat? She sends her love."

A ripple of laughter flutters across the kitchen. I notice that for once, Van isn't pulling his ear.

Chip and Taylor approach me, eyes downcast.

"Grandma," Chip says. "We're really sorry."

"Yeah," adds Taylor. "We didn't mean to get you in trouble with Mom."

I try to hide my smile with my hand. They obviously believe the wrath of Katya is something not to be trifled with. "I appreciate that, boys, and while I don't like that you went through my things, I'm the one who's sorry. I had no business bringing that stuff in the house when you were coming."

They start to shuffle away, and I stop Chip by his shoulder. In a low voice I tell him, "It's not all fun and games, you know. I saw some kids get pretty messed up in my day, and saw some bad things happen to them. Don't be fooled into thinking it's a joke because it's not."

I have no idea if what I said meant anything to him, because he only nods and gently extracts his shoulder from my hand before turning back to the living room. He pours an orange juice from the carafe that someone set out and stands next to his father. The resemblance is startling. If not for the buttery amber color of his hair, like Katya's, he'd be the very image of his father.

Charles looks like he's about to throw up.

"Thanks for trying," Katya says, energetically whipping the pancake batter. "If he doesn't listen to me, he's not going to listen to you. Especially when you do it yourself."

"I had to say something."

Katya stirs a few more times, and I say, "You're going to whip it into a mousse if you keep that up."

"How are you feeling, Mom?" She doesn't take her eyes off the batter, but tilts her head in my direction.

I go back to playing with my braid. "Okay for now. Hard to believe there's anything wrong with me."

"There is, though. You know that, right?" Katya abandons the pancake batter and regards me with a hand on her hip. "You can't pretend it's not happening. And you know" — she drops her voice low so the children won't hear — "it's not like you'll go gracefully if you just let it run wild inside you."

My breathing feels too shallow suddenly, and I clutch at my heart. I consciously slow it down, deepen my breath, *uijayi pranayama,* my yogi would say.

"I'm sorry," she says. "I don't mean to sound harsh. But I can't feel good about you making these decisions until I know you have all the information."

The family is talking in groups of two and three. The boys are asking Darius about the BMWs he sells. Kit and Reenie are talking about babies, Kit carrying on about how much she wants a baby cousin, preferably a girl, and suggests a name that sounds like Areola. Max works away trying to light the camp stove, which he finally does, putting on a pot of perk coffee.

No one's talking to me at all.

"Do you ever wonder why you're here?" I ask, not really to anyone in particular.

Katya has been washing her hands at the sink. "What?"

"I sometimes wonder what I'm really doing here, anyway."

No one else seems to have heard. Katya comes closer, drying her hands on a towel. She approaches warily. "Is that what this is? You think you're pointless?"

"The university doesn't want me anymore. You kids don't need me; in fact, sometimes I wonder if what I ever said sank in at all."

"What does that mean?" She tosses the

towel on the counter.

"I tried so hard to raise you the best way I knew how. To not be trapped by material desires." Now I turn my gaze at Ivan, giggling with Jenny. "To have self-confidence to pursue your dreams, to treat yourself with respect." At this I look at Irina, now in a chair with Darius massaging her shoulders. She's staring at her new wedding band.

"You could have done worse," she says wryly, snapping out the towel to fold it again. "We turned out more or less okay."

I shake my head; she took that far more personally than I meant. "I'm very proud of all of you, what you've accomplished. But I sometimes think it was all innate within you, and my influence was nil."

Kat leans against the counter next to me, facing the family. "Do you remember when we had that big fight about the dress?"

"Oh Lord, not that again."

"You were trying to force me to be a nonconformist. Do you get the irony in that? You wanted me to conform to your ideals of being a rebel. So, I rebelled by being as conformist as I possibly could. We were no different than millions of other mother-daughters in the world, only you were the one smoking pot and dressing like a hippie."

"I wasn't smoking then." Not much, anyway.

"You know what I mean."

"So my influence has been opposite of what I intended? That's not something to treasure on Mother's Day."

She moves around to stand in front of me. "You influenced us more than you know, but you didn't do it with slogans and granola. You did it just by existing. And anyway, you're still needed. Look at Reenie, she's about to go to pieces as it is."

Katya doesn't know about the bleeding, and I'd like to tell her, but it's not my place to do so. "So, it's only Reenie who needs me?"

Katya turns back to the kitchen counter and starts mopping up stray bits of pancake mix. "I need you," she says in such a low voice, it's like she's speaking to herself. "I might need you much more pretty soon."

I catch her eye and raise my eyebrows. She looks over her shoulder at Charles and gestures with her head.

Ah. I see. I can also see the tan line on her left hand where her wedding ring used to be.

In the quietest whisper I can manage, I ask, "Are you splitting up?"

Her only answer is a tiny shake of her head.

I'm distracted from Katya by a loud chorus from the family. I look up to see Ivan, pulling his ear and turning pink in the center of a crowd. They are all exhorting him to do something, but what I don't know.

I pick up on it when Jenny says, "I'll go get your guitar. You don't show off your talent enough." She skips away up the stairs, like she's been running up those steps her entire life. It's remarkable sometimes how easily someone slips into a family.

"Oh, I showed off my talent enough in college," Van says, grimacing. "Parking myself under a tree outside and playing sensitive folk songs. You know I didn't get one single person stopping to listen? Not even the old man who dug cans out of the trash to return them for the deposit."

Katya remarks, "You probably picked a really poor location, full of people too busy to stop. You always were crap at marketing."

"It's a fair cop," says Ivan in a foppish British accent, winking at Jenny, now presenting his guitar. I don't know what the hell he's talking about, but Jenny seems to think it's funny.

"Coffee's ready," says Max, as Ivan arranges himself on a kitchen chair. Even

Chip and Taylor drift in from the living room. Ivan strums and hums and tunes up for a minute, and takes a breath to start.

A cell phone goes off, playing "Ride of the Valkyries."

Katya whips around and glares at her husband. Charles takes the phone out of his pocket, punches a button, and it goes silent.

Ivan clears his throat as Jenny announces, "He just wrote this. Like just now, this weekend."

And so he begins. As he sings, he stares down at his guitar, never once glancing up at the rest of us. I never knew his voice was so nice; a pleasant, easy tenor. As long as he's fiddled with that guitar and scribbled down lyrics, I'd never heard him do more than hum.

She has a pretty linen suit
And a fresh unlined face
Staring at her diamond
Everything is in its place
What am I supposed to do
If all this is not enough?
I've been climbing all my life
But still there's more above.
She tells me
You know there is no perfect
Only real life and liars

All anybody's trying to do
Is keep putting out the fires
What's perfection anyway
But lifeless symmetry
To hell then with perfect
Give me real life and liars

The last notes ring away, and no one speaks for a moment. I steal a look at Katya. Her mouth is open slightly as she stares at her brother unblinking, her hands are — for once — completely still.

Ivan breaks the silence. "It's not finished obviously, and it's not very good, I'm not sure about the line about putting out the fires and I think the melody is —"

"Oh, shut up," Jenny says cheerfully. "It's marvelous."

"Wow, Van." Katya, next to me in her unfamiliar stillness, hasn't taken her eyes off him yet. "That's . . . wow. Really good." She shoots a quick look at her husband, then down at the floor.

"Yeah!" chirps Kit. "I bet the radio would play it. That oldies station anyway."

"Oldies!" scoffs Chip. "How can it be an oldie if Uncle Van just now wrote it?"

Kit scowls at him. "You know what I mean! Simple listening music, whatever."

"Easy listening," says Van, smirking.

"Thanks, Kit."

Van searches out his older sister's eyes, but she has turned back to the counter, again stirring that batter to within an inch of its life.

Max abandons his post at the camp stove and grabs Ivan's hand in both of his for a healthy shake. "Wonderful, son. That's the best you've done yet."

Van laughs. "Sure, Dad. I don't think I've ever played one for you before."

"I bet it's your best, anyway."

"Yeah, it probably is," he says, getting up from the chair. "I'm going to put this away." He gestures with his guitar.

"I think he should go to Nashville," pipes up Jenny. Van stops in his tracks. "Break into the music scene. That's where all the songwriters go, so he tells me."

"Really? You would go?" asks Irina, her eyes shiny as she looks up at him, now halfway up the stairs.

"No. I don't know. Well, maybe. We'll see. Probably . . ." Van continues muttering as he goes up the stairs. Jenny winks in our direction and follows him up.

Well, I'll be damned.

My phone rings, and I almost jump out of my skin. It's been so quiet with no power. I answer because I'm closest.

It's Paul.

"Is everyone okay over there?" he asks.

"We're fine. That big tree is down, but it fell across the street, not onto the house."

"That is lucky."

"Yes, we are very lucky."

For a moment I forget that I'm on the phone. We are lucky, aren't we?

"Mira?"

"Sorry, Paul. What about you and yours? Is the homestead okay?"

"My porch got crushed by some limbs, but nothing that can't be fixed. Still looking for the dogs, but I think they're fine, just spooked by the thunder."

I usually look forward to Paul's calls, even when they're just business, because he can usually be counted on to say something complimentary or funny. Something that makes me smile bigger and feel warm. But now, I just want him off the phone to get back to my family. I rush through remaining pleasantries and hang up before he's even finished saying good-bye.

Katya's kids elbow each other as they sit around the kitchen table, laughing with goofy good nature, making a big show of fighting over the pancakes. Chip and Tay look none the worse for wear, considering their shenanigans last night. Darius and

Charles sip coffee, leaning against the wall near the dining room, and their posture is so similar that I do a double take: both have ankles lightly crossed, the hand without the coffee casually hooked in a front pants pocket. Irina doesn't notice; she listens to Katya over by the kitchen window. I can't hear them, but I can guess by that sweet glow over Katya's face — normally so severe, now soft and open — that she's reminiscing about the baby days. Jenny and Van are deep in conversation in the living room, just outside the kitchen, until Van takes a shift at the camp stove to let Max eat some pancakes. I perch on the kitchen counter to crunch my muesli.

The cool breeze stirs the cooking smells through the house, and my family's chatter warms me like an afghan, and if I remain in this very moment, this moment alone, everything seems bliss.

They talk about road conditions, and the Detroit Tigers, then Katya squashes a burgeoning argument about the war in Iraq between Darius and Charles, by asking, "Mom? When do you see the doctor next?"

I wipe my fingers on my pants. "I don't know."

"You don't remember?" she prompts.

"I don't know. I haven't made another appointment." I remember Dr. Graham thrusting a card toward me, telling me in her soft, kind voice to come back when I've had a few days to think. When I didn't take it — my vision was shrinking and I felt like I was in a tunnel, I just kept stepping backward — I saw Max's hand take it from her.

The room grows quiet again, and the silence seems sharp in contrast to the happy buzz that came before. I stare down at my cereal, going to mush in my bowl. I don't want to see Katya's face, hard in judgment, or Irina, prematurely mourning.

I catch myself thinking, why me? And I wonder who I'm talking to.

"I'll call the doctor in the morning," I tell them, and I'm surprised to realize that I actually mean that.

I raise my eyes from my cereal bowl and find my family exchanging glances with each other, sending those telegraphic messages that families do. Darius squeezes Irina's shoulders, and she puts a hand over one of his and squeezes his hand in return.

I tell them, "I can't promise anything, but I'll listen to the doctor and see what my options are."

"Good," says Katya, through a mouthful of pancakes. "Glad to know you're being so sensible."

"Watch it, or I might change my mind," I say, grinning at her. "I'd hate to go all sensible on you."

The timbre in the room changes, and the conversation bubbles up like champagne in a flute. I catch Irina and Darius holding hands tightly, and though her face still looks pale, she's smiling. Jenny and Van are openly cracking jokes about dead parrots, and Katya ruffles little Kit's hair. In profile, I realize how much those two look alike, and I wonder if they'll fight through her adolescence as much as her mother and I did.

I was forcing her to be nonconformist, I suppose, but it made so much sense at the time, wanting to impress my ideals upon her. Was that so different than a dad teaching his son to play football because he played in high school? It didn't help matters that by the time Irina came along I didn't have the same energy or time to comb the thrift stores for recycled clothes, and I relied more on packaged food for lunches. Irina got to fit in, just because she was last, and I was worn down. But to Katya it must have seemed brutally unfair.

For the moment though, my family looks fairly content, nearly happy, if not for the sadness in Irina's smile as she worries about the baby she didn't know she wanted. And Charles still looks like he might throw up. Still, a better-than-average mealtime gathering.

Was that all it took? Me agreeing to call the doctor? They must think they know what I'm going to do, that I'll run in there and get my tit cut off.

We'll see about that.

But then, no one is insisting that I do anything. They seem honestly contented, for now anyway, that I'm just going to listen. Keep an open mind.

Isn't that what a flower child is supposed to be? Open-minded?

Saying good-bye to my children is always bittersweet, and this morning the bitter wins out. My mortality looms over their departures, as I imagine it will for every parting from now until the final one.

Katya gives me the tightest hug I can remember receiving in years, and she hangs on for an extra second. This chills me; she hasn't shown me this much genuine need since before puberty. What has Charles done?

Their family parades out into the rented Ford Explorer, and the house feels ten times bigger without the grandchildren and all their noisy electronic stuff. My hit of relief at having the extra space back is followed by a sinking feeling of despair and guilt, because how many more times will I get to see them visit and stand in the driveway waving at them as they go?

Tears leak onto the bridge of my nose, and I sniff hard, watching their car retreat until it rounds the corner, out of view.

Darius and Irina leave next. Irina whispers into my ear, "No more blood so far." I tell her to call me tomorrow. She doesn't tell me if she's sticking it out with Darius, and maybe she doesn't even know yet, herself. But they've been in constant physical contact since they came down for brunch. Darius himself is unreadable. I wonder if I'll get the chance to know him better; if he'll drop his walls and relax around us. He can't be this placid all the time, it's inhuman.

He shakes my hand, then pulls me in for a light embrace. "Stay well, Mrs. Zielinski," he says.

I smile up at him. "I won't expect you to call me mom, but really, Mira is just fine. And I mean it about dinner. Please come again to see us."

He nods and guides Irina out by the shoulder.

Ivan and Jenny stay to help us do the

dishes. The radio tells us power might be out tomorrow, too. I don't mind. I like being off the grid. It's like the real world is suspended, and that feels very good, especially right now.

Ivan plans to drive Jenny back to her car, which they arranged to have towed to a nearby gas station, once they finally got a cellphone signal. They might have some time to wait for that tow truck, which is busy after the stormy night. They plan to walk on the shores of Lake Charlevoix to kill time, while they wait. Something tells me they will have lots to talk about.

"Don't disappear to Nashville without sending at least a postcard," I say, stretching up on tiptoe to hug him around the shoulders. Where did the little boy go who didn't even reach my shoulders? The toddler who liked to hang on to my pinky finger as we walked?

"When have you ever known me to make a snap decision?"

"Snap decisions never killed anybody," I say. He holds me at arm's length for a moment and smirks. "Well, okay, so some snap decisions are ill-advised. Still, you could do with a little more spontaneity."

Ivan shifts his guitar on his shoulder and picks up his duffel bag. "I don't know.

Seems pretty foolish to give up a tenured position and go dashing off to wait tables and harass people with my songs in a strange city."

Jenny appears beside him, having collected her things. "I think it would be worse never to have tried, to be lying there on your deathbed thinking, what if it'd worked?"

Van bites his lip and exhales sharply. I think the word "deathbed" has upset him.

I kiss him on the cheek. "That was a lovely song. You really have a knack."

I fold Jenny into my arms. She feels like a daughter-in-law already, and I could get used to this. I hope it's not an either-or choice: staying with Jenny or pursuing his dream. Maybe they need French teachers in Nashville, too.

And then they're all gone with all their trappings and clothes and noise, except for the crumpled wreck of the Escalade that awaits a tow truck.

Max and I sprawl on the couch. I lean into his side, using him like my own personal lounge chair. As morning warms to afternoon, it's starting to feel like summer again: the warmth presses in through the windows, especially those at the front of the house, where leafy branches used to filter the harsh light.

A metallic buzz and click announces the return of electricity. The television upstairs starts blathering. I want my silence back, but I'm too lazy to get up.

"I'll get it," Max says, "but you have to get off my leg."

I peel myself up, and my spine feels stiff with just the few minutes I was resting there. I need some yoga, but first I'd like some proper tea.

I nearly drop my teacup on the counter when a horrific whining noise begins just outside my front door. I carry my teacup and saucer out to my front porch, facing the gaping hole in the yard and the muddy circle of upended roots.

Workers are sawing apart the tree limbs that are splayed across the street.

"Hey, babe," says Patty, approaching from across the street, coming around the tree. "Not going out the window this time, I see."

"Oh, you saw that, did you?" So that was how my family knew where to go looking. Patty saw me sneak out. Thank God she did, or I might have slipped off the pier in my marijuana haze. I'm too old for that shit anymore.

I park my butt on the porch's top step. The morning sun, now moved to the side of the house, has already dried off last night's monsoon rain. Patty comes along and plops down uninvited. But not unwelcome.

"Your house seems okay," I say, sipping my tea, though it's really too hot yet.

"Yep, just some shingles flying off. I might even have my stepson fix it rather than calling the insurance company. Seems like a lot of bother when he's a roofer and all, anyway."

I wonder if she's heard about my foolishness on the pier.

"You wanna come to church with me next week?" she says, and I'm startled by the question. She knows I'm only a hair away from atheist, and she has never, in all our lives as neighbors and friends, asked me that.

"You think because I'm sick I need some churching up? Why, am I going to hell?"

"Just thought it might be nice."

I shake my head and try to hide my disappointment by drinking more tea. I never would have thought Patty would try this, using my illness to evangelize.

She says, "There was this one lady in my church. Lung cancer. One of those people like Superman's wife, who never smoked ever, but she got cancer anyhow."

"Superman? Oh, Dana Reeve. Right."

"She had the whole church praying for

her, and she always had people giving her hugs, driving her places, helping her do stuff when she was feeling weak. It was a lovely thing to see."

"I'm sure. And you're about to tell me that she was cured, and it's all due to all that praying and church."

"No, she died, actually." Patty turns to me and her face — etched by years of laughter and jokes and winks — is still and serious. "But I never saw anybody more serene. I'm sure she had her fearful moments, but man. She floated through the world, right up to the end."

I can't answer her, because to speak would break the dam loose. I set my teacup down because it's started to rattle against the saucer.

"Well. You think about it." Patty rubs my arm and squeezes my hand before getting up with an audible groan. I don't watch her go back into her house. Instead I'm staring at the floorboards between my feet. The paint is peeling. The last time Max painted it, Van was just graduating from high school.

The buzzing pauses, and the silence makes me look up. The workers are pulling away great hunks of tree, leaving trails of wet leaves behind them as they pull the branches down the road to a truck. I wince as they haul the pieces up, and they land with a great rattling boom in the truck bed.

The saws roar to life again, deepening in pitch as they bite into the fallen maple. I can feel the grinding, chewing noise in my chest it's so loud, and I put my hand over my heart, then cross both hands across my body, as if to protect it.

A fluttering catches my eye, to my left. I turn to see a butterfly dancing a circle in the air. It cartwheels by, between me and the muddy ball of roots.

That's when I look down in the hole left by the fallen tree. Tiny green shoots push up from the dirt, already reaching for the light.

■ ■ ■ ■

A^+

Author Insights, Extras, & More . . .

FROM KRISTINA RIGGLE

■ ■ ■ ■

DISCUSSION GROUP QUESTIONS

1. Does Mira's reluctance to have surgery for her breast cancer seem understandable?

2. What other reasons might she have for this reluctance beyond what she shares directly with the reader in the opening chapter?

3. Which significant life changes are facing Mira, and how might those changes be affecting her state of mind regarding the cancer diagnosis?

4. How would you describe the relationship of Mira to each of her children? How do these relationships affect the plot of the novel?

5. How do you react to Mira's marijuana use? How much does it affect her decision-

making throughout the book?

6. How would you describe the marriage of Mira and Max? How do you think their relationship plays into her reaction to her cancer diagnosis?

7. How does birth order affect the three grown siblings and how they fit into the family?

8. Which main character — Mira, Katya, Ivan, or Irina — do you understand the most? What parallels can you draw to your own life?

9. Mira observes in the book that children grow up any way they want to, despite a parent's best efforts. Do you agree with this?

10. Why does Katya find herself driving by her old boyfriend's house and secretly calling him? Have you ever felt drawn to a romance from your past?

11. What is the source of the friction between Mira and Katya, and does it seem justified to you? Do you have old childhood fights with your parents that still

echo in your adulthood?

12. Do you think Katya and Charles's marriage will endure? Do you think Katya will truly change her life? If so, in what ways?

13. Do you agree with Katya's decision to stay with Charles? How else might she have reacted?

14. Why is Ivan so clueless about romance?

15. Do you think Jenny and Ivan have a future together? Why or why not?

16. Why do you think Irina engages in reckless romantic behavior?

17. What do you think Irina should do about Darius and the baby?

18. Do you believe Mira will change her mind about the surgery when she sees the doctor again? Why or why not?

19. What role does the Big Tree play in the novel?

20. How does Mira's lack of formal religion play into the story? Do you believe her

view has changed by the end?

21. How does the setting affect each of the characters?

22. Do you think the Zielinskis are a happy family at the beginning? How about at the end of the novel?

AUTHOR Q&A

Why did you choose to write this novel using four points of view, and with Mira's point of view in first person, the others in third person?

I wanted to write the kind of book I love to read. I love a good family drama with a big cast of characters and colorful personalities. Also, it's fun for me as a writer to get into different voices. It's hard to get bored when you switch perspectives regularly. It did make for some tricky logistical issues sometimes. It was hard for me to remember what each character knew at any given point and where all the rest of them were, since the progression from chapter to chapter is not always precisely linear. But that was part of the fun, too. I put Mira's voice in first person because I wanted to leave no doubt that this is her story, first and foremost. Also, she's such a bold character. It would have seemed strange to speak for her, instead of letting her speak for herself.

What inspired this story?

I'd been trying to get published for a while, and that effort to be commercial had wrung all the joy out of my writing. I finally decided that I should write to entertain myself, and even if rejections rolled in, I could at least enjoy the process and be proud of the result. Happily, this book was received very well. I suspect this manuscript was the most authentic I'd ever produced.

What kind of research did you do for the novel?

I did some reading, and contacted Susan G. Komen for the Cure, but the best research of all came from interviewing local doctors. A prominent oncologist told me that women of Mira's age often discover a lump in their breasts while holding their grandbabies. I found that detail so poignant that I worked it into the book. Another doctor walked me through a "diagnosis talk" just as she would give a real patient. She also told me how patient reactions to breast-cancer diagnosis have ranged all over the map and didn't always follow what seemed logical or reasonable. This bolstered my faith in Mira as a genuine character, even if her reactions might not be "correct" or "expected."

Your novel's epigraph is the famous first line from *Anna Karenina,* "All happy families are alike; each unhappy family is unhappy in its own way." How do you think that quote applies to your book?

I'm sure happy families are alike — all two of them! I'm being glib here, but my point is that every family has its problems, the Zielinskis included. It's funny, some people who have read the manuscript seem amazed at how screwed up these characters are, when to me they don't seem that far out of bounds. Maybe people are reacting to how all these problems seem to be coming to a head all on one weekend. That's the way novels work, though. More drama that way.

Is the story autobiographical?

No. Mira is diagnosed with cancer before the story even begins, and that diagnosis drives much of the plot, but that's not a reaction to anything that's happened in my life. Everyone has someone in their circle of family and friends touched by cancer, but that's not why I wrote about it. I needed a crisis to drive the story, and breast cancer is singularly terrifying to women. As for the other plot elements, I can relate to each of my characters on some level, but no one character represents me in the book.

There's one male voice in the book: the middle child, Ivan. Was it hard to write from a male point of view?

Not especially. I can relate to Ivan quite a lot, in fact. He's a struggling songwriter and at the time I wrote the book, I was an aspiring novelist. It wasn't hard to convey his feelings of frustration over trying to break into a creative profession. Also, he and I share a love of Monty Python.

Why did you set the book in Charlevoix, Michigan?

This little town in northern lower Michigan is known as "Charlevoix the Beautiful" and it fits. I spent many summer weekends there visiting my grandparents, and some of my happiest memories come from walks on the dune at Mt. McSauba, or taking in a sunset from the pier. Mira and Max's house is loosely based on the home on Dixon Avenue where my grandmother grew up.

Charlevoix (pronounced SHAR-le-voy) is one of my favorite places in all the world, and I figured if I had to spend a year or more writing a book, I should at least dedicate the hours in my imagination to someplace beautiful.

ABOUT THE AUTHOR

Kristina Riggle lives and writes in Grand Rapids, Michigan, with her husband, two kids, and dog. She's a freelance journalist, published short story writer, and co-editor for fiction at the e-zine *Literary Mama.* Though she doesn't live at the shore, Lake Michigan makes her heart happy whenever she can get there.

The employees of Thorndike Press hope you have enjoyed this Large Print book. All our Thorndike, Wheeler, and Kennebec Large Print titles are designed for easy reading, and all our books are made to last. Other Thorndike Press Large Print books are available at your library, through selected bookstores, or directly from us.

For information about titles, please call:
(800) 223-1244

or visit our Web site at:
http://gale.cengage.com/thorndike

To share your comments, please write:
Publisher
Thorndike Press
295 Kennedy Memorial Drive
Waterville, ME 04901